JUST ANOTHER SATURDAY NIGHT
ON THE STREETS OF BORDERTOWN

"Wolfboy!" I called, and his long nose swung our way.

He grinned, which can put you off if you've just met him. When you get used to it, he looks pretty good, actually. He's lean and rangy and muscle-y, and covered all over with short coarse red-brown fur. That night he wore a black t-shirt with the sleeves ripped out, tight black jeans, and black hi-top sneakers. His ears end in pointed tufts, the lower half of his face is lengthened, and his canine teeth are . . . well, about what you would expect. He has claws, thick and slate-colored, on his fingers. When he types, he sounds like a dog on a kitchen floor.

"Wolfboy," I said, "I'd like you to meet Caramel."

Give the kid credit; she held out her hand. Wolfboy took it and inclined his head. Pretty courtly for a guy with a dog nose.

—from "Danceland" by Emma Bull and Will Shetterly

Other anthologies edited by Terri Windling

Life on the Border
Elsewhere 1 (with Mark Alan Arnold)
Elsewhere 2 (with Mark Alan Arnold)
Elsewhere 3 (with Mark Alan Arnold)

Faery

Borderland (with Mark Alan Arnold)
Bordertown (with Mark Alan Arnold)

The Year's Best Fantasy, First Annual Collection
    (with Ellen Datlow)
The Year's Best Fantasy, Second Annual Collection
    (with Ellen Datlow)
The Year's Best Fantasy and Horror, Third Annual
    Collection (with Ellen Datlow)

The Fairy Tales series, edited by Terri Windling

The Sun, The Moon, And The Stars by Steven Brust
Jack the Giant-Killer by Charles de Lint
The Nightingale by Kara Dalkey
Snow White and Rose Red by Patricia C. Wrede*
Tam Lin by Pamela Dean*

**Available from Tor Books*

BORDERTOWN

Edited by
Terri Windling & Mark Alan Arnold

TOR
fantasy

A TOM DOHERTY ASSOCIATES BOOK
NEW YORK

This is a work of fiction. All the characters and events portrayed in this book are fictitious, and any resemblance to real people or events is purely coincidental.

Bordertown and the Borderlands were created by Terri Windling of the Endicott Studio, with creative input from Mark Alan Arnold, Phil Hale, and the authors of the stories in this volume.

"Danceland" copyright © 1986 by Emma Bull and Will Shetterly.
"Demon" copyright © 1986 by Midori Snyder.
"Exile" copyright © 1986 by Bellamy Bach.
"Mockery" copyright © 1986 by Ellen Kushner and Bellamy Bach.

BORDERTOWN

Copyright © 1986 by Terri Windling.

Cover illustration by Thomas Canty, from a photograph by Robin Hardy and Terri Windling.

A Tor Book
Published by Tom Doherty Associates, Inc.
175 Fifth Avenue
New York, N.Y. 10010

Tor Books on the World-Wide Web:
http://www.tor.com

Tor® is a registered trademark of Tom Doherty Associates, Inc.

ISBN: 0-812-52262-1

First Tor edition: January 1996

Printed in the United States of America

0 9 8 7 6 5 4 3 2 1

CONTENTS

Introduction

Come away, O human child!
To the waters and the wild . . .

—William Butler Yeats
"The Stolen Child"

I hear that out in your World, mothers warn their little ones that if they misbehave, the fairies will come and steal them away. . . .

What a load of crap. Let me tell you what really happens.

Most humans go about their daily lives completely unconcerned about what goes on in the distant realm known as the Elflands. Since Elfland first reappeared in the World, you've made it clear we're not exactly welcome here—and truth to tell we don't want you in Faerie either. You stick to your side of the Border and we'll stick to ours, and that suits about everybody just fine.

But every once in a while a child is born who can't seem

1

to fit in anywhere in the World. A misfit, a malcontent, with an itch in his soul, a wild look in her eyes. We don't have to steal these kids away—they come of their own accord. Hell, we couldn't keep them away if we tried.

Being human, they cannot cross the Border into Faerie. So they come to the Borderlands—that no-man's land between Elfland and the World. Where magic bleeding from out side of the Border has warped and twisted into unpredictable shapes. Where our spells and your technology work sporadically—or not at all.

In the infamous city of Bordertown, elves and humans mingle in an uneasy truce, vying for dominance in the High Council chambers, the marketplace—and, most of all, the rock'n'roll clubs in the slums south of Ho Street. Clubs like mine, the Dancing Ferret: cheap beer, good wine, and the best bands in town.

Down in Soho, the runaways have claimed the abandoned buildings as their own. The gangs cruise at night on spell-powered bikes: the elvin Bloods in red leather, the human Pack—dark and dangerous, the Rats from under the docks, the rich kids from Dragon's Tooth Hill.

You have to be crazy, or desperate, to come here. But if you make it across the waters and the wilds to Bordertown, come on over to the Ferret. The first beer's on me; after that, kid, you're on your own.

                                   —Farrel Din
                                   The Dancing Ferret
                                   18 Carnival Street
                                   Bordertown

EMMA BULL & WILL SHETTERLY
Danceland

Friday night started, for me and for all of us I suppose, in the street outside Danceland. I was sitting in the sidecar, waiting for Tick-Tick. She'd parked the bike outside Danceland and made her usual arrow-like way across the street to Snappin' Wizard's Surplus and Salvage ("More Bang for the Buck, More Spell for the Silver").

Snappin' Wizard's is the only other thing on that end of Ho Street that's still lit up late at night. And oh, is it lit. Pre-Change cartop revolving lights flash rude and red in the windows. Between them, will-o'-the-wisps bop back and forth in rhythm. Signs on the window glass, in paint and fairy dust, shout about solar cells and self-bored stones and logic boards and clock spells, and how they're cheap cheap cheap!

The Queen of bloody Faerie couldn't keep Tick-Tick out of there. She'd left with a mumble about being just a minute, and she'd be right back. Or maybe she didn't say it this time, and I only supplied it from the memory of all the other times she had. Whatever. I didn't expect the Ticker back inside half an hour.

I slid way down in the sidecar so I could prop my head against the back padding, and shook an herbal cig out of its box. They're big stuff with the elves, who don't much like tobacco. I think they like them because it makes them all feel like old vid stars, dragging moodily on a cigarette. I'm not poking fun. Why do you think *I* smoke them?

I rolled the coltsfoot-and-comfrey smoke over my tongue like wine and watched the crowd in front of Danceland. People were milling on the sidewalk, waiting for the band to start. Four elvin Bloods in poet's red clustered near the doors, looking sharp (and aware of it, I'll bet) against the building's black-patent paint job. A halfie woman with a lion's mane haircut dyed black and white was practicing some synched dance step. She was coached by a black human woman with silver bells in her elflocks. An elf kid had his seedybox balanced on one shoulder, and people were dancing to its music. Four members of the Pack pulled up on two cycles, their jackets trailing bright motley streamers. One of them asked the crowd at large if the music had started. One of the Bloods by the door shook her head, not really friendly but not like anyone expected war, and the Pack kids drove off again.

Danceland's double doors were arched over with row after row of white lights that flashed in sequence and seemed to chase each other forever. DANCELAND was written in script over the doors in pink-red neon—the genuine pre-Change article, but the gas was rattled around now with a spell. (I know this only from the Ticker's explanation. The business of How Things Work is her specialty, not mine.) When I squinted, the whole front of the building became a blaze of bright fog.

It's at the very end of Ho, but it's worth the trip. The Factory is older, the Dancing Ferret is trendier, and the Wheat Sheaf is more exclusive. But Danceland has the *old* magic, the kind you don't have to be an elf to make. The old magic is made with loud music and sweat and colored light. But the best thing about it is that stinging feeling at the back of your head that says *anything* could happen tonight.

Which is, come to think of it, the most pervasive magic in Bordertown. But keep in mind that magic doesn't always work the way you expect in the Borderlands.

"Uh . . . hi," somebody said behind me, breathy and excited-scared.

I leaned my head back a little more and looked up into big round brown eyes under a heavy thatch of brown bangs. Her skin was tan, too, or maybe just evenly grubby. She wore a gray denim jacket and jeans that weren't ruined yet, and a black cap with a pheasant feather tucked in its band. The cap looked new. The whole ensemble was the quintessential Worldly kid's idea of What They Wear In The Borderlands. You could start a mail-order company selling outfits like that and clean up: Halfie Frankie's Faerie Fashions. I hate runaways. They make me hurt all over, just under the skin.

There's always been places that called to people. Even before the Change, there were cities that shone in the back of the mind like Faerie gold. You knew, *knew*, that if you could just run away to one of those places, you'd become someone else, someone wonderful, and wonderful things would happen to you. I heard a list of those magical cities once. I remember London, Liverpool (interesting name, but a disgusting concept), New York, and something with two words that started with an S. I've forgotten the rest.

"Are . . . you elvish?" she asked, smiling and biting her lip.

There's nothing ambiguous about the roundness of my ears, and yes, I'm pale, but it's because I hate going to sleep as much as I hate waking up. I remember being her age, though, and being about as long in town. I tilted up one lens of my riding goggles, showing her a dark-blue eye, and said kindly, "No, I'm Jewish."

"Oh," she said, crestfallen. I hoped she'd be gone by the time Tick-Tick came back; one sight of the Ticker and the kid would be offering to lick the Genuine Faerie Mud off her motorcycle boots.

"My name's Orient," I told her, as something of a peace offering, and stuck my hand out. She shook it.

"I'm Camilla." She sighed, and wrinkled her nose. "It's a stupid name."

That gave my stomach a little twist. Camilla means "attendant at a sacrifice." There were too many things of value to sacrifice in Bordertown if you were young, scared, and not scared enough.

"That's okay. Everybody in Bordertown has a nickname." She looked hopeful. Oh, I hate runaways. "Yours is . . ." I thought for a second. ". . . Caramel."

She was disappointed, though she tried to hide it. I knew what she'd been hoping for: something like Firebird, or Starwind. The sort of name no one could live with, or up to. So I gave her one of my lopsided grins that Sai says looks rakish even without my eyes to help. I said, "Burnt sugar. Sweet, but smoky, and it's been through the fire."

Okay, it was hokey, but it cheered her up. "I guess that's pretty good," she admitted.

"Where you from?"

"Bellinbroke."

"Pretty far away?"

"Took me nine days to get here, and I got good rides the whole way."

It was too far; she'd never go back home, even if she wanted to. When she wanted to. I dragged hard on the cigarette to loosen the lump in my throat.

"Want some water?" Caramel asked me, and there was a coyness in her voice that made me raise both sides of my goggles this time. She held out a beer bottle, half full of beautiful, translucent crimson. Mad River water.

I took it from her. I wanted to peg the thing into the alley and hear it shatter. But that would be no help in the long run.

"Have you had any of this yet?" A nice, calm voice—I was impressed with myself.

"A little." She was defiant at first. Then a sheepish look crept across her face, and she shrugged. "It tastes kind of gross."

"This is elf stuff, Caramel. To them, it's just water. The sort of humans who drink river water are . . . not in style." Which was true enough, if you only counted the Wharf Rats. But there were humans and halfies who thought money was a license to be stupid in public, who wore crystal or silver cups on chains or silk cords around their necks. Maybe this kid hadn't seen any of those yet. "I'll make you a trade," I said, swinging the bottle a little.

She looked at it, and at me. "What kind of trade?"

I balanced the bottle between us on the sidecar's rim. Then I slid one of the silver bracelets, not the thinnest, off my left wrist and held it out. "I'll give you this for it. On the condition," I added, as she reached, "that you use it to pay your way into there," and I nodded at Danceland. "You can keep the change. Whoever gives it to you, tell 'em Orient sent you, and you want to talk to Goldy. Deal?"

Her eyes were practically rolling, from me to the bottle to Danceland's front doors.

"Straight," I said. "It's just a dance club, and Goldy's just a bouncer." Goldy would disagree, of course. "He's a good guy to talk to when you need to."

She bit her lip—no smile this time—and finally took the bracelet. "Why this Goldy? Why not you, if you're so concerned about me?"

I grinned, which was harder than it sounds. "Because I come and go. But I'll find you if I need you." Which was a joke of sorts, but of course she didn't get it.

She turned to go, and we both saw him at once. You might think he was wearing a full-head mask, a good one of the sort that outfits like the Horn Dance wear. And once you wrote off the head as a mask, you could come up with something to explain away the pelt on the rest of him, too, like a fur suit in spite of the weather. But Caramel was new in town, had never seen the Horn Dance or anything else, and hadn't developed that cynical turn for explanations. She not only stopped when she saw him, she stepped back a pace or two.

"Wolfboy!" I called, and his long nose swung our way. He grinned, which can put you off if you've just met him. He headed toward the sidecar, that long swinging walk earning a jealous scowl from one of the Bloods.

When you get used to it, he looks pretty good, actually. He's lean and rangy and muscle-y, and covered all over with short coarse red-brown fur. He shaved his face once, and we all hated it. I think he decided never to do it again when the Ticker said, "It makes you look so . . . young." That night he wore a black T-shirt with the sleeves ripped out, tight black jeans, and black hi-top sneakers. His ears end in pointed tufts, the lower half of his face is lengthened, and his canine teeth are . . . well, about what you would expect. He has claws, thick and slate-colored, on his fingers. When he types, he sounds like a dog on the kitchen floor.

"Wolfboy," I said, "I'd like you to meet Caramel."

Give the kid credit; she held out her hand. Wolfboy took it and inclined his head. Pretty courtly for a guy with a dog nose.

"Pleased to meet you," Caramel breathed. She turned and looked at me sideways. "Guess I should go . . ."

I gave her a nod. "You don't want to miss the first song."

Wolfboy and I watched her go. I said, "Lord, lord. Perfectly nice Friday night, and I have to get pinned down in the street by some little thing with the dust of the World still behind her ears.''

Wolfboy chuckled deep in his throat and patted my head.

"Oh, go chase cats." I shook out another cigarette and held it out. I lit it, too, since paper matches are a nuisance for him.

"You been out of town?" I asked after his first mouthful of smoke.

He grinned like a fiend from hell, and pulled a many-folded leather wallet out of his back jeans pocket. With a flourish, he let the folds fall open in a sort of waterfall. Neatly flattened inside and preserved with a bought spell were something like twenty four-leaf clovers.

"Oh my stars and garters," I breathed. "Well, if I need to borrow money I'll sure 'nuff come to you. You gonna sell 'em inside?" I asked him, pointing to Danceland.

He refolded the wallet with a practiced flip and nodded.

"Offer one to Goldy. He's going to need it." When Wolfboy raised his eyebrows, I said, "I just sent that runaway to him."

He giggled in a voice low enough to make a couple of Packies nervous and shook his head.

"I don't suppose you'd trade one of those little green beauties for the latest copy of *Stick Wizard*, would you?" I squinted speculatively at him.

He looked down at me with an expression that even on his face was easy to read: You've got to be kidding.

I pulled my copy out of the map pocket in the sidecar (after all, what else am I going to use the map pocket for? Not maps, anyway). The stick-figure characters on the cover were block-printed with ink and fairy dust, and moved when you looked at them. On this issue, the Wizard was flying off his beat-up cycle as it hit a trip-wire. At each end of the wire were, of course, his arch-nuisances. Tater and Bert, the cigar-smoking elf delinquents. I could almost see Wolfboy salivating. Tater and Bert are favorites of his. He thinks they should have their own book. I don't know about Wolfboy sometimes.

But he shook his head finally. I didn't really expect him to deal—by the end of the night someone might *give* him a copy, after all. So I smiled and put it away.

"Here's a fine convocation of riffraff," Tick-Tick said behind me.

"Boil me in lead," I cried, and turned. "She's back before morning!"

"Oh, shut up. Hi, Lobo." She smiled at Wolfboy. He smiled back and dropped his gaze. He loves being called Lobo.

The Ticker was loading a paper-wrapped parcel into the bike's top cargo box.

"Goodies?" I asked.

"Well, not that you'd think so. A little replacement stock, wire connectors and that sort of thing. And a toy or two."

"Or eight or ten," I said, but she didn't answer me.

Tick-Tick is pure elf, and looks it. Pointed ears, luminous pale skin, shining silver eyes. Slender and almost oppressively tall. She'd never fit in the sidecar, so it's a good thing she owns the bike. She usually dyes her hair dandelion-yellow and wears it short, with a single long lock at the very front and center of her hairline that hangs fine as milkweed fluff to her eyebrows. In spite of her height, she looks delicate as spun sugar. It surprises people to find that her favorite perfume is Eau de Bearing Grease and Hot Solder.

She was wearing her idea of power dressing tonight: a long gray leather coat and tight pants of the same, low red leather boots, a dark gray suit coat, white shirt, a red leather tie, and three garnet earrings in her right ear. I've tried to tell her that this is *not* what they wear in the boardrooms of the World's corporations, but she points out (and rightly) that I can't be sure, can I, and they might if they had the good taste to think of it, mightn't they?

"So," she said, "anyone here want to rock the moon down?"

"Me! Me!" said I, and leaped out of the sidecar. Wolf-boy, sober lad that he is, let out a yell that made the whole street shudder. I left my goggles in the sidecar, and checked my hair in the rear-view mirror. The Ticker had done my dye job the week before, and I was still nervous about it: the spikes of red around my face showed like lit matches against the natural black of the rest. It's been years since I left the World, but it has its fangs in me yet. There's a limit to how conspicuous I can be and still feel safe.

"Yes, yes, you're just breathtaking." Tick-Tick sighed. "Come along."

The crowd outside had turned into crowd inside, we found. Danceland's insides are all black cinder block walls, from which they wash the fairy dust graffiti every night. "After all," the club's owner, Dancer, says, "this place is supposed to be *different*, for Zeus' sake."

The stage lights were still out, but the band's equipment was set up, and the spell boxes that ran the amps were glowing gently. The Ticker headed for the pool tables to fleece a few unsuspecting Bloods, and Wolfboy and I pushed through to the bar.

Valda was already clunking bottles of beer down on the counter three at a time. "Val, precious Val," I bellowed across three feet of noisy space, "did the coffee come in yet?"

She looked at me as if about to say no, then smiled and said, "You're a lucky boy." I blew her a kiss, and she headed for the other end of the bar to pour me a cup. Not, mind you, that I don't like beer. I adore beer. But I can get that anywhere.

She set the cup in front of me and a bottle of beer in front of Wolfboy. I pried a silver stud out of my wristband and told Valda, "That's for both," before Wolfboy could pay.

He raised his bushy eyebrows at me, and I shrugged. "So pay me back when you've made your killing in good luck," I said, meaning the clovers, of course. He winked and hoisted his bottle.

I let the steam and the coffee smell wash over my face for a second before I actually sipped any. Coffee is shortage-prone in the Borderlands, and expensive since most of what passes through is doing just that: passing through to Faerie. But, oh, it's worth the price.

Someone tapped me on the shoulder and said in my ear, "Watch that stuff, young man."

I turned and found Goldy shaking his head at me. Goldy is black and not tall, even for a human. But he's built like a pyramid standing on its head. His hair is plush-short and metallic gold—thus the nickname, of course. He was in uniform, which is a green long-sleeved Danceland t-shirt. It's not that conspicuous, since Dancer sells the things, and there are always a few in the club on any night.

"Goldy. What it is. Watch what stuff?"

He narrowed his eyes at my coffee cup. "That's a dangerous intoxicant. You may get high as the Tooth and tear the place up before the night is out."

I rolled my eyes. "Call me Mr. Coffee Nerves."

"Or perhaps I might toss you out now and save myself a bit of trouble. It'd be no more than you deserve."

"Me? Oh, you got my present, then."

"If you mean your runaway, yes, you snot-nosed little mutant, I did. What am I to do with her?"

"Talk her out of doing all the stupid things we did at her age."

"Except for continuing my acquaintance with you, I've never done anything stupid. I assume you found her?"

I could hear the capital *F* he meant to put on "found." " 'Course not. Though I suppose you could say I found her nickname," I mused. I wondered what she would have been called if she hadn't met me.

The colored lights in the ceiling spat and swirled. "Back

to the fray.'' Goldy sighed and disappeared into the crowd. Then the stage lights came up, and Dancer, the owner, walked across the stage. I saw the way she did it, sort of lazy, as if there was no audience at all, and I shot a look at Wolfboy. When Dancer introduces the band, it's something special. But when Dancer walks to the mike like that . . . Wolfboy gave me the thumbs-up, and we started moving toward the stage.

So did everyone else, of course, but we made it to the middle of the dance floor, at least. Somewhere ahead of us I thought I caught a glimpse of a black cap with a pheasant feather that vibrated with its wearer's excitement.

Dancer stood at the mike for a second, during which you could hear every breath that was drawn in Danceland. Twice she began to move her hands, as if to preface words that didn't come. Then she threw back her head and laughed, and said, ''I give up. Ladies and gentlemen, Wild Hunt!''

The roar of the audience shook those black walls, and I helped. I doubt there was anyone in Danceland who didn't know the name. Bordertown had been full of the sound of Wild Hunt all summer. The recordings came out once a week, a song at a time, on mag tape, or in an impression ball, or digitally coded. But there were no pictures of the band. No one had ever seen them in concert, and nobody seemed to know someone who worked in the studio where they'd recorded—you know the sort of thing. So we'd play the recordings, the tearing, heart-shaking music pouring over us, and we'd pretend that we could tell from the sound how they looked.

We were wrong. All of us. They took us by surprise, and she most of all, because all the poets and painters and visionaries in Bordertown could never have imagined her.

It's not that she was the archetypal elf. Strider, the third of the Danceland bouncers, is the archetypal elf, a real flipping Prince of Faerie sort. No, this was the Snow

Queen from out of that old tale, the beautiful White Lady
of any romantic ghost story.

She was tall, of course, and pale, paler than Strider or
the Ticker or any other elf I'd ever seen. Her eyes were
the color of silver in the sun. Her hair was white as new
snow, or expensive paper, or the fiery-white highlights on
silver. Again the word silver—white as she was, she was
a rich-looking white, and demanded rich words to describe.

Her hair was clipped close to her head on the left side,
lengthening as it went over her head until it looked like a
white wave cresting over her right ear. Her left eye was
caught up in a bar of light blue paint that ran from her
nose to her hairline, where it became a streak of pale blue
dye across the short white hair. The dye ended in a curling
tail above her left ear. It's difficult for a human to judge
elvin features—by human standards, there's no such thing
as a homely elf, I think—but I would swear that hers was
the most beautiful face that Bordertown had ever seen.

She wore white leather leggings and a white sleeveless
thing that shimmered like the silk that comes from the
Elflands. She played a Fender Witchfire bass the blue of
midnight. Fairy dust swirled in the paint job in galaxies
and nebulae, suns that formed and flashed and died as you
watched. Light strobed off the rings on her fingers as she
chorded and slammed down on all four strings, then
scraped her pick down the E. It was the opening riff of
"Shake the Wall Down," and suddenly everybody was
dancing.

Wolfboy got snagged by an elf-girl with pale green hair,
a wicked grin, and a red jewel on her cheek like a birth-
mark or a tear. He picked her up by her waist, whirled her
around, and they were both gone into the crowd.

The hyperharpist played a Fairlight, one of the Sorcerer
series judging from the stuff he got out of it. Waveforms
so clean you could have eaten off them. The lead guitarist
had a topknot of burgundy hair, an eight-stringed ax, and

six fingers on each hand to play it with. The drummer was insane, but drummers often are. They just aren't all as precise and tasteful in their madness as this elvin woman was. I won't even try to describe what the halfie on elfpipes did with that instrument, but it wasn't anything that an Elflands elf would have thought of, or approved of. The total effect was wonderful and impossible and, all right, magical.

And they sang, of course. All of them, in close, twisting harmony; or just her, the White Lady, with a pure clear voice that made every word a projectile into the head and heart. They segued straight into "Heart's Desire," a modified version that was somehow as creepy as it was driving.

Suddenly Sai appeared before me. She was grinning and shaking her head, and I realized that I'd been dancing by myself, gaping at the band ever since the music started.

"What are you doing, letting your tongue dry?" she yelled.

I gave her my best I'm-an-idiot shrug.

Sai is another Danceland bouncer, the middle member of the Terrible Trio. She's a halfie, tall, plump, with a round pink face and rainy gray eyes. She has Oriental hair, uncompromisingly straight, heavy, and black. She wears it shoulder-length to show it off. Not that she liked her father, mind, or even knew him. She just hopes that someday some elvin bigot will smart off about it, and she can loosen his teeth. When an elf makes trouble in Danceland, Goldy and Strider let Sai throw him out, whenever possible. It makes her so happy.

"When did Dancer score this coup?" I shouted at her, and pointed at the band.

"Two days ago. She was half crazy with it, I tell ya. Didn't know whether to bless her luck, or cuss it for not leaving time to advertise."

"Poor baby."

She shrugged and grinned at the same time. "Word gets

around.'' And it was true that the place was full. Advertising would have only meant the Terrible Trio would have to turn away tourists.

Strider slid gracefully through the crowd and put an arm lock around Sai's neck. She rolled her eyes and pinched his thigh.

''Owoo! Halfie scum,'' he said affectionately, loosening his grip and giving her a quick kiss behind the ear.

''Pointy-eared creep,'' she replied in kind, and put her hand in one of his back pockets.

Strider, as I said, is a veritable Lord of Elflands. He has the fine mane of silver hair to the middle of his back, the regal carriage, the elegant long-fingered gestures that melt the hearts of human girls.

Someday I'm going to ask how such an unlikely pair as Sai and Strider became sweethearts. Not anytime soon, mind you—but someday.

''Dance with this jerk,'' Strider told her, nodding at me. ''He looks brain dead standing there by himself.''

''I'm on duty,'' Sai protested.

Strider shrugged. ''Nothing's goin' down. Goldy and I can handle it for half a song, girl.''

''You can't handle your—''

He stopped her by smacking a kiss on her lips. ''You've got the dirtiest mouth on Ho Street.''

I didn't hear her response, but I think he blushed. Then he smiled lazily and drifted off through the dancers.

Sai dances well. You wouldn't think, looking at her, that she'd have that elvin grace, but she does. She says it comes from her boxing days. I put some effort into trying to match her, and ended the song pleasantly winded.

Wild Hunt swept on into ''Running on the Border.'' It's not really a dance number, but it has too much intensity, too much a sense of headlong motion, to be a ballad. It's a showpiece for the guitarist and lead vocalist. They're out in front for the whole song, weaving in and out of each other's work with only breathing space between verses.

People stayed on their feet and on the dance floor, swaying in place and singing along, doing double handclaps just like on the tape.

Then someone pushed past me, so hard that I would have fallen if Sai hadn't caught me. I got a ragged view of him as he went by, and a better one from the back once he was past: an elf, and from the clothes not a Border-townie. He wore a full-skirted coat that fit close to his waist and stopped at mid-thigh, in a brocade of some magical weave that changed pattern restlessly. His hair was uncolored, and worn in a moon-white braid that reached his waist.

"My, my," Sai said happily. "Weeds of Elfland he doth wear."

I hung on to her upper arm. "Calm down, he hasn't done anything."

"Couldn't I just warn him a little?"

"No."

I realized a moment later that Sai might get her chance yet. The elf in brocade pushed his way to the edge of the stage and shouted something at the band. It might have been a name; the Elflands accent throws me off until I get used to it.

Wild Hunt tried to keep going, but you could tell they were all rattled. When he shouted again and pounded a fist on the stage, the White Lady faltered and stopped, and the rest of the band came to a ragged halt behind her.

She turned off her mike, but I could still hear her in the silence that followed the music's death. "Leave me alone," she said. She had the Elflands accent, too, but not as thick.

The elf down front balled his fists and said something furiously in Elvish.

"No! I told you no. I am not—I *will* not go." She was hanging on to the neck of the bass as if she was afraid someone would try to take it away.

Sai had begun moving forward, which was tough. The

crowd had pressed itself away from the stage and back
toward us, and they were packed as tight as a new brick
wall. I followed along behind her as best I could.

More Elvish from the guy in brocade; I recognized the
words for "clan" and, I think, "Border."

The White Lady was turning away from him, as if to
walk offstage, but she stopped when she heard his little
speech. "Are you, now?" she said with scorn that would
crack metal. "Well, not me. Maybe all *those* pretty
sheep—"and she pointed in the general direction of the
Elflands "—but not me." And this time she did walk
away, taking off her bass as she went.

The elf grabbed the edge of the stage, to vault onto it.
Then Strider was there, a defending knight in a ragged
Danceland t-shirt, as if he'd appeared out of the air. He
set those long white hands of his on the guy's shoulders,
spun him around, and gripped his lapels.

Suddenly Strider let go and took a step backward. For
a moment I felt a dropping feeling in my guts, wondering
if he was hurt, if the Elflander had done something to him.
But they each took a step sideways, and I could see wari-
ness and surprise in Strider's face, but no pain.

The Elflander had a long, angular face, with thin lips,
a high-bridged nose, and slender eyebrows that winged up
at the ends. He was looking at Strider as if the latter were
something found growing on the floor of a public rest-
room.

Strider spoke an elvish name, rather cautiously. I won't
try to transcribe it.

The Elflander raised his chin a notch and let his upper
lip curl just a little. "You are not permitted to be free with
my name," he said.

"You're over the Border now. That name doesn't mean
piss-all here." Strider was usually politer than that, especially in a situation like this, where he's supposed to be
just doing his job. I don't know whether the Elflander had
meant to insult Strider or if the man was naturally arro-

gant—or naturally foolish. But Strider *always* knows exactly what he's said.

After a quick up-and-down look at Strider's habitual attire—the green Danceland shirt that looked as if someone had driven over it several times (which, in fact, Strider had), the blue jeans that seemed to be held together with patches and optimism—the Elflander said, "Little more than a savage. It is pitiful to know you are an elf."

"Yeah, well, you set a fine example for the race, rich boy. Go make trouble in somebody else's place." Strider took a step toward him, to make his point a little plainer.

The elf drew something from under the skirt of his coat. At first I thought it was one of the retractable metal antennas that gang members duel with sometimes. But he snapped it to its full length and slashed the tip across Strider's face with one quick motion, and it didn't leave a welt. It left a gash.

In front of me I heard Sai cry out, and I wondered where Goldy was. Trapped in the crowd, most likely. People were scrambling away in that mad, mindless fashion that tells you something has happened and no one knows what. Strider stumbled back against the stage, blood on the lower half of his face like a bandit's kerchief, and the Elflander pressed the attack grimly. A lunge caught Strider in the upper arm. Another pass sliced his t-shirt through the middle of the Danceland logo. It was too precise to be coincidence. I caught a glimpse of the bloody stripe across the skin beneath.

I was sticking my elbows into people, trying to get through to help. What I intended to do when I got there, I don't know. My motions seemed horribly slow, and the Elflander horribly fast. I had an awful vision of reaching Strider only to find him in bits on the floor.

He was, in fact, on his knees, one arm clutched over his middle, his other hand in a fist. Sai had broken through and was nearly in reach of that damn Faerie blade when Strider gasped, "No."

Sai stopped instantly, to my surprise, and looked to Strider for an explanation. The Elflander drew back a pace and lowered the tip of his blade just a little. Behind him Goldy stepped out of the crowd like a black phantom, ready to nail the stranger if he didn't like Strider's reason for not doing so. He had snatched a baseball bat from under some counter, and it hung loose at his side.

Strider shook the hair out of his face and turned cold, narrowed eyes on the Elflander. "This is an honor fight. Nobody gets this son of a bitch but me."

Sai stiffened and looked as if she would have objected, but Strider ignored her.

"And I *will*," he spat out.

The Elflander turned his back (a fine gesture of contempt, but *I* wouldn't have turned my back on Sai just then, whatever Strider's stated preference was). He saw Goldy for the first time, and was obviously startled. But Goldy smiled evilly and bowed him through the crowd, which parted grudgingly. Every face I saw among them was turned to the Elflander, hard with hate. Strider is not always easy to like, but he's one of *ours*.

Just before the door, the Elflander turned. He had returned his cutter into his gaudy jacket, and he drew himself up with, I'll admit, a certain elegance. Addressing Strider, the stage, or us all, he said, "We shall continue this matter sometime soon."

"Damn straight," Strider grunted.

The two locked eyes. Then the Elflander glanced away and smiled thinly. He bowed as though we had all come to pay court to him, swirled, and was gone.

Sai and I helped Strider to his feet. I remembered the band only then, but they had left the stage. I was glad of it.

Wolfboy was holding the door to the back hall open for us. He looked impassive, even for him. We got Strider into the office and made him sit on the couch, but he refused to lie down. Sai got the first aid kit.

Strider pulled the shirt off over his head, with a fair quantity of teeth-gritting. The Elflander had gotten in a few licks that I hadn't seen. It always looks bad when an elf is wounded; it's the combination of gore on that pale skin and elvin blood's tendency to clot slower than human. And of course, it looks worse when the elf is a friend.

I filled a bowl with water at the office sink and brought it, with a couple of towels, to Sai. She started with Strider's face. The water in the bowl changed color quickly. There was a lot of silence, broken only by Strider's occasional swearing. I wanted to say something cheerful. Plenty of things came to mind, all of them abysmally stupid. I kept quiet.

Goldy stuck his head in. "Is it as bad as it looks?" he asked.

Sai frowned, but Strider shook his head. "I'll live. Mostly slashes, and none of them deep. The bastard knew what he was doing." He grinned suddenly, which was almost frightening. "When he drew on me, he'd lost it for a second. But when he started cutting . . ."

"What was that objectionable little tool of his? Any idea?"

"It's a goddamn dueling toy in the Elflands," Strider replied.

I think we were all equally startled. After Strider's near-silence on the subject of his life in Faerie, a sentence like that one sounded like the whole Alexandrian library.

Sai rummaged in the first aid kit, found a tube of Gold-N-Rod Creme, and began to streak it across the slashes on Strider's skin. Though she was careful, he said some remarkably inventive things, and when she did his face she had to hold him by the hair to keep his head still. I watched the stuff draw the edges of the skin together, appreciating that miracle more than I ever had. In the Elflands, of course, it works instantly and prevents scars from forming at all. That probably explained the Elflander's perfect face, given his habits. But maybe he was just very good with his fencing gadget. Lucky him.

Goldy looked helplessly at Wolfboy and me. We shrugged, about in unison. "Strider, my lad," he said finally, "are you quite sure you don't want me to find him, cut off his pretty braid, and see that he eats it?"

"The hell you will!" Sai said, and her voice made us all jump, even Strider. "If he doesn't want to do it himself, I'm gonna, you hear me? Oh, shit." She turned away and banged her fist against her thigh.

Strider squeezed her shoulder. "Hey, all of you, why don't you take a walk? I don't exactly feel like talking right now. Okay?"

Sai looked up at him.

"Yeah," he said gently, "you too."

She nodded and stood. Wolfboy and I were already on our way out. Sai followed, closed the door behind her, and we all stood in the hall feeling useless.

At last Goldy said, "Ah, well. Friday night, a band that will draw half of Bordertown when the word gets out, and only two of us on the floor. Nothing we can't manage, yes?" He looked at Sai.

Sai pursed her lips, then shook her head slowly. She held up one finger.

"Oh dear," said Goldy.

"Please, Goldy? I gotta get out of here. I'd just take this out on some poor jerk out front."

Goldy sighed. "Very well. Don't do anything foolish, will you?"

Sai grinned wearily at him, and went down the hall toward the back door.

As we went the other way, back to the main room, Wolfboy tapped his chest, and Goldy said, "You'll fill in?" Wolfboy nodded. Goldy shook his head. "If there's any more trouble, wait for me, hmm? You may look like Captain Fangs'n'Fur, but you're a pussycat in real life." Wolfboy growled at him, and we all felt a little bit better.

Dancer had obviously held things together in the aftermath. The crowd had stayed, the band was onstage powering up and tuning, though the White Lady wasn't back on yet. I wondered how *I* would feel, knowing that someone who'd sliced up Strider with no great provocation was very, very angry with me. I began to wonder if she'd like someone to walk her home. . . .

Tick-Tick met us by the door. "I'll buy," she offered.

"Thank you, but no." Goldy said. "I'm going to need every wit I have left. And as of this moment, all my breaks are canceled." He gave us a little salute and went back to work. Wolfboy glanced at Goldy's back as if thinking how rarely the Ticker offered to buy, then shook his head sadly and left us to get a shirt from Val so everyone would know he was on duty. I think Wolfboy likes uniforms more than the rest of us.

"Well, *I'll* let you buy me something," I said. Maybe I should've offered to watch the place, too, but I look bad in green.

"Good. I refuse to get drunk alone, just now."

We didn't actually get drunk. Valda set dark bottles down for both of us and let us drink some before she asked, "Is he okay?"

I thought about it. "That depends on your definition of 'okay.' Emotionally, no comment. Physically, he'll be fine in a while, though he'll have a peachy dueling scar."

"Dueling," Val spat. "That wasn't goddamn dueling." she wiped a glass with a furious motion. "He cut up Strider the way you'd cut the head off a weed. And Strider without even a pocket knife on him . . ."

That was when my body and mind caught up with each other. I found myself tight all over and inclined to shake.

"Drink up," the Ticker said solemnly. "We're all alive, and in a year this'll be nothing but an anecdote."

"Only if something worse happens in the meantime," Valda muttered.

The White Lady came back onstage then, and the band

started up. Even Wild Hunt couldn't get me to dance any more that night. But I let the music erode the tension in me, and clear my head a little. Watching that white elvin woman helped me too; the very sight of her was like a cold compress to the forehead.

I was halfway through my second bottle before I said, "Ticker?"

"Mm-hm?"

"Why are the Trio the way they are?"

She raised her eyebrows. "Which way?"

I struggled with the answer—I hadn't had quite enough beer to loosen my tongue. "Goldy and Sai have suddenly gone a little bloodthirsty. And Strider, for that matter. If someone cut you up like that, how would you react?"

"I'd lie down and moan for a week."

"Well, of course. But would you . . ."

"Swear vengeance, and insist that I be allowed first crack at the beggar? I don't *think* so."

"Would you expect me to do it for you?"

"Heavens, no!"

"Good. Though I don't know what I *would* do. And yet, we're as close as Goldy and Strider are."

"Closer." She finished her beer. "Where is all this going?"

I shrugged. "I'm not sure. But I don't like the Terrible Trio's reaction any more than I like what they're reacting to."

Tick-Tick thought about that for a while. "I think it's just steam. They've been playing their parts for so long— you know, Borderland's baddest—and this reminds them that they're mortal." She looked at the empty bottle. "My, two beers do make me profound."

"Chatty, anyway." I beamed at her. She slugged me.

After a minute, I asked her, "You think he knew him?"

She blinked. "Strider and the pretty boy?"

I nodded.

"You think he didn't?"

I hated not knowing what had really gone on out there on the dance floor. I hated worse knowing that I probably never would. If Strider didn't want to talk about it, he wouldn't. We all have secrets in Bordertown; I suppose everyone has secrets in the World and in Faerie, but their secrets are smaller—and maybe more desperate. At least we can think of ourselves as—well, what's that line from the song by Locas Tambien? "We're tragic, romantic figures / We're so much cooler than you!"

From then until closing, we did nothing more demanding than listen to the music and spend the Ticker's money.

Wild Hunt came back for an encore, and then had to come back for another one even after Dancer turned the lights on. They finally got people settled down and ready to go home by resorting to a ballad, "Jenny on the Hill." The White Lady put down her bass and sang it, in a style that was brutally simple and wonderfully effective. It took the melodrama out of the ending and made it seem that lost love and premature death were simply the way of the tragic world. I had to pretend to sneeze when the song was over, so I'd have an excuse to blow my nose.

Tick-Tick went to help herd people out the door.

"Orient!" Valda called.

I turned and found her holding up a push broom. "So you want to stay after closing like the employees?"

"Oh, lord," I sighed, and took the broom. Wolfboy joined me in stacking chairs—all except the one Goldy dropped into and refused to leave.

He looked more drained than I'd ever seen him, and a little tense around the mouth.

"That bad?" I asked him.

"I doubted I'd live to see this moment. I don't suppose you'd be so kind as to fetch me a beer?"

"The dying bouncer's last request," I said, and handed Wolfboy the broom. He snarled at me.

When I came back with the sweating bottle, Goldy said, "Seen your little runaway lately?"

I'd forgotten Caramel, frankly. "No."

Goldy shook his head. "We may have lost her, then. I'm afraid that the events of the evening scared her away."

"Can't blame her for that." I remembered my last sight of her jaunty, foolish pheasant feather. I'd felt a sneaking smug pleasure, one I hadn't admitted to myself then, that thanks to me she'd gotten into what might prove to be the concert of the year. I felt dreary suddenly, and very, very old.

Wolfboy looked up then, and Goldy and I followed his gaze. The White Lady was crossing the dance floor toward us. She was even more of an apparition in the dusty setting of Danceland with the houselights on. Once there were angels, and they must have looked like that.

She smiled, a lovely curving of her carved alabaster lips. "May I sit?" Her right hand moved in a fluid arc toward the stacked chairs, and her rings all flickered.

Wolfboy grabbed a chair and set it out for her with a little bow. "Thank you," she said with a grave smile. I wondered if she'd like one to rest her feet on. Hell, why use a chair? I'd get down on all fours and she could rest 'em on my back.

"You—all of you—were wonderful," I said, and felt like an idiot.

She laughed. She had the kind of laugh that made you want to say a lot of amusing things. "That's very sweet of you."

"And very true," Goldy said solemnly.

She smiled and tucked her chin. It was a charming gesture. "We don't often play in concert, and it's difficult for me—I feel very shy in front of an audience. But everyone here was so excited, so kind to us. . . ." She fluttered her white hands. She had three rings on her right hand, all of elf-silver and sapphires, with only her middle finger and thumb bare of them. She wore none on her left hand;

they're hard on the guitar neck. A sapphire swung from each of her earlobes.

"There was a little too much excitement tonight, I'm afraid," Goldy said, "for which I am heartily sorry."

The smile fell off her face, chased away by something that might have been fright. She looked down. "I'm sorry, too," she said softly. "The one who made the trouble . . . he was my fault, I think."

"Your fault?" I asked. It was startled out of me, I suppose.

"He . . . we were lovers, for a short time. He is not willing to leave it at that."

So that was half of the night's mystery solved. I felt a little sorry for the Elflander, even as I felt alarmed for her. It wouldn't be easy to accept the loss of the White Lady with anything like grace.

We all fell silent, not wanting to pry, but not sure how to change the subject. In Bordertown, even more than in the World, you tread very lightly around personal matters—your own or someone else's.

The pressure was relieved when Dancer came up to us, Tick-Tick dawdling along behind. "Good show," Dancer said to the White Lady. "Damn good show." Then I realized that she was carrying the bag that held the night's receipts. Business with the band leader, of course. We all scattered to various jobs.

I managed to be the one by the door, though, when the White Lady was ready to leave.

"Will you be all right?" I asked her.

"What? Oh, yes, of course. You mustn't worry about me." She offered me a lovely smile, a little tinged with sadness. I don't care if she *was* half a head taller than me. I felt protective.

"If he's out there waiting for Strider, you could be in trouble."

She shook her head. "He won't hurt me. But I'll watch

for him, and be careful.'' She touched my hand lightly, and added, "You are very kind."

I was struck quite dumb, of course, in both the original and the more corrupt sense of the word.

"Perhaps I will see you again?"

"I'd like that," I said finally, getting my tongue loose from the roof of my mouth. "People around here usually know where I am."

She looked amused. "But who would I ask them for?"

Oh. Right. "My name's Orient."

"Orient. And mine is Linden." She touched me again, a fingertip to my hand, and slipped out into the street and the dark.

I leaned against the door for a moment to catch my breath. Wolfboy was watching me from the bar; he grinned when I met his eyes.

I walked over to him. "I was only asking if she'd be all right," I muttered. He treated me to one of his hair-raising giggles.

Valda called down the counter to us. "Guys? One more favor? Can you take the bottles back to the alley?"

Wolfboy spread his hands out, as if to imply that we would do anything for her. I wasn't feeling quite *that* generous, but I wasn't above hauling a box or two.

Val had already loaded the empties into the crates. The brewer would pick them up in the morning from the alley. Wolfboy and I shouldered a few each and headed for the back.

The way led past the office door, and I wondered if I should knock, see if Strider was all right. From the way Wolfboy slowed down, I suspected he was wondering the same thing.

"Oh, hell," I said, "why not? If he objects, he'll just break my face, right?" I knocked. There was no answer. I tried again, a little louder, and when nothing happened, I opened the door a little. Then I stuck my head in.

The room was just as we'd left it, but Strider wasn't in

it. I pulled my head back out and shut the door. "He must be all right," I said. "He's gone."

Wolfboy thought about that for a second, then shrugged. We went on, through the door at the end of the hall that opened into Danceland's private garage, and through that to the alley door.

All right, it's not really an alley, it's a very small cul-de-sac, with the building's back door located near the closed end. So it's black as the inside of an intestine out there on any night except when the moon is bright. Tonight, unfortunately, the moon was bright.

He was lying in a grotesque parody of ease, hands folded over his stomach, legs straight. He looked like a tomb statue in white marble. It was a long and horrible moment before I realized it was not Strider. Then I saw the braid and recognized it, and knew whose corpse it was in Danceland's alley.

I've been staring at that last sentence for fifteen minutes. I've tried to go on and describe the body, and failing that, to simply recount, in order, who did what. After all, this is why I'm writing, this is the event I'm trying to make some tentative sense out of. But even though I can see, in my mind, the Elflander's body—all too well, in fact, which may have as much to do with why I haven't slept yet as this narrative does—I can't write it down. It makes me shake.

Dancer sent Val to alert the coppers, and Tick-Tick to Strider's and Sai's place to warn them. The Ticker came back and reported that they weren't there. Just as we were trying to decide if we were relieved by that, Strider came in the front doors. I wish now that one of us had thought to ask what he'd come back for, but I don't suppose the answer would have been of any use. It's just a loose end, like where he'd gone in the first place, like where Sai had gone when she'd left the club, like whether anyone could swear that Goldy and Wolfboy had been inside Danceland *all* night, like whether Linden was bothered enough by her old boyfriend that she'd want him dead. Even the Ticker's alibi is low-grade. Hell, maybe they all did it. The only person whose innocence I'm certain of is me. And if this goes on, I'll be asking people to corroborate my memories.

So the cops arrived and did all the investigative things we'd done and a great many more besides, and finally took Strider away with them to the lock-up. It was the obvious thing to do, but it didn't make it any easier to watch.

The sun's been up for three hours. I'd forgotten this particular time of day existed. I went back to Danceland after writing the last paragraph. I wanted a cig, and I wanted my damn copy of *Stick Wizard*, because I knew I wasn't going to sleep. Both things were still in the sidecar. The Ticker had parked the bike in Danceland's garage for safekeeping and gone home with Sai, to keep her from being alone and from doing something stupid.

I went to see if someone was around to let me in, or if I could get in by myself. I had to go through the cul-de-sac, of course. I didn't get in the garage, didn't even try, because I found something on the ground near the street end of the cul-de-sac, and it distracted me.

So I don't have my cigs. I have a pheasant feather with a distinctive nick out of one edge, dirty now from lying in the mud. I've been picking it up and twirling it or sliding it through my fingers, as if it's an impression ball, ready to pour out its stored song at a touch. I'll sleep now. I have to, whatever I might dream. But I want to know what it means. Caramel, where are you now?

Doesn't seem right to scribble in Orient's diary. I look at my writing on his pages, and it's like I came to Orient's grave to make a speech (pretty silly idea, huh?) and found myself puking on the funeral flowers. Too late now. Should've tried this in pencil maybe, and erased it if I didn't like it. Sorry, Orient.

I want to say that this is Lone Wolf's writing that you're

reading now, but Orient calls me Wolfboy, like most people. Could be worse. Guess I'm grateful I don't have to say it's Dogbreath writing this.

It's not easy. I look at all those pages Orient wrote, and I'm jealous, and I'm sad. He began with last night, but I'll begin earlier. Orient's my friend, or maybe, was my friend. That's why I'm doing this, continuing what he started. Even if my written words aren't much better than my spoken ones. Orient and I are a bit alike, you see, so it's more than just finishing something a friend began.

That looks stupid: Orient and I are a bit alike. But it's true. Maybe he's not as quiet as I am, but he watches more than he talks. He likes to read, 'cause he thinks there's more to living than most people do. He—

I hate writing this. God, I hope he's all right.

He and I, we've both been changed by the Change. I don't know who had it worse. Orient's fey. That means "touched by Faerie." He grew up in the World, and people always thought he was strange 'cause he could find things. Things he'd never seen. All he needed to know was that something existed, and—

Shit. I'm writing about him in the past tense. I won't do that anymore, until we know something. And if he's dead, I'm sorry. This stupid journal will be my tribute to him. Maybe I'll burn it, or throw it in the Big Bloody, or see if I can get it published. Something. If he's alive, he'll get to read this. If he gets to read this, I want him to know that he's a pissbrain and the only reason I wrote this was to mess up his stupid diary. The Human Compass writes about me as Wolfboy. What a pissbrain.

I hope he's okay.

All Orient needs to know is that something exists, and he can find it. He told me about driving through some strange city with his Mom when he was eight. She wanted Greek olives for some reason. Maybe she was taking salad to a family get-together, or something. Orient pointed off in the distance, saying, "There." She laughed at first, but he got mad. I can imagine it: "There, Mom! There!" And she got mad at his insistence. And she followed his directions to prove that he was wrong, 'cause he had never been in this city, he could not know where to find Greek olives, he did not even know what Greek olives were since she had never made this salad before. She would prove her point to him, then she would spank him, and he would never mention this nonsense again.

Orient led her to a Greek grocery that had the most beautiful olives you could imagine. Big, purple—

All right, I'm making that part up. Maybe they were tiny, dried, bitter olives. The point is, they were there.

And the point is, she stared at Orient like he was what he wasn't.

And the point is, that's when he quit thinking of himself as a person and started thinking of himself as a freak.

And he never mentioned that nonsense again.

'Course, that didn't do any good. He couldn't stop finding stuff. People couldn't stop noticing. People don't like what they don't understand. People don't know that the trick is to try to understand what they don't like. Orient was a freak, and in spite of being a handsome, bright kid, he was fey. Everyone whispered it. Some people shouted it. Some people laughed at him. Some people beat him. After a while, he got tired of pretending he didn't hear and he didn't hurt. He did what almost all fey kids do. He ran away to beautiful Bordertown. Just like the kid last night, I imagine, and if it's different, it doesn't matter.

Started off completely differently for me. I wasn't bright and I wasn't unusual and I wasn't fey. I was a little geek with zits who wanted all the pretty girls, and none of the pretty girls wanted me. Not because I was fey. Because I was nothing special. What I would have given then to be fey. . . .

So I did what all kids do who want to be special. I ran away. Just like the kid last night, maybe. And I ran with a couple of gangs in B-town, and I found that one way to be special was to develop a rep for a smart mouth. I was extremely high one night in the Dancing Ferret and some elf woman was talking too loudly about short-lived humans and their habits. So I said, "Yap, yap, yap. What a—" Well, you can guess what I called her by what she turned me into.

She stared at me at first. She obviously expected something more. Even elves forget sometimes about the way magic ebbs and flows in the Borderlands. Then she laughed, and everyone else laughed, even the Packies I had come with. I turned and ran. Loped, maybe. I could see my hands and arms, and I felt my body hurting and changing. I got my lifelong wish then. Even in Bordertown, I was no longer like anyone else.

There's a million stories in the big city, and . . . Nah.

The thing is, Orient and I went through the same things, even if we did them in reverse order, for different reasons. The same past. We both knew too much about being outsiders. Maybe that's part of the reason he became friends with me. Doesn't explain the rest of our friends, or maybe it does. Orient said I liked playing dress-up better than most of our crowd, and that's true so far as it goes. I like feeling a little less like something waiting for a silver bullet and feeling more like part of a community. But I could join any of the thousands of little gangs that form the greater gangs of the Pack, the Rats, the Bloods. Or even one of the independent gangs: Dragonfire, the Horn Dance, Commander X's Kids . . . I don't want it. Orient forgets that he was the one who once suggested we pick a name for ourselves, and I was the one who vetoed it with a chopping motion.

I'm not writing about it. I ought to. Somebody reading this is going to wonder what the hell happened, so I'll be nice.

The early part of Friday night went pretty much like Orient told it. He was a little more taken with the White Lady, Linden, than I was. I thought she was too fond of playing tricks with her voice, and I've seen elf and human and halfie women who did more for me. I thought the real talent in the Wild Hunt was the drummer and the hyper-harpist and the halfie on elfpipe. Big deal. The band's good and deserves its fame.

I heard a little more of the argument between the Elf-lander and the White Lady than Orient did. I hear a lot better than I did before I was changed. And I know a little more Elvish than Orient, so the argument was clearer to me. The Elflander wanted Linden to come back with him, he wanted her to come back now, it was important, and her life in Bordertown wasn't. I'll bet that really endeared him to her.

I can't add anything else up until the end. Orient went into the alley first, moving awkwardly with three crates of empties. I knew something was wrong first. I smelled blood. I'm not as good as my rep; I didn't know what kind of blood it was. I smelled a lot of things, most of them alley things, and some of them things that the Elflander did as he died. I attributed those to the alley, too, at first.

It was the stupid Faeriecloth coat that tipped me off. It caught the light from the back door. I wondered why the stranger ditched it, then I grinned, thinking someone had swiped it from him to teach him a lesson about Soho. I was still grinning when I saw that he was still in his coat. I was still grinning when I saw what had been done with him while he was in his coat. I made a grunting sound and set down my load of crates.

Orient turned. Then he saw what I was looking at, and we both stared for a little longer, then he went to the side and threw up. I don't think he left that part out because he was ashamed. I think it wasn't important to him.

The Elflander's coat was in ribbons, like his skin, and the light made him all shiny with elfblood. I don't know why I didn't vomit. Maybe dogs can vomit for emotional reasons. The Elflander's long white braid had been stuffed into his mouth, and a part of my mind was saying that wasn't very original while another part stared in horror. His dueling toy was still in his hand.

Orient and I went into the back room without having to suggest it to each other. Neither of us wanted to have to look at the corpse. Orient leaned against a stack of whiskey kegs and brought up both hands to push back his black, red-tipped hair. Or maybe just to massage his temples. He said, "Strider's in trouble."

I grunted.

"Can we cover it up?" That was phrased as a question more out of habit, I think, of being considerate of me. He answered it himself. "No way. Might get Dancer in trouble with the coppers, if we wait. Might get Strider in more trouble. Shit." He looked at me then, face pale and controlled. "I'll tell Dancer. It's her alley, after all."

I nodded. I was as happy to pass on the decision. Now I wish to god I'd sat down with Orient and talked about what we saw, him babbling, me scribbling on something. Maybe he wouldn't be missing now if we had.

Having read what Orient wrote, I can guess what thoughts were going through his head as we went to tell Dancer. Strider did it. No, Strider'd meet the Elflander near the river or in a bombed-out house or in a deserted theater, and they'd fight until honor was satisfied or Strider was dead. That's how Strider thinks, the simple git.

Sai did it then, to protect Strider from the stranger who had cut her lover for fun. No, Sai wouldn't jump someone in the alley, and Sai wouldn't go after him until she knew Strider was fine. Then she'd arrange for the stranger to be without his little dueling toy—have some friends surround him, or something. And she'd show him why she was So-Ho's middleweight champion for a season and a half, until she decided she was too pretty to stay a boxer. Sai wouldn't kill. Not like this, anyway.

That meant Goldy did it, because he was frustrated that he couldn't do anything else to show he cared for Strider, because he felt that he should have stopped the stranger sooner somehow, because he stepped outside to grab a breath of fresh air and saw the Elflander waiting for Strider— And that didn't work either, because Goldy's not like that, no more than the rest of us are. In fact, Goldy might take a certain delight in tossing the Elflander to the cops for a night in the B-town jail. Wouldn't do that with a local, but with a Faerie lord in a silly coat . . .

And that left Orient with one last suspect, his White Lady. He wouldn't like that, 'cause he had a crazy crush on Linden. But Orient's smart. He'd weigh the possibility, and it wouldn't work any better than any of the rest. You don't carve up a crazy boyfriend. You just wait patiently until he finds someone else to pester. No wonder Orient seemed so frustrated in his last notes.

We stepped into the main room and Orient said, ''The elf that made trouble tonight . . .'' I was the only one who knew why he stopped, but everyone could tell something was wrong.

Val came over and put her arm around his back. ''What?'' she said.

''He's dead. In the back alley. He's all . . .'' Orient winced. ''. . . cut up.''

''Fuck,'' Goldy said. Goldy never swears.

Dancer and the Ticker went back to look while Orient tried to describe it to Goldy and Val. His words didn't do much to tell it, but his tone did. I was actually glad I couldn't talk, myself.

''We call the cops,'' Dancer said when she came back.

''No,'' Goldy whispered, and I thought there was going to be worse trouble.

Dancer didn't hear, or maybe she's wise enough to know when to pretend she didn't. ''Val, go tell Strider and Sai what happened. Tick-Tick will go tell the cops.'' She glanced at the Ticker. ''Better take the avenues to the cop shop, 'cause the short cuts might not be safe this time of night. And I wouldn't be surprised if you didn't even leave for another five minutes or so. Bikes can be so hard to start, sometimes.''

The Ticker smiled a tiny bit, more in recognition than in humor. Goldy nodded, said, ''Yes. That's right.''

Dancer brewed a pot of coffee while we sat around, not really talking about anything important, people saying things like ''Good band,'' and ''Bastard deserved it,'' and ''Fuckin' *hell*!'' and no one bothering to answer any of the things. Dancer poured coffee for us all, and I realized that was another first. Not the freebies, 'cause Dancer can be so generous I sometimes wonder how she stays in business. But she never worked behind the counter. Val usually made decent coffee, and Goldy brewed great coffee. Dancer's tasted like she was the one who taught Goldy, but even Orient's ''good coffee'' seemed perfunctory.

Val came back and said Sai and Strider weren't home. I didn't like that. Then Strider came in. I liked that less. He was pocketing his key to the place and saying, ''Anybody seen Sai?'' He stopped, stared at us staring at him. ''What'd I say?'' And when no one answered immediately, he added, ''Hey, if my part's crooked, I'm sorry, I lost my comb.'' His hair, as usual, was a perfect white mane.

Goldy shook his head.

''That's a joke,'' Strider said, moving toward the bar where we had gathered. Then he stopped and said quietly, ''Something happened to Sai.''

''No, Strider,'' Goldy said. ''Not that we know of.''

''It's that elf,'' Dancer said. ''He's dead back by the empties. Cut up bad, like someone hated him.'' That was obviously a warning, not an accusation. ''Tick-Tick's gone for the cops. I told her to. If I didn't, they'd shut me down.''

Strider's pale face went paler, which is some trick. The new scar was like a lightning flash on his cheek. He sat on a stool and whispered, ''Oh, to sail a sunless sea.'' It took me a minute to realize that was a Faerie oath, and before I did, Strider sounded more like himself. "It's all right, Dancer."

"I told her to stall. You could get out—"

He shook his head. "And go where? This is Border-town. I'm Strider. I don't want anything else."

"Don't be a bigger fool!" Goldy hit the table with the flat of his chocolate-brown hand, and our cups danced.

Strider smiled slightly. "Hey, Goldy, don't give me that. You know."

"Yeah, you bastard." Goldy turned his back on us all. His broad shoulders shook, and no one spoke for a minute or two.

"He's dead," Strider said, not quite asking.

"Yes," Orient said.

"Fine. Then I don't have to see him." He glanced at Dancer. "Coffee, please?"

"Yeah, sure." She slid him a cup.

"Goldy?" he asked, lifting the cup to his lips.

Goldy grunted, sounding like me, I suppose. He didn't turn around.

"Tell Sai I love her. Tell her not to do anything stupid. And don't you do anything stupid, either."

Goldy's bright head bobbed in a nod.

"Got any poems for me, Wolfboy?"

I shook my head. I hadn't written anything in three weeks, but I knew I'd write something soon.

"You're innocent," Orient said, and his voice was accusing and angry.

"Maybe."

Orient looked upward in exasperation. "You could say so, then."

Goldy said, "He doesn't have to."

"No," said Orient. "I guess not."

Tick-Tick came back with the cops soon after that. I didn't recognize them as cops, not immediately. There's not a lot of law in B-town, and you almost never see the Silver Suits in uniform in SoHo. Law only comes in for important things, like an ugly killing that too many people will hear of. The woman was about Dancer's age. Her hair was a sun-bleached brown with flecks of white, combed straight back from her forehead. Her skin was lighter than Goldy's and darker than Tick-Tick's. She wore a loose cotton jacket cut from a pattern of tropic flowers, black slacks, and black loafers. Her eyes were hidden behind silver glasses, probably Night Peepers. She kept one hand in her slacks pocket, maybe 'cause there was a weapon there, maybe 'cause it made her jacket hang better. The elf was less conspicuous, with his white hair cut very close to his skull and dressed in a sea-green suit.

"Name's Rico," the human said, not smiling. "My partner's Detective Linn. Anyone want to see a copper card?" I've always wondered about that name, 'cause the only c-card I ever saw was brass.

"It's all right, Sunny," Dancer said, and Goldy snickered.

"Good," Rico replied, looking at Dancer. "Sorry you're in this." Her head didn't move at all as she asked Goldy, "Something amusing?"

"Yeah," he said. "Sunny." Once we had a talk about why cops were called coppers. Goldy said that was because you could buy them cheap.

"For my cheerful disposition," Rico said. So far her face hadn't been any more expressive than her silver glasses. "Think it's funny, Walter?" Goldy didn't answer. At another time, the whole exchange would have been amusing, but it wasn't now. I think Rico agreed. She said, "Everyone stick around, okay? You—" she pointed at me. "—show me the body while Linn takes statements."

I can't say that she did anything more significant than we did. She lit the place with a torch spell, which impressed me until I saw that it only made everything more obvious, and more ugly. Rico whistled a low note as she looked at the Elflander. She walked around and studied things, not touching anything. Then she stood quietly, and

I figured she was doing what I was doing: trying to imagine it.

When she was ready to go, I stepped in front of her. I pointed at the body, pointed at the alley, and shrugged. Rico's about my height, so she looked straight at me in that way they must teach at cop school and said, "Aren't I going to do something more? What do you want? I should take fingerprints? I should try a spell to sense what happened here?"

I nodded.

"Right. Look, Lobo—" I realized it must have been the Ticker who told her my name."—even if we had the murder weapon, we probably wouldn't sense anything more than rage, quick heartbeats, and a real sick pleasure. And that last is a guess, so don't quote me. As for fingerprints, make me laugh. No murder weapon. In an alley, anything else is circumstantial. The whole case would probably end right here if it wasn't for two things." She held the back of her hand toward me and lifted her index finger. "Your friend made some crazy threats in front of three hundred people." She raised the next finger. "Someone killed Tejorinin Yorl."

I tucked my chin slightly, showing her I didn't understand.

"I don't know either," Rico admitted. "Not exactly. Some elf kid who just inherited something important in Faerie. Don't know why he came out here; maybe on vacation or something. But he was rich and important, and we've gotta get someone for his murder."

I almost hit her.

"I don't like it," Rico said. "Not at all. Dancer's told me about most of you, and I asked questions of your friend at my office. Sounds like you're all okay, for B-town kids. But facts are facts, Lobo. If we can find who's responsible, everything'll be fine. If we can't . . ." She shrugged and headed back into Danceland.

I stood there and thought about it, until she called back,

"C'mon, Lobo. I know you write. Linn'll want your statement too."

I just realized one of the reasons Orient might have started writing this account. It's a testimony. I thought it was a diary, or what he said: he couldn't sleep. Then I thought maybe he wanted to publish his version of the story in one of the street papers, maybe try to sell a book to one of the World presses: *I Ran with a Bordertown Gang* by "Orient." Yeah, sure. Orient's smarter than that.

Consciously or subconsciously, Orient was thinking about the same things Rico made me think about. Questions are being asked, and the answers have to go a long way. This Yorl was an Elflander, so there'll be reports going to Faerie at least, and maybe to the World as well. Which means, just maybe, this thing we're writing is going to be read by people who don't know dick about B-town.

I went in and listened to the last couple of stories. The elf cop had a notebook, and he wrote everything in. Strider claimed to have been walking around, just thinking. Goldy was moving around the floor all the time, he said, but the cops knew he could have ducked out for a few minutes while claiming to be in a back room or on the balconies. They wrote down the names of the members of Wild Hunt, but didn't seem too excited about getting anything from them. About the only time no one was watching them was while Yorl was slicing Strider, and Yorl was still alive when the band reassembled.

"What about Sai?" asked Rico.

"She went walking, too," said Goldy, not too happy.

Rico nodded. "It's a houseful of great alibis."

I sat there, scribbling on some paper that Dancer lent me. I could have interrupted the statements, I suppose, but I wanted to write out my theory in full. So I did, and it was short, only a paragraph like the following:

The killing was the work of a gang, three at least and probably more. I saw Yorl when he was cutting Strider on

*the dance floor. Yorl was good, like he'd studied that du-
eling gadget for years. He was too good to let himself be
carved all over, even by Strider. And this work was done
mostly for the fun of the carvers. You saw that. The business with the braid. Even if Strider killed Yorl, Strider
wouldn't do that. Yorl had to have been surrounded, and
as one kid distracted him, another cut him. Some sickies
probably heard talk about Strider and the Elflander and
decided to kill an outsider for fun, figuring Strider would
get the blame. Everyone on Ho Street had to be talking
about what happened in Danceland.*

"A gang," Rico said, when she joined me at a table.

I nodded.

"You're the only one with this gang theory."

I nodded again and gestured for her to give me back the
paper. When she did, I wrote something like:

*Orient doesn't know much about knife fights. He didn't
think about the cuts. Or about what it means, doing that
thing with the braid to a corpse. You blame him?*

I think she smiled a tiny bit, and that was worse than
the absence of expression.

"No, I don't. You want to pin this on the Bloods, the
Pack, or the Rats?"

I snorted in disgust and wrote:

*You think there's only a few gangs here? There are hun-
dreds. There are some really twisted bunches that hide
within the bigger gangs. They wear the colors of the Bloods
or the Pack or the Rats. They claim allegiance to the bigger gang and act like the rest of that gang is behind them.
Could be any of them.*

That little smile came back. "Dancer and I ran with the
Go-boys when I was your age. We were part of the Pack.
So, who do you favor?"

That made me stop, not because of what I wanted to
say, but because of the fact I was writing this for a cop.
Then I wrote: *You hear of an idiot named Fineagh Steel
who styled himself the leader of the Bloods?* Fineagh built

a little army of elf morons—they may live longer than us, but they can come just as stupid—then jackbooted around Soho for all of a week or two. Some kid took him out in a duel. I imagine a few of the bigger Blood gangs would've done something about him if the kid hadn't.

Rico nodded. "I hear he's dead. I hear his gang's scattered. You think this was the work of one of his lieutenants maybe?"

I shrugged.

"Doesn't work, Lobo." She took off her glasses and grinned at me. Her eyes weren't any friendlier than the glasses. "Why carve a strange elf? If they were jealous of him, they'd rough him up and steal his money, that's all. No need to get the cops down on everyone."

I nodded, wishing I had someone better to point at.

Rico folded up the page I'd written on and replaced her glasses. "Nice theory," she said. "No evidence to back it up." When she said that, it was like she'd kicked me, even though her voice sounded kind, for her. "Sorry." Then she tore up my statement and handed me the shreds. I stared at it. She said, "If I convinced anyone that Strider couldn't have done it by himself, we'd just have to lock up a couple of his friends, too." She patted the back of my hand and left me sitting at the table.

I decided not to tell anyone about it until I knew more. Maybe Orient would still be around if I'd showed the pieces of my statement to him.

Rico and Linn left with Strider when a van and a few Silver Suits showed up. The Silver Suits poked around and fingerprinted us all and did some mystical juju that obviously had as much effect as Rico expected, but now their report would be nice and fat. When they were done, one of them said none of us should disappear. Goldy laughed at that, but it's a little ominous, now that Orient's gone. The Silver Suits took away Yorl's body in a shiny black bag, and finally, Dancer said, "To hell with it. Good night, everybody.'' And we all wandered out into the good night.

It's Sunday. Still no Orient. I woke, went away, heard some interesting news, drank a whole lot of coffee. Now I have to do something while I wait, so I'll keep abusing Orient's journal.

I woke up around noon Saturday and didn't want to get out of bed. I lay there, thinking it was time to change the sheets and wishing I lived with somebody and wondered if maybe Strider did it. Time does that, lets you see things differently, sometimes in ways you wish it didn't. Whether he did or didn't, I like Strider. But what do I know about him? What do I know about myself? Maybe the killing was an accident, and then Strider had to figure out how to cover it up. If you accept that, it's not too hard to imagine him doing the rest, forcing himself to do something so atypical that no one would believe he had killed Yorl. Under normal circumstances, all he would need was a reasonable amount of doubt in the situation and charges would probably be dropped. He may never have known that he'd killed someone as important as Tejorinin Yorl.

Or maybe he knew exactly who he'd killed. What was Strider in the Elflands, before he was Strider?

The day was cooler than the day before, but that doesn't bother me. I found my other jeans and a corduroy jacket and decided not to bother with shoes. There's enough broken glass in B-town that that isn't the smartest thing to do, I suppose, but it makes people think I'm tough. The fact is I tended to run from trouble before I was changed. Now that I'm stronger and more perceptive, I run even faster.

I went to Sai's. She makes great huevos rancheros without the least provocation. And if she didn't feel like cooking for a stray, she might need some company.

She had company. Tick-Tick was there, sitting a little stiffly on a purple beanbag, maybe aware that it clashed with the red leather outfit that she wore. Sai wore a faded man's undershirt and cut-offs. Under her black bangs, her eyes were almost as red as Tick-Tick's leather. I made a little circular motion with my hand, and Sai smiled a tiny bit, saying, "Hi, Wolfboy. C'mon in. The Ticker toasted bagels, but I'm not too hungry."

I suppose I should mention that Sai was almost always hungry, but you probably get the idea that Friday night's events had everyone acting out of character.

Tick-Tick said, "Rico and her faithful elvin companion came by earlier."

I nodded and stuffed a bagel in my face.

"They didn't have anything useful to say," she said, and shrugged. "We didn't have anything useful to tell them."

"She said I could visit Strider," Sai said. "You want to come, too?"

I grabbed two bagels and followed. Sai took her bike, a beautiful blue thing that she called the Bat-cycle for some reason. I hopped into Orient's usual place in Tick-Tick's sidecar, which made me wonder where he was. I pointed at the seat and frowned, and the Ticker said, "I haven't seen him around. We were supposed to meet. We can swing by his place after seeing Strider."

The B-town Jail isn't particularly better or worse than most jails, I imagine, but I wouldn't want to stay there. Rico had left a note at the front desk, so we didn't have any trouble getting in. I wasn't too crazy about the man at the front desk, who shook his head as he looked at me and said, "You kids are getting weirder every year."

A couple of Silver Suits walked Strider into the waiting room and leaned up against the wall as if they were bored enough to sleep. One was bored by each door, and they both had three-foot sting-rods dangling from straps around their right wrists.

"Nice place," Tick-Tick said.

"You should try their breakfast," Strider answered.

"You're such an asshole," Sai said.

"I'm glad to see you, too, love."

They kissed, and the Ticker and I tried to pretend we were as bored as the guards.

"We're getting you out of here," Sai said quietly.

"No whispering," one guard called. "Besides, you aren't."

"He's innocent!" Sai said.

"You're confessing?" the guard asked. Before Sai could say anything more, he said, "Look, kids. Behave yourselves, and we won't bug you."

"Yeah," Strider said, seconding the guard's advice.

"Okay," Sai said. "Okay. But I don't like this, Strider. I want you out of here."

"No chance for bail," Strider said. "I just hope I don't lose my tan."

"Don't be a pain," Tick-Tick said. "You just make it worse for Sai when you act like that."

Sai quickly shook her head. "No. I understand."

"Hey," Strider said softly, and he stroked her chin with his forefinger. "I'm okay. Maybe I'll get a lot of reading done."

"Rico said the charge is Murder One," Sai said. "I don't want you to get that much reading done."

Tick-Tick's elvin features were very grim as she said, "You won't get any reading done if they opt for a memory-wipe, Strider. Not until you learn how again. And if they pick death—"

Strider turned away suddenly. "Trial's weeks away. 'Sides, they'll do what they'll do, okay? You guys better leave now."

"No," the Ticker said.

"I can go back to my cell anytime," Strider said.

"You certainly could," the Ticker admitted. "That won't help you, and it won't help Sai. Is that what you want?"

"I want out," Strider said.

The Ticker nodded. "I know. We have to find who did

it. The cops need someone to hang for this one. Maybe literally.''

Strider glanced at Sai. She looked at her lap, and I suddenly knew why Strider was being so stupid. I suspected it earlier, but I knew it then. He thought Sai did it. He was too stupid to realize that if she had and he'd been arrested, she would've confessed immediately. I wondered if she'd already considered confessing anyway, just to save Strider. I decided to ask Tick-Tick or Orient later. No point in giving Sai the idea.

I pulled out a sheet of scrap paper and wrote out something like what I'd written for Rico about my theory, then added: *Problem is, we don't have anyone likely. Any ideas?*

One of the guards read it before letting Strider have it. Strider read it and his eyes flicked wide from their usual squint. "You sure about this, Wolfboy?"

I held my hands wide, like: Who's ever *sure*? Then I nodded.

Sai and Tick-Tick read the note together. Tick-Tick said, "You should've said something—Oops."

I waved downward to show I'd let that pass, then grabbed the note back and scribbled: *Rico didn't like it. Where's a suspect? Who'd want to carve a stranger, even one as bad as Yorl?*

"Wharf Rats, perhaps," Tick-Tick mused. "A chance for fun, and a chance to blame someone else."

"Not all the Rats are like that," Sai said. Her brother's a Rat.

"It only takes three or four like that," Tick-Tick said.

"There were five Rats in Danceland last night," Strider said, and we all got very quiet.

"Is it my turn to call you an idiot?" Tick-Tick asked.

"No," Strider said. "Hers." He pointed at Sai.

"I'll save it for later," Sai said. "What about these Rats?"

"They had a table up on the left balcony. Near the wom-

en's room. I was watching them before Yorl decided I was
a fencing dummy."

I lifted my hand. Tick-Tick glanced at me, then told
Strider and Sai, "After you two left, Lobo filled in on the
floor."

"Did you see the Rats?" Strider asked, surprisingly
hopeful for Strider. "One was a little brown-haired guy
with tiny round glasses. Wire rims. The rest were, well,
Rats."

Rats aren't usually distinctive as anything more than
Rats. Sai's brother is a nice guy, but he's a River addict
like most of them, and he dresses poorly and smells a little
funny. . . . I didn't think about any of that. I just shook
my head.

"You went by that corner," Tick-Tick said to me, 'cause
she likes things very clear. "After Strider and Yorl fought.
And the Rats weren't there." I nodded. I'd remember Rats.
The Ticker added, "Was this when you and Goldy first
made the rounds?" I nodded again. Tick-Tick smiled.
"Rico might like your theory a little better, now."

"Yeah," said Strider without any emotion at all. "Some
Rats did it. She'll love that."

"Still . . ." Tick-Tick said.

"We'll find them," Sai announced.

Strider nodded, not particularly hopeful, and said to Sai,
"I thought . . ."

"I know," she said, and the Ticker and I looked away
again. We talked for another couple of minutes about
nothing particularly promising. When it was time to go, I
gave Strider a poem I wrote late the night before. It was
a stupid thing about owls flying over dark forests, but he
read it and said, "Nice. I'll put it on my wall."

His own damn wall. That was when I could've cried.

Tick-Tick watched me give him the poem, then suddenly began patting her pockets. She came up with the
new *Stick Wizard* and passed it on, saying, "From Orient
and me."

Sai looked sad. "I didn't bring you anything."

"Yes, you did," he said, and kissed her lightly on the lips. Then his mouth quavered a fraction, and he turned and said to the guards, "Let's go."

Sai watched him leave, then said, "Where to?"

"Orient," Tick-Tick announced.

"He can find a Rat with round glasses?"

"I don't know," the Ticker admitted. "But it's worth a try."

And it would have been, if we could have found Orient. We went to his flat, then to Danceland, where we told Goldy and Dancer and Val what we'd learned. None of them had seen Orient. Val was annoyed because he'd promised to buy her lunch at Taco Hell. So we went back to Orient's apartment. The Ticker had a spare key, so we went in and bitched about him being out of anything worth drinking. Then Sai saw his diary open on the kitchen table.

"You shouldn't read that," Tick-Tick said.

"It's about last night," Sai replied.

"Ah," Tick-Tick said, and she read over Sai's left shoulder while I read over Sai's right. Tick-Tick finished first. She moved away and said, "Why didn't he come get me?"

"He didn't want to wake you," Sai said hesitantly: "Maybe he didn't want to wake me."

Tick-Tick didn't answer. She looked out the window, then said, "I'm spreading the word. I'll tell Horn Dance, I'll tell Scully, I'll tell Commander X's Kids. Somebody must have seen him somewhere."

"I'll go too,' Sai said.

"Someone should wait here, in case he returns."

They both stared at me until I volunteered with a nod. I reread Orient's entry, then began my own. No Orient. I woke up this morning on his rug—which needs to be swept or beaten. Goldy came by with a turkey sandwich and a quart of orange juice. He brought coffee beans. (I write that hoping Orient will read this and suffer a little for troubling his friends.) Goldy made a big pot of coffee and told me that the gangs are turning B-town inside out. Everyone was calling in favors. Sai has her brother's friends cruising the wharfs. Goldy talked to a few Pack leaders who hope he'll join their gangs someday. Tick-Tick spread the word among the Bloods; what with the ones who like her and the ones who admire Strider, there'll be a lot of elves in red leather cruising B-town. She even made a run up the Tooth to speak with Scully and some of the Hill kids. Dancer and Val went to talk with Farrel Din and other old-timers. Goldy says the streets are alive. We'll find Orient and we'll find the Rats who were in Danceland Friday night, and maybe we'll even find who killed the Elflander. Sometimes I'm rather proud of this stupid town.

Reading Wolfboy's entry, I almost felt as if I *was* dead. Are there ghosts? If they walk, do they suffer from the guilty looking-over-someone's-shoulder feeling that I got from Wolfboy's introduction?

There's a lot of comfort, for me, in reading his account of what happened. The knowledge that Wolfboy and the Ticker were at work on the other end of the puzzle and that we eventually met in the middle—it puts everything in context. I wasn't alone, I wasn't isolated; I was helping to solve the larger problem in my own inimitable nitwitted fashion. But that's not what it felt like in that room.

As soon as I'd written, "Caramel, where are you now?" I felt the pull. It's not as if it grids itself out nicely in my head: here's all the compass points marked with little red letters, and here's the dotted line drawn over the street map with the big star at the end marked "You win!" I'm a finder, not a cartographer.

"Pull" is the best description I have for it. When I'm trying to find something, whether it's running water or someone's glasses, I can feel it drawing me toward it as if I was on the end of a string. The string, unfortunately, can go straight through furniture, buildings, or a dozen feet of solid earth, which is more than can be said for me. I also don't know where the thing is until I've found it, which is why you can't walk across town, knock on my door, say, "Orient, I've lost my pink socks," and expect me to tell you they're on the floor of your closet. But if you ask me to find them for you, I'll feel the pull, and if I follow it, I'll be led eventually to your place, your closet, and your socks. Payment in advance, please.

So Caramel felt like Thataway, and I left the journal and the feather behind and followed my feelings.

I dodged around a lot. The way led through Soho, where fallen buildings or contumacious gangs will sometimes block off streets or even whole neighborhoods. There are also a few gangs who wouldn't dream of keeping strangers out—the local economy would collapse if they did. I triangulated around anything I couldn't walk through, and ended up near the river.

Caramel was in what remained of a warehouse-loft a few blocks from the wharf. It had been brownstone once, with a frosting of terra-cotta details: garlands and vases and things, and elaborate moldings around the windows. Some of the terra-cotta remained, though much was either scavenged or broken. The whole building had been painted by the simple expedient of getting on the roof and pouring cans of paint down the walls. No one had thought to mask the windows, apparently.

I could hear harsh-voiced bells from a distant boat. I smelled fish, machine oil, and the sweet-and-musty odor of the Mad River. An orange cat slid from a windowsill and into hiding as I watched. Nothing else moved. It was too late in the morning for the fish markets, and too early for anyone else in this neighborhood. Hell, it was too early for me. I was hungry, and raw all over from lack of sleep. I felt as if I'd left my eyeballs in talcum powder overnight. My finding talent, which doesn't turn off and fades only slowly, had begun to feel like a rhythmic yanking, mostly at my back teeth. And, of course, I was solidly in the middle of Wharf Rat territory. My day was made.

I circled the building once, just to make sure Caramel was in it and not in something past it. The possibility that she'd done the murder had crossed my mind. It must have been on its way to someplace else, because it didn't stay long. But it made me nervous to find her in Rat City. It reminded me of that bottle of river water I'd taken from her. The water of the Big Bloody can, among other things, produce multiple personalities in a human being, all with a remarkable talent for disguise. Many of the Rats are raving psychotics in lamb suits.

If she didn't kill the Elflander—which, nervous or not, I was betting—then the evidence pointed to her as a witness. If I could get her out of hiding and convince her to talk . . . well. I was counting on her clearing Strider. But if she convicted him instead, then that was right, it was justice, and I'd see it done and get the hell out of town because I wouldn't be able to stand the sight of the place anymore.

There was no security on the front door, of course. I followed my talent up the stairs, through a hall whose walls might have been held up by the binding action of the spray paint on them. Then in midhallway I stopped, and stepped back into an alcove where a radiator had once stood.

The Ticker would have had my skin, I realized, long before that. She's tried for years to instill a sense of self-preservation in me, and after all her work, it's only rudimentary. In this case, for instance, it kicked in much too late.

Sin Number One: I'd arrived unarmed, unprovisioned, and unaccompanied. I could just hear her. Orient, my dear boy, we have a *body count* already. This is Condition Red. I don't care if you're only going down the hall to take a *leak*. . . .

Sin Number Two: Having already committed number

one, I'd compounded it by walking into a strange building in hostile territory without noticing what was, literally, right under my nose.

There are a lot of ways for an inhabited building to smell. Infants. Boiled cabbage. Sex. Disinfectants. Lamb chops. Perfume. Wood stoves. I haven't got the Wolf's nose, but I didn't need it. This building was lived in by a group of people with nasty personal habits. Drinking river water gives human sweat and urine a characteristic odor, and that odor haunted the halls and clanked its chains at me. Oh, I knew those chains.

I stood in the alcove cussing myself out for maybe three-quarters of a minute. Then I continued down the hall. What else could I do? If they had a sentry hidden, I'd already been seen, and there'd be someone waiting for me on the stairs. If there wasn't a sentry, I had nothing to worry about anyway.

There were only two doors in the hall, and one of those was a rusty sliding one for an old dumbwaiter system. My trail led through the wall between them. I put my ear to the clammy plaster and heard voices, but none of them was Caramel.

I heard a sound behind me and turned. I was just in time to see that the rusty dumbwaiter door hid a nice renovated *quiet* lift mechanism, and that the woman stepping out of it had a tire iron. Her first swing caught the wrist of the arm I'd blocked with. Her second landed where the first had been meant to: the side of my head. Lightning flash. And nothing.

Coming back was slow, and I suspect intermittent. That last is hard to be sure of, since I wasn't a reliable observer through much of it. But I know when I woke up more or less in earnest.

I didn't know where I was. I don't mean I didn't recognize it—I'm talking about with my eyes still closed. I couldn't find north. I couldn't find anything.

It was like waking up to discover you're lying on the

ceiling. A scream worked its way into my throat and stuck there.

I don't know if it was the vertigo or the blow to the head—I haven't had a lot of experience with being knocked out—but stage two involved being violently sick. I got myself propped up on my elbows afterward, in the process discovering the grinding pain in my wrist. I was cold and sweating and trembling, and I wanted to wash my mouth out with something. I lifted my head, very carefully, and saw what the Welcome Wagon had left.

A big glass jar of water. In red.

A little despairing noise got out of my mouth before I could stop it, and I rolled over and covered my eyes with my good arm. Welcome back, Orient.

I heard a door open; then someone kicked my foot solidly. The little seismograph recently installed in my skull went to the top end of its scale. When I dared open my eyes, I found a brown-haired man in wire-rimmed glasses bending over me. He smiled kindly when he saw I was conscious. All his teeth were bad.

"Hello. Are you feeling better now?"

I felt much worse. He had the gentle voice and sweet manner that I associate with genuine maniacs.

"Good. You know," he said with a birdlike turn of his head, "if you meant to ride in like The Borderland Kid and rescue your little friend, you didn't do a very good job."

His eyes went quickly to the other side of the room, and I got my head up enough to look there. Caramel was sitting hunched in the corner staring mournfully from under her tousled brown hair. Big miserable brown eyes. I lowered my head. "Thank you. I know," I said. I felt very much like hell.

He smiled meditatively down at me, massaging his fingers. "Well, you'll have to stay here now. She'll pull her weight just fine, once she gets used to things—" and he grinned at the jar of river water next to me. "You—we'll find a place for you too, I'm sure. Make yourself comfortable.'' He nodded and left the room. The bolt slid home.

I heard Caramel scramble across the floor to me. "Are you—'' she began in a whisper. "Oh, shit, of course you're not okay. Can I do anything to help?''

"No. Thanks.'' I wasn't whispering to keep them from hearing us. I was whispering to keep *me* from hearing us.

A moment later she lifted my head, very carefully, and put something soft under it. "My jacket,'' she explained.

The cloth smelled like soap and clean cotton. And I'd thought she lived in a building like this?

"When they brought you in . . . I thought you were dead. There's blood on your face.'' She paused, then said, "I know you shouldn't drink this stuff, but is it safe to wash in?''

"Yeah. Better wash it now, though, before we get desperate.''

"Desperate?''

"Before long we're going to be very thirsty. That's why it's there.''

"Should we throw it out, then?''

"They'll bring us more.''

She didn't answer that. After a moment I felt damp cloth against my cheek and smelled the water. I opened my eyes finally.

She looked older than she had last night. That's not quite true; she still looked sixteen. It was just an older sixteen. Ah, Bordertown, with its little rites of passage.

"You have a concussion, I think,'' she said.

"How do you—''

"Your right pupil looks a little bigger than the left. What are you doing here?''

That last sentence sounded yanked out of her. I smiled, sort of. "I told you I'd find you if I needed you.''

"How?''

I told her about my talent. It was a little perfunctory,

since I felt out of breath the whole time. But when I finished, her eyes were round and wondering.

"That's marvelous!"

"Not always," I said.

She was startled. Then she looked down and seemed very intent on wringing out her scarf. "I guess this is one of those times."

"No!" I reached toward her with my right hand. She was on my left side so it didn't quite make it. "That's not what I meant."

I now know what a searching look is; she fastened one on me. "You're a nice guy," she said, as if it was not a compliment but a simple observation of fact.

My conscious mind was beginning to go out with the tide. "Not always," I repeated, and went off into the dark again.

Waking up was much simpler the second time. I shifted position in my sleep, and my left wrist hit the floor. I made some noises, some of them profane. I had the good sense to raise my head to look at it, rather than raising the arm. My wrist was plum-colored where the tire iron had connected, and impressively swollen. "Should splint it," I muttered to myself.

"Working on it," Caramel said. She sat down next to me and held up two pieces of wood. "Dividers from the desk drawers," she said cheerfully.

Neither of us really knew how to apply a splint, but I helped by lying still and gritting my teeth. When she was done, I felt like a seal with a wooden flipper, but the joint was immobile.

I hadn't known there *was* a desk in the room until then. I got my right elbow under me and checked out the cell.

It had been someone's library once, high-ceilinged, with tall windows and decorative plaster friezes at the tops of the walls. Most of the wall were fitted with built-in shelves, all of them empty now. There were water stains on the plaster from leaks in the roof. One window had been inexpertly bricked up, probably right after the Change. The other window was barred, and the light came dimly through a layer of pea-green paint. There was a fireplace between two tiers of shelves, closed up with a sheet of plywood wedged into the opening. The floor must have been handsome once, but damp and neglect had weathered the planks gray. A heap of what looked like bedding occupied one corner, and the aforementioned desk, one drawer missing, stood in another.

"All the comforts of home," I muttered. Caramel didn't answer.

"Are you okay?" I asked.

She snorted. "Yeah."

"They . . . didn't hurt you, did they?"

She shook her head, then realized what I was really trying to say. "No. A couple of them thought about it, but I talked them out of it."

"You talked them out of it?"

She grinned. "This is kind of embarrassing."

"I won't laugh. I'm not sure I can."

"Well, I told them something from an old story I heard once. I told them I was fey, and that everybody in my family turned into tigers when they lost their virginity, and ate their lovers. And that I was still a virgin."

I had to laugh after all. "That's really dumb."

"I know." She was laughing, too. "But they were all pretty high. I don't think they'd have swallowed it otherwise." She folded her knees up under her chin. "I hadn't been in here long before they brought you in."

"Did they bring you here?"

She shook her head. "I followed them from Danceland. I managed to get myself locked in the garage downstairs. That's where they found me."

"You shouldn't have followed them."

Caramel fell silent for a little, then said, "They killed that guy."

That was hard to reply to. So I didn't.

"I think they were waiting for him. I saw him turn the corner into the alley, walking with one of them, and when I got to the corner, the rest were there. The guy with the glasses held out something in his hand and said, 'Looking for this?' and the elf went for his sword thing. Then they closed in on him and started sticking him, and . . . and cut off his braid. And . . ." She covered her face with both hands. I thought she wouldn't go on, but she said, "The one with the glasses said something about the river, that it was the blood of Elfland. And that if it was good, what would the blood of an elf be like?"

Then she stopped. I was glad of it.

I wanted desperately to know where Wolfboy and Tick-Tick were. Wanting should have been enough to give me a bearing on them. Nothing happened.

The jar of river water was beginning to stick in my thoughts. I wondered how Caramel was feeling. My mouth was dry and still sour-tasting, and my throat scratched a little. When *had* I last drunk something? At Danceland? I'd had coffee and beer there, both good for drying you out eventually.

"Why did you follow them here?" I asked Caramel.

"What was I supposed to do, go home and stick my head under the pillow?" she snapped.

"I would have."

She looked at me for a long moment. "Would you have? When they started splitting up to leave, and you knew you were the only person who could find out where they were going?" She looked like an empty-handed person who wanted something to throw. Then her eyes got wide and a little bleak and she turned back to me. "You could have done it, couldn't you?"

"What?"

"You could have tracked them down. You could have found them."

"No. Not unless I'd seen them. Otherwise I wouldn't know who I was looking for, and I couldn't do it."

"Really?"

"Really."

She rubbed her face and swept her hair back. She had a very high forehead. "Well," she said, "Well. Like I say, they split up when they left, to cover their tracks, I guess. The guy with glasses had a bike, and he drove off on that. But before he left I saw him put whatever it was he held out to the elf in his saddlebag. So I followed one of the ones who were on foot, and got here. I snuck into the garage, to find that thing. It seemed important, and I was afraid that if I didn't take it, the glasses guy would get rid of it before anyone could get back here. And I found it, and hid it—and then they caught me."

"But you said you hadn't been here long before they brought me in."

Caramel looked rueful. "It took me a long time to get up the nerve to break into the garage."

That made me laugh a little, which made her do the same. "So what was it?" I said. "The thing in the saddlebag."

She nodded and began to unlace one of her sneakers. That puzzled me, until she pulled it off and shook something out into her hand. "I don't think he knows it's gone yet," she said, and held it out to me.

I didn't take it from her. It was temporarily beyond me to raise my hand and reach for it. Such an unassuming little object, however valuable it might be. . . .

It was a ring of elf-silver set with a sapphire. My teeth chattered.

"Hide it again," I said, when I could. "It's important."

Linden was never offstage long enough to have done it. No, we knew who'd done it—Glasses and Friends. But if the deed had been bought. . . ? Oh, I wanted something cold to drink, and I wanted a nice herbal cig with it, and I wanted to bang my head against the wall until all my problems went away. I had a witness, and a missing puzzle piece, and no way in the World or elsewhere that I could deliver either of them.

The pea-green light grew steadily weaker. I crawled across the room and propped myself against a wall. Caramel took a nap, curled up on the heap of bedding. I looked at the jar of river water. I tried to remember every band I'd ever seen play. I counted the number of times I'd seen Tick-Tick blow something up. I looked at the jar of river water. Caramel shifted position. I looked at the jar of . . .

The door lock made noise, and I tapped Caramel's ankle to wake her up. Glasses came in with a flashlight and blazed it at us. None of the kindly light of a Faerie lamp here. I doubted there had ever been magic in this room, beyond the twisted magic that the river worked on humans.

I couldn't see him in the glare, until he turned the beam on the jar of water.

He made a clucking noise. "Maybe I should leave you some crackers," he said. He turned the flashlight back on us. "It's not so bad, you know. They'll tell you out there that it's dangerous, but they always say that. That's wisdom in that jar, strength, inspiration. They don't want you to be smart or strong or great. They want to step on you. That's why they're afraid."

I blinked and shook my head, and the light came closer.

"Really?" his sweet voice came out of the flashlight beam. "I'm stronger than you, right now. And you're afraid of me, aren't you?"

I could see him, finally; he squatted companionably next to me. He took my chin in his fingers. Then he drew his hand back and slapped me casually. A lot of little bells rang in my head, and I slid further down the wall.

"Leave him alone," said Caramel, in a surprisingly steady voice.

He looked at me, then toward her, as if considering the merits of her suggestion. Then he got to his feet. "All right, dear, I can do that for a little while. But you can help, you know. Just get him to drink up, and all the unhappy times are over, okay?" He smiled at her, and went out the door.

"D'you think you could knock him out the next time he comes in?" I said thinly.

"Hmm." A moment of silence. "I could hit him with a desk drawer . . . No, I don't think I could hit him hard enough. I'm not very big."

True, she wasn't. I sat in the dark and remembered what she looked like. Once, in the World, they would have called her elfin. That was before they discovered that the elves were a lot bigger than they'd made them out to be.

I wanted something to goddamn *drink*.

"You want to sleep?" she asked.

"No. I want to talk. What's Bellinbroke like?"

She chuckled a little. Have you ever noticed how much laughter can sound like crying? Bubbles of air coming out, and a little inhalation at the end like a sniff? "I'll get homesick, and it'll serve you right."

But she told me about her father, who taught at the university; and about her mother, private and self-possessed as a feral cat, who left her husband for one of his younger colleagues. Caramel told me how her father seemed to forget that his daughter existed, except when she forced him to remember. There are a lot of ways to get your father's attention forcibly, most of them unpleasant. Caramel had worked her way through, she figured, about half of them before she realized that the effect was never permanent. So she ran away to the Borderlands.

"What about you?" she said at last.

"Me?"

"Yeah, you. Come on, I told you mine."

So I told her, which is a measure of how out of touch I'd become. There was a terrible pain in my head that made all of my thoughts rattle around loose, I didn't know where anything was, and I was so dry I was afraid I'd crack if I moved. No, let's be honest. I was too far gone for witty descriptions. Drink the damn water, I told myself. Drink it now, get out of here, and you can kick it later. I wasn't so fuzzy-minded that I couldn't spot the two basic errors in that sentence.

I told Caramel almost all of it. I told her about the stupid olives, I told her about my mother watching me out of the corner of her eye when she thought I didn't see. Believe me, you can live with getting beat up in the parking lot at school dances. You can put up with opening your locker and finding a dead cat in it. You can even bear it when the next-door neighbor, usually distant but kind, gets drunk on night and tries to run you down with his car. But when you realize that your mother never touches you except when she has to . . .

I think I was semiconscious some of the time. I discovered that Caramel was holding my hand at one point, and couldn't remember when she'd first taken it.

I didn't tell her about my early life in Bordentown. I told her I did some pretty despicable things, and left it at that. Safe enough, since I know I've forgotten many of them. The river will do that. It *does* make you feel strong and smart, but only because it takes away all the things you've ever measured strength and smarts by. Everything, even your own well-being, is set at a distance and devalued. You can do the most appalling things and forget them a moment later, because they simply aren't significant. And then even the river begins to slip away and forsake you, and you need more and more of it to make you strong and smart, to make you forget your freakish talent that's the real cause of your fall, not the river, not your own asshole self-pity. That much I remember.

And I remember not being allowed to sleep, being stuck under cold running water until I was awake enough to scream and claw, being made to walk, walk, walk with a fierce voice alternately cursing me and bursting into tears.

If we didn't get out of there soon, I would drink that

water, I would take my faithless mistress back. In the dark of that room where magic never came, I was certain that this time no one would be there to make sure I kept walking.

I should have told her about some of the good things. I didn't. I fell asleep.

When I woke up, it was still dark. Caramel had her head on my knee, probably napping again. My mind was full of the exquisite clarity that is often the leading edge of hallucination. My mouth felt glued shut.

I thought, reveling in the ability to do so. Escape. Not for me; I wouldn't get a block away in this condition, even if every Rat in the building went to Faerie on holiday. For Caramel. Camilla. Attendant at a sacrifice. In hiding behind Danceland, watching five Rats let the blood out of a fairy tale, for the greater glory of whatever they worshiped. I'd taken away her name, but the destiny seemed to have stuck. Well, she wouldn't have to attend mine.

The door was no good—solid, locked, raving lunatics on the other side of it anyway. Neither of us was strong enough to get the bars out of the window. The floor was old, but in good shape—Glasses had crossed the room with nary a creak. The ceiling was also solid, and fifteen feet away. How to get one small girl out of a top-floor room . . .

The fireplace. Oh, god, the fireplace.

I shook Caramel awake and pried my lips apart. To her eternal credit, she woke up fast and without a fuss.

"Go see if you can get the plywood out of the fireplace opening," I whispered. Even that made me feel as if I'd been breathing thumbtacks. "If you can't do it without making a racket, come back here and tell me."

I waited alone in the dark while she made scrabbling noises at the other end of the room. "Can't," she said finally in my ear. "Not without a noise."

"Help me over there."

I worked on one end, with my one good hand, and she

worked on the other. I felt all my fingernails break and bleed, and kept clawing away. Finally I got desperate enough to give the bottom of the plywood a kick. With a scraping sound that nearly made me swallow my tongue, it tilted. We grabbed the now-grabbable top edge and pulled the board free.

Maybe they were asleep. Nobody came in. I stuck my head into the fireplace opening, trying not to think of all the things that might accumulate in a disused fireplace. Far above me I saw a square of dark blue shot with stars. The flue had rusted and fallen out, along with an ominous lot of crumbling firebrick. Still, if I hadn't been so dehydrated, I would have cried.

"Take a look," I whispered. "Can you get up that?"

She brushed by me; I felt her hair against my face. "I think so."

"Careful. There'll be loose brick. Watch out for a guard on the roof." It was staccato and disconnected, but I knew I couldn't keep talking for long.

"Where do I go for help?"

I shook my head, which, of course, she couldn't see in the dark.

She grabbed the front of my shirt and hissed, "Where? Come on!"

I didn't know where. I didn't know where anything was. Or anybody. People might be at Danceland; more likely it was closed. She could try a dozen different places and not find anybody. I couldn't find anybody. Delirium was setting in.

"Please!" I could hear her crying. "I don't know people in Bordertown, and by the time I get help, it could be too late for you. Where can I find help?"

And it came, like a couple of notes from a familiar song, just enough to recognize it by. Thataway.

Not enough. What the hell was it? Where was north? I felt for it and called for it, until the dark in front of me was shot with colored sparks. That was north. There.

Still not enough. This time I couldn't just follow until I got there. I had to figure it out from here.

I found them all, in the midst of pain and madness—Danceland, Tick-Tick's place, Wolfboy's. They were all too far south to be the trace I'd gotten when Caramel asked me to find help. Then I tried my place. It matched.

I told her. She sobbed, and kissed me on the mouth, and lowered me gently to the floor. Then she scrambled around me and went to work.

I reconstructed it later, with no small quantity of admiration. She piled the bedding up to look as if she was in it, all except a couple of pillows. Those she put in the bottom of the fireplace, so any loose brick that she dislodged would make no sound when they hit. Then she leaned over me again.

"Can you get the plywood back up once I'm in?" She had a hand on my face, so I could nod in answer. "Okay. Hold the fort, Orient."

I heard her at first in the chimney, until I fought the plywood back into place. I think anyone who was looking for something amiss would find it—but that was my job, to keep anyone from looking. Just long enough for Caramel to get away.

I dragged myself away from the fireplace and let go of consciousness for a while.

I have large, merciful gaps in my memory where the rest of it should go. I remember waking up to find the window an oblong of gray-green in the shadowed room, and discovering that I'd dragged myself most of the way to the water jar. Instinct is a wonderful thing.

I remember Glasses coming in, casting a cursory glance toward the pile of inhabited-looking blankets, and giving me the benefit of his conversation for a few minutes. He drank some out of the jar. I could hear him swallowing, seeing his throat working. A little of it trickled down his chin and shone there, until he saw me staring at it. He wiped it away very slowly. I tried not to cry until the door closed behind him.

Many gray intervals later, something boomed, not far away. The second time it happened, I identified it as an explosion. It happened a third time.

These, I knew, were significant. I decided to stay awake, on the off chance that I'd remember why.

The gunshot brought me fully conscious, though. It came from the next room. Then the door burst inward, and Glasses stood in the opening, eyes wild. He had a sawed-off shotgun, and he was leveling it at me. The whole scene seemed remarkably clear, and I had time to wonder why, after years of haphazard observation, I should suddenly be able to count the hairs on the backs of my murderer's hands.

I thought the roaring noise was the sound of the shotgun, and me dying. But some of Glasses' chest blew into the room, and so did he. A second later the Ticker came through the door, all scarlet leather and bared teeth, an immense handgun in a two-fisted grip.

She looked to me, saw the water jar, and stooped on it like a hawk. It broke against the wall with a splash, and I whimpered.

"Shh, shh," she said, and held me against her. It was Tick-Tick, you see, who wouldn't let me quit walking and die all those years ago.

I felt her start to shake, and remembered that, for all her skill with things that go boom, I'd never seen her do what she'd just done. "Lobo!" she shouted. "All clear. Get your ass in here!"

He had the water, a cloth soaked with it. They'd known I wouldn't be able to swallow at first. Wolf's brown-furred face was contorted, as if he'd be crying if his tear ducts worked that way. They carried me out between them, through the smell of fired weapons.

Someone had thought to bring a stretcher, and it was

waiting in the hall, along with Goldy and Sai and—dear grinning god, was that Scully, from up the Tooth? The wet cloth had given me back the use of my tongue and lips, if not my throat, exactly. I whispered to the Ticker, "How big a party is this, kid?"

She shrugged as best she could, carrying me. "We had to get you back. We've all lost our house keys." And then, for only the second time in as long as I've known her, I saw her cry.

No point in going over the rescue. There are enough pieces of it in Orient's part of the story. It was your basic arrival of the cavalry, I suppose, but none of it was fun. Too much worry about what could go wrong, for us and for Orient, and whether we could free him before the Rats realized that we were there. The worst part was when their sentry spotted us from the roof, right after Tick-Tick's first smoke bomb went off. The Rat had a gun, and we were all pinned down until the Ticker said, "We need to lower the technology level around here." She closed her eyes and mumbled something, and there was an explosion from the roof that was almost as loud as one of hers. She nodded grimly, and we went in. Afterwards, there wasn't much happiness in our success. Orient was a mess, and we all knew we wouldn't have found him at all if Caramel hadn't escaped. Still, we thanked everyone who had shown up and watched the Gathering of the Gangs disperse.

We took Orient home while a couple members of the Horn Dance fetched Doc. Doc cleaned and splinted and bandaged as Orient gasped and winced and looked extremely unhappy. He wrote out a short version of his stay at Glasses' place. I wanted to make a joke about having two mutes in our little group, but I couldn't think of anything funny. People had died. Nobody important enough that the cops would come around, but people nonetheless. Orient drank a lot of water while he wrote it. The Doc said, "That's enough. You got your story from him, now go away and let him sleep."

"What do we owe?" Tick-Tick asked.

"Ah, forget it. Wasn't interesting enough to charge you for."

I fetched Doc's coat. Next time she puts her hand in her pocket, she'll find seven four-leaf clovers.

We all went out and sat on the steps so we wouldn't disturb Orient. No one spoke. Tick-Tick's face was drawn and tired, almost gray under her dandelion hairdye, and one pointed ear was bruised and slightly bloody. Sai squinted in the distance, her eyes very Oriental and very elvin at the same time. She wasn't watching anything that I could see. Goldy rubbed his strong, brown hands over his metallic hair and stared at the sidewalk. It was just after noon of a beautiful day, we'd saved Orient, and I expected us all to pass out from exhaustion.

Caramel stood nearby, looking like she didn't know whether to stay or leave. Sai noticed her and said, "Hey, c'mon. Sit and rest. You could use it. We all could."

"Thanks," Caramel said as she sat cross-legged beside me. She glanced at Sai, then at the rest of us. "What're you going to do now?"

"We're going to talk too much," Goldy said. "As usual."

Tick-Tick nodded. "And maybe we'll figure it all out. What have we got?"

I held up the ring that Caramel had found. A sapphire set in Faerie silver. Orient had winced when he said who wore sapphire and silver rings.

"We have the ring," Tick-Tick said. "And a witness." She nodded at Caramel. "That'll clear Strider."

"It's not enough," Sai said.

"It'll free him," Tick-Tick said.

"It's not enough," Sai repeated with a shake of her thick, black hair.

Goldy nodded. "The singer would've let Strider die for her. The Rats were just Rats, but she's the one who used them."

"We could go to Rico with what we've got," Tick-Tick said. "Maybe Rico could help."

Goldy said, "Rico can't do a thing. Linden will say the ring was stolen by the Rats, and that'll be that."

"Even if we do nothing," Tick-Tick said, "Linden will have to live with it." I wondered if she was thinking about the Rat she shot, or the one whose rifle had exploded in his grip.

I raised my hand, then started scribbling while they waited: *Why the ring? Why was it important to Yorl? Why would Linden kill someone who meant little to her? Why were the Rats at Danceland that night?*

"Very good questions," Goldy said. "But do you have very good answers?"

Why did Yorl come here from Elflands? Who is Yorl? Who is Linden?

Goldy said, "No, no, no, my friend. Good *answers*."

No one laughed.

"I doubt Linden's in Rico's files," Tick-Tick said. I agreed with a nod. Records in B-town are pretty thin. The coppers get reports on runaways sometimes, and they're building a file on people they've arrested, but that's about it. Rico would need a better reason than "we think she hired some Rats" to go through the trouble of tracing a SoHo musician.

Where's Linden? I wrote last, and Tick-Tick shook her head sadly. "We're going to have to wake poor Orient."

Orient woke violently, scattering his bedcovers. Tick-Tick put her hand on his brow and he settled down.

"Sorry, kid," he whispered.

"It's all right. Lobo's got some questions for you."

Orient nodded sleepily. "You guys can't do anything without me." He looked bad, pale enough to be an elf, but he sounded pleased. I was still sorry we woke him.

I wrote: *Where's Linden?*

He closed his eyes, which turned into a wince. After a second he pointed toward the hotel area in SoHo. "That-away," he croaked.

Then I wrote the tricky one. *Where's an elf named Yorl, a relative of Tejorinin Yorl?*

Orient frowned at me. I wasn't sure he understood, and even if he did, the question might be too vague for him. A worse possibility occurred to me: what if there were as many Yorls among the elves as Joneses among us? But Orient grinned weakly.

"If there's more than one of them, I'm gonna have a migraine, Wolf." He bit his lip and closed his eyes. Then he opened them again, wide. "Same way," he whispered, nodding toward the hotel area. "Same damn way."

We talked a lot more after that, sitting in the street. Everyone liked my theory and no one like my plan. No one came up with a better one, so finally we scattered to the various bikes. The Ticker stayed with Orient because someone had to—and because she thought this last part was unnecessary, I think. Or maybe she didn't want to get in a position where she might have to hurt someone else. Caramel was willing to play the part I wanted the Ticker to take, so the B-town Players were ready for their first bit of improv.

Finding Linden wasn't hard. We asked at a couple places for the lead singer of Wild Hunt, and somebody said she was staying at the Roses of Elfland. Sai and Goldy weren't happy about waiting in the street, but they agreed. They thought they were there in case the plan fell apart. They were there because I didn't trust them to keep to the script with Linden.

Caramel and I knocked at Linden's door. She answered, opening it enough that we could see sunlight and expensive furniture behind her. The room smelled of herbal cigarettes, perfume, and something tart that was her own scent. She wore a sea-green dress with billowing sleeves.

It was cut on one side to reveal golden stockings set with tiny diamonds. Her hair fell over her right shoulder like a moon-lit avalanche of virgin snow. I understood why Orient was so taken with her. I thought she was reasonably attractive, even. ''Yes?'' she said, and then, catching my gaze with her silver eyes, she said, ''You helped pack up after the gig at Danceland. We appreciated that.'' She smiled kindly.

I wanted to bow and say something gracious. Caramel and I looked odd in the clean hall of the Roses of Elfland. My jacket and jeans hadn't looked good before this morning's adventure, and Caramel's gray traveling clothes were smudged with grease, mud, soot, and half-a-dozen things less easy to identify. Then I almost laughed, realizing that the clothes were the least of our oddness. Caramel seemed very shy and very young as she stood before Linden, and I was hardly the boy-next-door. I nudged Caramel, who said, ''Uh, we have something you'll want.''

''I beg your pardon?'' asked Linden.

''A ring,'' said Caramel, growing more sure of herself. ''Belongs to Ms. Yorl. Is it yours?'' She showed the silver and sapphire ring. It was almost identical to the three on Linden's right hand.

''No,'' Linden said, blinking at us. ''But it looks just like mine. Your Ms. Yorl and I have remarkably similar taste.'' When neither of us said anything immediately, she smiled thinly and said, ''Good day.'' She began to close the door.

Okay, it was a stupid plan. I had an impression ball in my pocket, recording since we came up the stairs. Nothing we recorded would be proof, not in court, but I'd hoped we'd get something that would convince Rico to probe into Linden's past. That was shot now.

Then Caramel said, just before the door closed, ''So you won't care if we take it to the cops.'' Something about the way she said it reminded me that she'd watched Tejorinin Yorl get cut up.

The door stopped swinging. Linden's face was framed in it, a porcelain face haloed in sunlight. "Why should I?" she said, sounding suddenly short of breath. I almost felt sorry for her.

"No reason." Caramel stroked the ring between her thumb and forefinger. "What do you think a wizard could learn from this? Betcha one could find its owner at least. Betcha we'd get a good reward."

Linden's lips pressed together, and she shook her head slightly. Silver strands of hair drifted freely, and I suddenly knew we'd won. She said, "What do you think you're doing? What do you want from me?"

I grinned at her. I doubt I could've put my whole face into it. Baring the teeth was probably enough.

"Do you want money?" she said quickly, her voice going up the scale. "Is that it? It is a nice ring." She reached for it, and Caramel stepped back. "I had nothing to do with it!" Linden cried. "Nothing!"

I nodded and looked at Caramel until she asked the obvious question: "Nothing to do with what?"

Linden stood in the doorway and stared as if she was seeing something besides us. Then she slammed the door.

Rico liked the impression ball. Linn preferred the ring—he coaxed all the magic out of it and found not just Linden-as-owner, but a little trick that made it seem that where the ring was, Linden was, too. Just in case somebody being led into an alley should need a little magical reassurance that this was a safe place to go. Combined with Caramel's statement, it made Linden look bad.

Rico looked for female members of the Yorl family. I had wondered why someone with a new inheritance would suddenly come to Bordertown, especially someone who seemed to despise B-town the way Yorl had seemed to. I expected that Yorl had a sister. Rico found that Yorl had a wife who had left him a couple of years before his mother died. Mom's death left him the head of the family and a rich guy. Now that he was dead too, the missing wife stood to inherit a nice piece of whatever it is that elves consider valuable, if only she would reappear in Faerie. There were no photos or fingerprints of this wife; elves don't photograph, and they don't seem fond of the latter. But, amusingly enough, her elvish name translated into English as Linden.

The rest was easy to put together. Yorl must have arrived inconveniently in B-town and insisted that Linden abandon the band and be a proper wife and lady because he had a position to uphold now. When Linden heard that the mom was dead, the temptation must have been too much. So the Rats came to Danceland to meet with her, and during the confusion between Yorl and Strider, she gave them their commission and the Yorl-decoy off her finger. Whose idea it was to do it in back of Danceland to frame Strider, we'll probably never know. Me, I bet Glasses thought the chance was too good to waste.

Today we all went to the Border to watch a couple of elvin Silver Suits escort Linden Yorl through the gate to Faerie. No matter what happened to her there, she wouldn't come through the Gate again. Rico told us that she was officially Not Welcome in Bordertown.

We dressed in our best, of course. Orient was up and around, maybe a little too pleased with the effect of his arm in a black sling. And Caramel stayed close to him; Tick-Tick thinks Orient doesn't need any more nursing, but Caramel is very protective of him still.

Linden saw us. We'd meant her to. I saw her give a quick look to Orient, but he didn't move an eyebrow.

As Linden went across the Border, Strider called out something in Elvish.

"What was that?" Sai asked him.

"Jealous, love? Never you mind."

But I know enough Elvish to recognize the proverb. At least, I'd always thought it was a proverb. Now I'm not sure. Loosely, it's "Love wealth above life itself, and starve in splendor." It might be a curse. My other suspicion I don't want to think about: that it might be part of Faene's penal code.

We went back to Danceland, Goldy made coffee, and Orient found Dancer's lost receipt book. And I wrote this.

MIDORI SNYDER
Demon

The wooden floor trembled as students tossed themselves to the ground, chests heaving and sweat filling the air with a damp stink. They sat around the four corners of the room, leaving an opening in the middle where Koga Sensei stood, legs apart, eyeing them, a cross section of Bordertown gathered in a sweaty mass: Soho gang members—Packs, Bloods; Dragons; a few from the Hill who were brave enough to venture to Dragontown; and even a handful of Rats, who paid for their training in odd jobs. In white gis one could almost ignore the differences that weighed so heavily when they wore their street clothes, uniforms of a different kind. Almost that is, for the silver eyes of the Bloods still unnerved the Sensei, though he didn't let them know that. He waited a moment until their breathing settled.

"Hai, okay." He turned about and saw Keno leaning forward on his knees, eager as a silver wolf. "Keno!" he called and the Blood was up, shaking out his shoulders and clenching his fists in anticipation.

"Hey, all right! Get him! Do it, Blood!" came the encouragement from the other students near him. Keno was a good fighter, quick and light, his kicks near lethal with their bone-cracking speed.

Sensei looked around for a suitable opponent. His eyes rested on another student. He knew by the way she sat, fidgeting with her gi, straightening the front, that she was avoiding his gaze. Inwardly he sighed, wishing she had more confidence in her ability. Sometimes you pull your students, coaxing them where they don't want to go, and sometimes you push. Time was for a push. "Laura," he called, and turned his back so he wouldn't see the stricken expression that flashed across her face.

Laura scrambled to her feet, her stomach cold and her mouth dry. Shit! she screamed to herself. Shit, shit! Why'd it have to be her? And why'd it have to be Keno? It wasn't the sparring that scared her, it was him. Huh. She gave a snort. Everyone in the dojo was afraid of him. He was the meanest fucking elf she knew. But there was no refusing in workout. She stepped into the opening and faced Keno, her hands opening and closing in small fists.

"Eeeasy! Aw man, no contest!" came the catcalls from behind Keno's back. He smiled at her, smug and nasty.

"Come on, girl," came a voice from behind her, "kick his nuts across the Border!" Laura looked over her shoulder into Jenny Jingle's elvin face. Jenny poked her sharp chin up in the air, eyes glittering. "You can do it!" Jenny whispered fiercely.

Laura nodded at her, feeling the encouragement like a lick of hot flame over her fear. She stared a moment longer in the woman's fey eyes and then felt herself grow more steady, Jenny's support reaching out to her. Gotta do it sometime, she thought to herself. Might as well be now. She turned and faced Keno, stuffing her fear in to the farthest corner of herself and making her face a cold stone.

Sensei stood next to them, noting with satisfaction the change in Laura. They bowed to each other. Sensei barked,

''Hagemai!'' and they dropped back into a crouched fighting stance. Sensei moved away from them, staying close enough to referee the fight but not intrude as the pair began to circle.

Laura kept her eyes on Keno's face as he seemed to push her, closing the space between them. The same nasty smile tugged at his lips. She felt her own lips clamped in a scowl. He jerked his fists up and she jumped back, startled, expecting a punch. There was none. She heard the others as they hooted and banged their palms to the floor. Calm down asshole, she told herself. You can't fight if you jump at everything! Sweat itched her shaved scalp and trickled down beside her ear. Keno moved again, this time springing off the back leg with a lunge punch. She saw it coming, and a spurt of courage thrust her forward—not away from the spinning fist, but in and under it. She blocked the punch from underneath his elbow and slammed a counterpunch to his open belly before he could change direction. It was a solid punch. She felt the air huff out of him.

''BREAK!'' Sensei charged between them, blocking the fight with his body. Laura stepped back quickly to her corner, never taking her eyes off Keno. Adrenaline roared in her ears, though behind her she could hear Jenny shouting, ''Atta way, girl,'' and from the Packs, ''Waste the fucker!''

Keno moved back to his corner, no longer smiling. His head was a skull, skin stretched white over the fine bone. Laura shivered, seeing the ugly twist of his mouth. That's it, she thought. He's gonna kill me now.

Sensei was talking, instructing. ''Good technique. This is Go-no-sen; attack just after opponent commits, then move in and break his timing with counterpunch. Good.'' He nodded at her. Laura hardly heard him, her concentration centered on Keno, whose eyes flickered with white rage. ''Again,'' Sensei instructed, and they moved to the center of the fighting space.

Laura stepped forward and faced Keno. She shivered inwardly, sensing his coming attack like a whisper of cold air on the backs of her hands. She could feel his attack as if he had already beaten her. No, she stopped herself short, he hasn't beat me, not yet. Laura exhaled slowly and let the muscles of her shoulders relax. As she did so, she could sense the kick Keno had formed in his mind; the kick he meant to crush her with, fold her in two like a wet rag. His strongest technique, she thought, amazed at how clearly she could read his intention, and he'll use it now because he's pissed off. He expects me to run, but I won't and won't that be a surprise? She might have smiled, for suddenly she knew the fight was hers.

They bowed again and Sensei looked from one to the other. The dojo was quiet, students intent on the fighters. "Hagemai!" he barked to begin the bout, but before he'd stepped back completely Laura sprang forward, bursting like a bullet. One solid punch landed square on Keno's face before he'd even a chance to think about stepping down into stance. Keno's head snapped back and blood spurted from his nose, now lying at an odd angle on his face like a flattened plum. Sensei jerked Laura back by the scruff of her gi before she could add a second punch to her attack.

"All right!" roared Jenny from the side. The Pack and a few of the Rats started cheering her, banging their fists on the floor in a drumroll.

"Head up, Keno!" Sensei ordered through the loud shouts. "Don't bleed on the floor!"

Keno, head back and bleeding, staggered to the side of the room. Sensei reached him with a towel and placed it over Keno's nose to staunch the flow of crimson blood that stained the white lips and chin. Fingers pressed to either side, he jerked the broken nose back to center as Keno shrieked in pain.

"I'll heal myself, goddamnit!" he shouted at Sensei.

"Okay, okay," Sensei answered, ignoring the cursing

elf and laying strips of tape across the nose to hold it where he had set it. "Just want to be sure it's on straight!"

Laura watched them from her corner, trying not to holler like a banshee with relief. Two years she'd waited to pay that fucker back for all the hurt he'd caused her in workout, and now his time had come. She held herself still, letting others do the rejoicing for her, but her blue eyes gleamed bright, and in her chest, her heart tapped out a victory tune.

Sensei came back to the center and motioned Laura and Keno over to the center. She went, trying to look sober, keeping the grin from her lips. Keno's face was mottled white and red, his eyes starting to puff and blacken. They bowed again, a formal ending to the match—though it had ended, she reminded herself, before it had started.

"Hai, line up," Sensei shouted. Students scurried to their feet, quick to form a line according to rank. He waited until they were standing, shoulder to shoulder, eyes forward. He bowed crisply and they returned the bow smartly with one of their own. "Good workout," he clipped, and released them.

The line fell out, dissolving into small groups, some heading for the changing rooms, others lingering to bang their fists on the makiwara board, sharpening their technique.

Laura headed for the changing rooms, already untying the brown belt that held her gi. She had to hurry; she was due to waitress at the Dancing Ferret in less than an hour.

"Laura," a voice commanded, and she stopped and turned.

"Hai, Sensei," she responded automatically.

He walked over to her and shook her belt. "When are you going to test for black belt?"

She didn't answer. It was an old question, one she didn't want to face.

"Next month," he said firmly so she wouldn't argue. "You pick the day, but it has to be next month."

"Hai," she answered, wondering why she felt queasy. Rank tests did that to her. She never felt ready.

As she left Koga watched her, shaking his head. Some you pull, some you push, and some, he thought, turning to watch the angry Keno and his circle of Bloods depart, you think about kicking out.

For ten years Koga had held together a karate school. Held it together against all the wildness, bigotry, and rowdiness of Bordertown. He didn't care if they were human, elves, or anything in between, they were his students. They came to him from every section of the city, and no matter what law applied outside, inside the dojo it was his world. He controlled it, he made the rules. Oh, he'd brought a few students into line, kicking and screaming and raising the roof with threats. But it hadn't been more than water to a duck's back. The school held and his name got passed around in the clubs of Soho. They'd come to respect him, respect the safety he provided in the dojo, and, in time, working out together, they'd even learned to respect each other.

Koga pursed his lips, thinking. Students like Keno threatened the safety of the dojo. His skill was good, maybe too good; he'd never struggled for anything, never been humbled by frustration. And he had a streak of meanness, a cruelty that wouldn't bend. Koga sighed and rubbed his eyes, suddenly feeling tired.

In the changing room Laura stripped off her gi and rolled it up in a tight bundle, tying it with the belt.

"Hey girl, score one for our side tonight," Jenny called from the other side of the small room. She was naked and wriggling into a red t-shirt, her body a long slender rope of pale elvin skin.

"Since when did I join the Bloods?" Laura shot back, pouring the bucket of water into the sink and splashing the water over her hot, sticky body. The dojo had no shower, and students had to content themselves with buck-

ets of tepid water poured into old porcelain sinks. Laura
had once tried turning on the ancient taps; nothing had
come out but a cold rusty trickle.

"I'm not talking about Bloods and humans. I'm talking
about females. Keno hates everything about women, no
matter what side of the Border they come from—or hadn't
you noticed?"

"Yeah, I noticed," answered Laura.

"That boy is bad business," Jenny said, pulling on a
pair of black jeans and fussing with the zippers that dec-
orated the ankles. "It's nice to see him taken down a
notch."

"Scared the shit out of me," Laura confessed, drying
herself with a small towel. She sniffed her armpit and
wrinkled her nose. Ah hell, at the Ferret nobody would
notice it over the smell of smoke and brew anyway.

"No kidding?" Jenny said, giving her a lilting smile.
"Well, you did all right. Must be you got those killer
instincts," she joked. "I couldn't believe it when you flattened his nose. What made you move so fast?"

"Fear." Laura laughed, pulling on her own t-shirt,
silk-screened with a picture of antlers and a fool's mask.
It was her favorite shirt and she was wearing it to honor
the Horn Dance, the band who would be gigging tonight
at the Dancing Ferret.

"Come to dinner with us?" Jenny asked. "A bunch of
us have finally convinced Sensei to join us. Nothing fancy,
just whatever's hot and fresh at the Traders."

"Can't. I gotta work tonight at the Ferret."

"Aw, too bad. Well look, maybe we can drag Sensei
over there later and have a little victory toast."

"Be nice," Laura answered, brushing the water from
the tips of her black Mohawk and putting the gold studs
back in her ears.

Jenny swung on her jacket, pulling the little flute she
always carried out of her pocket. With her gi tucked se-

curely under her elbow she whistled up a little "Buttered Peas" and then finished off with "Silver Street Lasses."

Laura put on black baggy trousers, tying strings around the ankles, and smiled up at Jenny Jingle's magic fingers.

"I'm off then dear-io, let's hope to see you cheer-io," the elvin girl chanted, and then disappeared through the battered door of the changing room.

Alone, Laura tried to hurry herself. "Come on, Laura," she groused out loud, "get a move on." She fished out her tennies from under a chair and laced them up, then took a last look at herself in the cracked mirror before heading out. Not bad, she thought, staring at the blue eyes brightened with the glitter of fairy-dust on the eyelids. She turned to the side and cocked her head back, her Mohawk like the crest of a black bird. Not bad at all, she told herself. Here's one for you Laura girl for giving the shit-head a bloody nose and raising the spirits of female-kind everywhere. She lifted an imaginary glass and drank to the happy face in the mirror.

The night was damp, mist forming wreaths around the dull spell-lamps of the street and clinging to Laura's face as she jigged her way down Water Street. On one side of her was a stone wall that shielded her from the old canal. Once it had sparkled with fresh water, twisting and snaking through Dragontown and the Scandal District. Laura's Gran had told her how they had skated on it in the winter and fished in the summer. The canal was little more than a muddy bank now that stank like a swamp in the summer and filled with a sluggish stream in the early spring. To the other side of her were the ramshackle buildings that made up the Asian neighborhood called Dragontown, sandwiched between the Scandal District and Soho. Laura always felt that she might be somewhere else other than Bordertown when she walked through Dragontown. It smelled different, it sounded different; even the elves complained that magic was more unpredictable in Dragontown than anywhere else in the city.

Though it was getting late in the evening, shops were still open, the amber lights from open doors forming rectangles on the broken pavement. Laura passed busy teahouses and noodle shops where men talked and gambled, throwing down the mah-jongg cubes while enveloped by the steam from hot food. The smell of noodle soup set Laura's stomach to growling. "Quiet beast!" She patted it. "You'll eat at the Ferret."

In one doorway she saw an old man, sitting on the doorstep and smoking his pipe. She stepped through the cloud of gray smoke and caught the sharp smell of his pipe. She stopped a moment to look in the window crammed with a wide assortment of martial-arts weapons: the glittering points of the shuriken, wooden nunchakus, and bamboo shinais. There were also a few fake swords, a naginata, and a Chinese halberd. Her eye caught on the sight of a bo leaning discreetly at the back of the window. She wanted one. The short staff made a good training tool, and a nice companion for the walk home.

"What'll you take for the bo?" she asked the old man casually, turning her head toward the canal as if only partially interested in an answer.

"What'cha got, sister?" he asked, pulling the pipe from his mouth.

She shrugged. Let him name a price.

Broken teeth gaped at her as he smiled. "Got any chocolate? Huh?"

She stared back at him and made a rude noise. "When's the last time you got chocolate for anything, you old fart? This whole fucking shop isn't worth a lick off a Hershey!"

He stood up, angry, shouting at her, throwing his arms forward to wave her away from the shop window. "Hey, fuck you too," she hollered back, bristling as his hands pushed her roughly toward the street. She dug in her heels, ready to push back, until she saw the Dragons appear suddenly in the doorway of the shop. Three of them leaned out, curious, checking out the commotion caused by the old man's yelling. The light from the store shone on the spiked wristlets and the thin chains they wore as belts. "Shit," she muttered, and backed away from the shop, turning quickly and heading down the street. She'd seen how the Dragons used those chains, spinning them over head with a high, eerie whistle. Wasn't wise to call up too much attention when traveling here. In the dark, with her black Mohawk, she'd pass from a distance. But close up, looking at her blue eyes, they'd know she didn't belong. Dragons were the one reason Asian merchants still traded down here instead of Traders Heaven. Heaven had the illusion of safety that came with numbers, shops, and stalls huddled together as the traders hawked their wares. But Dragontown kept to itself and the Dragons were its guardians and street warriors.

When she reached the Old Wall surrounding Soho at last, Laura hurried her steps, running lightly over the uneven cobblestones of the old streets toward Carnival Street. I better not be late, she sang to herself as she leaped the curb and turned onto Ho Street, or Farrel's gonna serve me up for lunch! The change between Dragontown and Soho was abrupt and exciting. From the shadows of the Asian district she emerged into the bright lights of the clubs, the crowds of kids and gangs parading in electric colors, and the ever-present traffic of cruising bikes. The line before the Dancing Ferret was long, a testament to the popularity of the Horn Dance. Friends called out to her from the line and she waved back, not stopping to talk but shouldering her way past the crowd into the alley, then up the fire escape, and in through the back door.

The club was packed. The smells of smoke and sweet homebrew stung her nose and her eyes started watering as she edged her way to the bar. Standing on tiptoe, she tried to peer over and around heads, looking about for signs of an angry Farrel Din. She spotted him in the only quiet corner in the club, having a chat with his old friend Stick. The two of them framed an odd picture to her, a chubby elf and a tall black man in dreadlocks, a ferret sleeping on Stick's knee. But she sighed with relief. If Stick was here, chances were Farrel wouldn't have noticed her lateness. She ducked beneath an opening in the bar counter and went to the back room for an apron.

"Hey giant, we were beginning to wonder if you were coming tonight," Liza Malone wisecracked as Laura stepped behind the bar, tying on the black apron.

"Hey yerself, small stuff," she hollered back over the general din. Laura was short, barely making it over five feet. But Liza was shorter still and it had been a joke between them ever since they'd first met. "Gods, has it been this crazy all night?"

"Even crazier. Look love, grab those tables over there, would you? I've got my hands full here." Liza scooped up three pints of homebrew in each hand, balancing them against each other, and then pushed her way through the crowd to a table, her fuchsia-dyed pony tail bobbing above her shoulders. The crowd opened grudgingly and then swallowed her up as she passed.

Laura sighed for a moment, thinking about the long night's work ahead. Then she ducked under the counter and headed out for the tables.

Three members of the Pack sprawled on their chairs, already looking as if they had a head start on the night. "What can I get you this evening?" She leaned down to the catch the words.

"What I want's not on the menu." One boy leaned forward, drunken eyebrows trying to wiggle meaningfully.

Laura rolled her eyes in disgust. How many times was she going to hear that line tonight? "Hey, if it ain't on the menu, then you don't get it, see?" she answered tartly.

His hand shot out to encircle her waist. "If you was better dressed, babe, I'd take you out."

"If I was better dressed, asshole, you couldn't afford

me,'' she shot back, and freed her wrist from his grasp.
The other two burst out laughing at their luckless friend
and, to save face, he found himself having to laugh along
with them. ''Now then, what's it gonna be; are you drinking or taking up space?'' That was a nice thing about
waitressing at the Ferret, thought Laura. You didn't have
to be nice to customers if they didn't behave. Which was
a good thing, since they usually didn't.

Liza was right; tonight the packed club was full of crazies. It seemed she never stopped making the trip from
bar to tables and back again. Always something in her
hands; pints, or a rag for washing up, or dirty glasses.
And it seemed a night for fending off mashers, dodging
gropes, and blocking unasked-for embraces. Gods, she
thought exhaustedly, I've used up every one of my good
comebacks and the night's not over. But a part of her found
the rush and tumble of the lively bar exciting. It helped
that the Horn Dance was playing the club tonight. Their
music had a way of setting up everyone's spirits, unknot-
ting the rivalries and breaking down the tension that was
always there between elves and humans. Too busy dancing
and singing to fight, Laura figured.

Near to midnight, Jenny Jingle caught her by the waist
and twirled her round during one of her endless trips to
the bar. Standing behind Jenny she saw the round face of
Terrible Tim and his mate Merriweather, then Sandy and
Robbin from the dojo. And over Robbin's shoulder, Koga
Sensei, who was looking about with amused puzzlement
at the frantic chaos of the club. He looked different to
Laura, seeing him for the first time outside the dojo.
Younger, she thought, and somehow more accessible. She
felt shy suddenly, as if she were meeting a stranger, and
an attractive one at that.

''How was dinner?'' she shouted over the pleasant roar
of music.

''Not bad; we copped some fish that was still fresh down

at market,'' Terrible Tim answered, ''and Jenny here managed to jingle us up some chips to go with.''

''I played them a tune they couldn't resist.'' She shrugged, smiling.

''Great! Let me see if I can find you a table in all this mess. C'mon, follow me!''

They twisted through the crowds, following Laura, and when she checked back to see if they were still with her, she saw Robbin take Sensei's arm, pulling him along as he gazed distractedly at the crowds.

She found them a table off to the side but near enough to the stage that they could see the sweat as it poured off the faces of the hardworking Horn Dance. Jenny was already swaying in her chair, unable to stop the flow of music in her body.

''What can I get you?'' she asked them.

''BEER!'' they all shouted at her, except Sensei, who was watching the nimble guitar work of Manda Woodsdatter.

''Sensei?'' she asked to get his attention. His head snapped around to look at her, and he flashed a smile with straight white teeth.

''No,'' he said, shaking his head. ''Not Sensei. In the dojo I am Sensei, but out here, I am Koga. Call me Koga.''

Laura flushed, the simple use of his name surprisingly intimate. Her stomach fluttered, and she felt tongue-tied. She knew where she stood with Sensei, but not with Koga.

''Good sparring tonight,'' he said, to fill in the gap.

''Oh, ah, thanks, Sens—'' She stopped, caught by old habits. ''What can I get you to drink, Koga?''

He looked at the others questioningly.

''Beers all around,'' answered Sandy, ''and soon, or I'll die parched and withered.''

''Not likely,'' she retorted. ''You're as steeped in the brew as my aunt Millie's rumcake.''

''Ah, 'tis mortally wounded I am,'' he cried theatrically, clutching his chest. "Quick now, a drink for a dying man!"

"I'm going! I'm going," she cried, and plunged through the crowds back to the bar.

Standing at the bar, waiting for the drinks to be served, Laura found herself staring at Koga. Silly goose, she muttered under her breath. You see the man nearly every day in the dojo, and one day he steps out and you get a crush on him. Just like that! Just like a bimbo! She watched as Koga got up from the table and crossed the club to the alcove where Stick and Farrel were still conversing. She craned her neck and, surprisingly, saw Stick stand up and shake Koga's hand. Well, why not? she thought. Why shouldn't they know each other? Koga was standing, arms crossed over his chest, legs apart. Always in stance, she thought amused. He looked different somehow, though, and Laura couldn't help staring. She had never paid much attention to his physique, for it was usually hidden by the generous cut of his gi. But now, in a T-shirt that pulled tight over his chest, it was impossible not to notice the compact and muscular body.

"Beer's up." The bartender nudged her and startled her out of her staring.

"Shit!" she said to no one in particular, and headed back to the table, grinning like an idiot.

The night flew and it seemed to Laura that she did too, moving swiftly between the rowdy crowd, snatching bits of conversation when work found her near their table, and all the while, the steady beat of the music keeping her going. She felt a crazy kind of happiness whenever she'd catch Koga's eye and he'd smile back. Goofy girl, she admonished herself. He might be Sensei in the dojo, distant and forbidding, but in the Dancing Ferret he was just Koga and she was beginning to learn how nice that could be.

Laura glanced at a corner near the stage where two human boys were standing, eyes squeezed shut and swaying drunkenly. They were singing along with the band at the top of their lungs, pretending to bang away at electric guitars. Laura watched them, laughing at their gyrations as they slid their fingers up and down the necks of imaginary guitars and wailed out the tune. But her smile froze and the laugh caught in her throat when she saw behind them the silver head of a high-born elf. He was standing almost in the shadows talking to someone, but she could still make out the hawklike profile limned by the stage lights and the white hair that draped to his shoulders.

He turned slightly, his eyes flicking over the crowd, and she dropped her gaze so as not to be noticed. She turned back for another quick look and shivered. Corwyn of Aldon House—though on the street he was known as Long Lankin, the murdering knight. Better tell Farrel, she thought grimly, and hurried through the crowd to find him.

She came to the alcove, breathless and nervous. "Farrel—" she started.

"You were late tonight, girl, don't think I didn't notice!" he interrupted her.

"Look, I'm sorry about that," she rushed, "but I've just seen Corwyn over there talking to some of the Bloods. Thought you should know."

The change on the elf's face was instant. From mock anger it darkened to a real angry scowl. "Damn him," he muttered, and charged out of his seat, moving with greater speed and grace than Laura would have thought possible of the portly elf. She rushed to catch up with him and was at his shoulder when Corwyn suddenly broke through the crowd, heading for the door.

"What are you doing here, Corwyn?" Farrel asked, his voice hard.

"What you should be doing, Farrel. Teaching a child of the True Blood."

Laura looked beyond Corwyn and recognized Keno as he slipped to one side of the doorway, trying to pass unseen. Though he flashed by quickly, she recognized the strips of white tape that still graced his nose.

"What you teach is bigotry. There's no welcome for you at the Dancing Ferret."

Corwyn drew himself up, his eyes gleaming white and fierce; a sharp tic rustled the otherwise smooth and perfect skin of his cheek. "Go back to Elfland, Farrel Din. Remember what it is to be high born and don't pollute yourself with the things of Men."

"Perhaps you should remember why Elfland returned, Corwyn. . . ."

Corwyn of Aldon House hissed. Laura watched as the two elves stood tense, locked in a private and bitter hatred. Around the pair there came a pungent smell like smoke from a gutted candle. Dimly Laura heard the music of the Horn Dance falter, a sudden, missed note that soured in the air. Then Corwyn smiled, cold and ruthless, as he pushed past Farrel and out of the Dancing Ferret.

Silently, Farrel watched him go and then went to the bar and reached for a bottle of vintage Amber and a glass. Somewhere the music caught itself again, and Laura heard the lively notes of Bramble's pushbutton accordian take control of the crowd. She went back to waiting tables, trying to put the memory of Corwyn's cold face from her mind.

"Go home girl, it's late," Farrel's tired voice called to her from the alcove where he sat finishing the last of the wine. The club was near empty and subdued. Those who remained conversed quietly as they sat hunched at tables. The Horn Dance was packing up their equipment and getting ready to leave. Laura was wiping down the bar, trying to clean the sticky remains of homebrew and a thousand fingerprints from the polished wood.

She stopped, feeling tired herself, and threw the cloth down in the laundry bag. "I'm gone. 'Night, Farrel, see you tomorrow."

''Right.''

She went to the back room, took off her apron, and gathered up her things for the walk home. She had said good night to Jenny Jingle and the others awhile ago. They were off in search of something sweet to eat. Koga, before heading back to his flat in Dragontown had offered to wait and walk Laura home. She wished now she'd said yes, wished she hadn't gotten so stupidly shy. But there it was. And she knew the other reason she didn't want him walking her home. Home was in the Scandal District just beyond Dragontown. Laura lived with her mother, who'd still be working at this hour. She knew she shouldn't be ashamed, her ma had worked hard so that they could manage, so who cared what she did? But some had cared, and Laura had heard enough of the taunts, ''flatbacker's daughter,'' in her eighteen years to make her wary.

Pulling on her old leather jacket, she left the club and headed back uptown to the Scandal District. Soho was still brightly lit with fairy-dust and guttering street lamps, but the crowds had scattered and there were few to be seen on the streets. It had rained while she worked, and the ground was slick with moisture. Puddles of black water caught the light and glimmered like abalone. Laura walked carefully, trying to avoid the puddles, and listening to the soft slapping of her tennies on the wet pavement. She breathed deeply, the air wet and cold but smelling better than the smoke of the Dancing Ferret. She'd wash when she got home. She couldn't sleep unless she did. She hated the smell of smoke and beer that clung to her after waitressing. It depressed her, for it reminded her of the stale smell on her mother's skin after a night's work.

Laura's head drooped, almost resting on her chest as she walked home, following a path so often taken that it required no thought to follow. Up to Ho Street, over to Third, up a few blocks, and then she'd be on Water Street. She'd follow the canal a ways past Dragontown and then turn onto Brick Street, which led her through the Scandal District to her home on Hideaway Road.

Laura wasn't certain when she became aware of the noise behind her. She didn't notice it right away, thinking the soft squelching sound was made by her own footfalls. But she slowed her step and suddenly thought she heard the uneven patter of someone else. She stopped, holding herself still. The footsteps stopped as well, but not before she had heard them clearly. "Shit!" she whispered to herself.

She started again, hoping that somehow the sound would not be there. But as soon as she moved, she heard it again, this time closer. "Shit," she cursed again. She had to make a decision. First choice, she could run. Looking up Third Street, she saw she was still a long block from Water. Water Street would be lit with the teahouses still open. She could take refuge there, stay all night if she had to; she had enough change in her pocket from waitressing to buy tea. Second choice, she could fight.

She turned around and peered down the dark street behind her. She couldn't see anything at first, and then a shadow moved along a building and she caught the flash of white hair in a stray shaft of light. Then another shadow darted beside it and she heard the footsteps moving in on her. So, there were two of them—not good. She turned and started sprinting up Third Street, and behind her she heard them break into a run.

One arm hugging her gi, the other pumping the air, she pushed herself for more speed. She chanced a glance over her shoulder as she ran and saw the Bloods closing in. She turned back, but too late—she saw a third Blood step from a doorway in front of her and block her path. A hand shot out and pushed her, throwing her off balance and sending her careening on the pavement. She tucked her body in a roll as she fell, but it did little to cushion her fall on the broken concrete. Her cheek was scraped open by the stones and the wind was knocked from her chest as she slammed into the ground. She rolled and landed faceup, dazed and staring at the burst of yellow stars in her eyes. A hand reached down and grabbed her by the front of her jacket, pulling her brusquely to a standing position.

She had been close to Water Street. So close. A street lamp at the corner cast a slim streak of light on her, but they had caught her while she still remained unseen in the shadowy side street. He pulled her close to his face so that she might see him clearly, elvin eyes burning whiter than the strips of tape across his nose. Her breath came hard and fast, forced through her throat constricted with fear.

"Hey, street meat, you're mine this time!" Keno hissed in her face.

Don't think, she screamed to herself, just act. Reflexes snapped to life in Laura's body, and she jerked her knee up into his groin. Ready for it, he twisted away and she followed through slamming a punch to his stomach. He grunted, surprised, but held on to her jacket with one hand and punched her face with his other fist. In the small second before the blow connected, she saw it coming and rolled her head to one side. Lights burst in her eyes again as pain exploded along her jaw, but she didn't go under. She returned with another strike aimed for his throat. Keno jerked his head back and her attack fell short.

"Get her arms, fuckheads!" he shouted to the other Bloods.

Laura's arms were wrenched back on either side and her head pushed forward. She leaned away from one of the Bloods, using his grip for support as she thrust out a side-kick to his knee. He jumped back out of range, dropping her arm, and she swung around to attack the other.

"I said hold her, you faggots!" Keno roared as he caught her free arm again and twisted it up high behind her back.

She cried out as the bone in her arm nearly snapped. Her lungs burned for air and her face bubbled and ached with the hits it had taken. Keno forced her away from the open street and deeper into the shadows. Her legs resisted, dragging and twisting against the ground. He slammed her into a wall and held her there, her cheek pressed hard against the wet brick.

Laura spat out the warm blood that filled her mouth. "Is that how you like it, Keno? Huh? Three against one? Or maybe Bloods don't have balls and it takes three of you to get it up."

He pulled her out from the wall and slammed her against it again. "Shut the fuck up! Give it to me," he ordered one of the Bloods standing next to him, and then he released her and turned her savagely about to face him. "Now hold her," he said, and they pinned Laura's shoulders back against the wall. "I wouldn't waste spit on you, street meat." He was breathing hard from their fight and Laura could see him struggle to regain his composure. He drew in a deep breath and then smiled malevolently. "Like I said, you're mine. I own you."

Laura thrashed against the wall and tried to kick out with her legs. Keno's hand shot out and caught her face in a cruel grip. His fingers dug into the sides of her cheeks and he forced her head back, her neck exposed. "You like to fight, don't you, street meat? Well, I got something that'll make you a real killer. Yessir, you're gonna be my weapon against the Dragons."

Laura didn't understand. She had expected to be beaten—not raped, gang honor forbade that, but beaten within an inch of her life for humbling him in the dojo. His words made no sense to her. With his free hand he raised a flask and uncorked it with his teeth. He held it up so she could see it, glittering with its own light, and then brought it close to her lips. Her eyes widened as she realized what it was. Fairy-dust. Mixed in some cheap wine that smelled cloying and sweet.

Laura thrashed and bucked wildly under the Bloods' grip. She didn't know what the fairy-dust would do to her, but she knew what kids looked like when they took too much of the stuff. She tried to escape the liquid as Keno forced it in her mouth. She choked and spit, trying not to swallow, but Keno held her fast, and the wine filled her mouth and trickled down her throat.

It tasted sour as it passed her throat and into her stomach. She retched and groaned as waves of heat and nausea billowed out from the center of her body. Keno's hand pulled away from her face and her head drooped forward; the Bloods let go of her and stepped back, slowly, eyeing her cautiously. She took a step forward and staggered, the ground rocking beneath her feet and the heat of the drug burning in her head.

"Step away from her." She heard Keno's voice hushed with excitement. They moved farther back and formed a wide semicircle in front of her. Through a haze she saw Keno pull a flute from his jacket. Odd, she thought, feeling like a detached spectator, Keno hardly struck her as the musical type. She looked again at the flute, and something about it made her recoil and start to whimper. It was made of bone, hollowed with five note holes and knobbed at either end like the tibia of a child. He lifted it to his lips and began to play.

She stared, transfixed by the white bone. The low, eerie sound echoed in her head and seemed to unravel the very moment in time on which she stood. Then a coldness, white and silver like the trees of Elfland, began to creep through her veins; a freezing cold that shook her teeth and shivered down her back; a sharp cold that excised all emotions save a bitter numbness. On her skin it seemed to Laura that the sweat froze and hardened into ice.

"It's working," an incredulous voice breathed.

Keno stopped playing. "Of course it works." He sneered. "It comes from Corwyn, not some hag of an Elftown witch-wife. It's one of the old spells of power. Corwyn gave it to me, just like he'll give me Dragontown when I'm done ridding it of Dragon scum." He put the flute to his lips again and began to blow the mournful notes.

Laura's head ached with the sound. It itched within her and stung her like a wasp. She jerked her head up and smelled the smoke of guttering candles. She felt a burst of longing, a perilous need to obey the music, do as it asked so it would not punish her with its maddening sting. She trembled and shook as a current of energy erupted in her body. She heard the snapping of bones and threw her head back to scream. From a throat now thick and furred she howled, long ears laid flat against her head. Two horns sprouted from her forehead and stabbed the misty air.

Keno stopped playing and watched breathless as she changed. Little snot-nosed Laura was gone, and now there waited a demon, *his* demon, his to command. She stared at him with baleful eyes glowing a bright orange. Her jaws snapped at the space between them, eating the last of the notes as the night grew quiet. Her Mohawk had grown into a shaggy pelt of pointed quills that hung down her back. She shook her head and they rattled like dry spears.

Keno pocketed the flute. "Right," he said to his Bloods. "Let's go hunting." He turned his back to her and headed into the hidden alleys of Dragontown. She followed him, the thick pads of her clawed feet landing silently on the pavement.

In the still dawn light Koga returned from the docks at Riverside with a mackerel wrapped in paper and a handful of potatoes in a sack. He liked the morning and even the usual stink rising from the wharves didn't dampen his good mood. Last night had been fun. Been a long time since he had allowed himself the pleasure of a night out. He'd kept himself at arm's length from his students. Had to, otherwise they might lose their fear of him, and that awe was necessary for their training. Still, he liked his students; liked their crazy energy, their creative rowdiness that bristled even in such a harsh life. And Laura. He liked her too. He had been surprised when she refused the offer of a walk home. Hadn't he seen sparks between them? He scratched his head with his free hand. Well, it'd been a long time since something like that too. Maybe he'd read the scene wrong.

He chuckled under his breath, remembering the sharp retorts she had flung at drunken kids as she scolded them into good behavior at the Dancing Ferret. Of all his students, he thought, she was easily the best. She had come to him two years ago full of spit and anger and thrown herself into the training. She had never lost the spirit that made her a good fighter, but she had grown more steady and more centered, the mark of a good karateka. He sighed and looked up at the gulls wheeling noisily overhead. She was good; he'd have to promote her to black belt soon and then hope that she didn't quit. Best thing to do, he thought, smiling, is to give her a good reason for hanging around.

Ahead Koga saw the small bustling figure of Miwako Fujimoto heading to market. Her feet scuffed softly over the cobblestones, and on her arm she carried a small basket for her shopping.

"Morning," he called out to her as she approached.

She jumped at the sound of his voice, and he could see now that she had been lost in thought.

"Ah, good morning, Koga-san. How are you?"

"Fine, there's a good catch in today," and he held up the mackerel for her to see.

"Good," she said, nodding back, still looking preoccupied. "Did you hear about Mrs. Chen's son?" she asked in a low voice.

He stopped and frowned. "No, what happened?"

"He was killed last night."

"Gangs?"

She shook her head. "Hard to say for certain. He was"—she groped for the right words to express her horror—"torn apart, they said. His head clean off." She shuddered, then her eyes widened. "They think maybe some animal did it, but what kind of animal does that and lives unseen in Dragontown?'' She looked at him, hopeful that he might have an answer. He didn't.

"So,'' he said, frowning at his shoes. "That's terrible.'' He looked up at her again. "I'll stop by Chen's place and see if I can help.'

"Hai.'' She smiled. "Let's hope this creature is not coming back, heh?''

"Yeah,'' he agreed.

She bowed briskly and they said good-bye. He watched her for a moment as she hustled to the market. Neither had said what they really thought. They both knew enough about magic in Bordertown to know that nothing unusual happened without a reason. And if it meant the killing of a Dragon, that couldn't be good news for Dragontown. He turned and hurried his steps toward home.

Laura's eyelids fluttered stickily as she tried to open them. When she did, she saw that dawn was just breaking and the sky was streaked with pink and gray. Her head was pounding and her tongue tasted like old leather. She paused, confused, trying to understand why she could see the sky from her bed. She turned her head, and it seemed her brain slid to one side and crashed into her skull. Brick and stone loomed over her, green with moss. She frowned and wiped a dirty hand over her dry mouth. At the sight of her hand she stopped, staring at the fingers as an image of claws sparkled before her. She struggled to sit up, fighting the vertigo that swept her head and spun the landscape.

"Shit!'' She exhaled and gazed stupidly around her. She was in the canal, sitting beneath a bridge on a damp muddied bank. She looked up at the underside of the bridge. "Like a fucking troll!'' she exclaimed out loud. She shuddered and rubbed her face with stiff hands. She was cold and her limbs felt numb. She looked down and saw her jacket was gone and her t-shirt hung in shredded rags. It was caked with something brown and hard. Her feet were bare and bleeding.

She stood up shaking, holding the slippery stones of the bridge for support as panic bubbled in her chest. What had happened last night? She struggled to remember, and nightmares began to form in her memory, hovering vague and wispy as ghosts. A clear image formed of Keno's face, and she heard the echo of a bone flute. She saw another face, contorted with fear and screaming wildly. There was blood, lots of blood, and the same maddening tune played over and over again. With a stab of pain, the nightmare reached into reality, and Laura remembered killing the Dragon. Horror shrouded her like a cold mist, and she hugged her arms around her chest, cut by an icy chill so deep that she was certain she could never be warm again.

She stared for a long time at the ocher mud of the canal, cold and trembling. Despair made her stand, afraid to move. But a sliver of stubbornness pricked at her, urged her through the terror to get going. She started walking along the side of the canal searching for a stairway that would lead her out. She found one and hoisted herself up the crumbling steps and crept out into Water Street. The street was quiet and nearly empty this early. It took her a moment to get her bearings, and when certain of her direction, she fled down the winding streets to the one place she knew she'd find help.

Laura climbed onto a trash can and peered through the grill covering an alley window. The lights were on in the Dancing Ferret, and she could just make out the white hair and broad back of Farrel Din. She checked the street to make sure no one could see her and then rapped at the window through the bars. He twirled about abruptly, quick on his feet for such a big man. He came to the window and scowled at Laura, but motioned her to the back door with his head.

"Laura, what the—" His rumbling voice stopped as he

took in her draggled state. He reached out and pulled Laura into the building and shut the door. Inside it smelled of stale beer and wood polish.

He guided her into the office behind the bar, a small room dominated by a huge desk that was covered with notes and memos, a spell box, old cups, and a half-eaten cheese sandwich on a blue plate. The walls of his office were covered with elvin abstracts, glimmering with shifting lights. He sat her down in an overstuffed chair and poured her a cup of strong tea.

"Here." He thrust the cup into Laura's hands and leaned back against the desk to watch as she drank it.

Laura swallowed some of the hot elvin tea, and it soothed her parched throat. Her nose started to run from the steam, and she sniffed noisily. The warm cup eased the ache out of her stiff fingers. She sighed and looked up at the elf. One eyebrow was cocked above pale eyes that stared back appraisingly. Laura knew that look; it was Farrel's specialty. If you'd done something wrong it made you feel like he'd caught you at it, naked. But if you needed help, it determined how much and what kind. Farrel was wearing his usual tattered coat marked by an odd stain or two. Laura noticed, with a flicker of amusement, that the usual cobalt blue ascot at his neck was a raving orange.

"Nice color," she said, giving a wan smile.

"Something new," Farrel answered, never taking his eyes off her.

Laura sighed and put the cup down. She wasn't ready to tell Farrel what happened, yet she needed his help. "I need some new clothes. Do you have anything you can spare me? I'll get it back to you."

"Sure; look through the costumes in the back room." He jerked his head in that direction. "There's hot water in the men's room. Why don't you wash up as well?"

Laura got up and went to the bathroom. Gingerly she stripped off the ragged clothes, not wanting to touch the brown stains. She turned on the taps and waited until the little basin was filled with steaming water. A mirror above the sink showed her just how bad she looked. The scrape on her cheek was dirty and crusted with dried blood. A purple bruise was swelling on the other cheek. Her eyes gazed back at her with a haunted expression. She shied away from the image and began to wash.

When she was done, she dressed in some clothes she found hanging on a peg in the back room. A pair of trousers that were too long, she rolled up. A t-shirt two sizes too big hung to her knees. It was a dark blue with the word "Antioch" in yellow letters across the chest. Laura wondered briefly if it was the name of a band. There was an old denim jacket with a pyramid and an eye embroidered in bright colors on the back. The shoes were all too big except for a pair of leather boots with square toes.

When she walked back into the office, Farrel smiled at her encouragingly. She realized then how seldom Farrel smiled. Laura stood there, rocking from foot to foot and chewing her lip.

"Wanna talk about it?" he asked.

Laura looked down at the square toes of the boots. "Can't," she answered, "not just yet."

The elf nodded. He leaned over, giving Laura one of those intense stares. "I want the t-shirt back in one piece. Got it? The rest you can have."

"Okay, I promise. I'll get it back to you as soon as I can."

Laura headed for the door, still feeling her employer's gaze on her back, intent with all the questions he had refrained from asking.

"Take it easy, kid," he said as she shut the door behind her. But Laura, deep in her own thoughts, didn't hear him.

Laura walked quickly through the winding streets of the old city to Dragontown. She was heading for the dojo where she knew Koga had a flat at the back. She needed to talk to him. She needed to explain to somebody what was going down in Dragontown, and it needed to be someone who'd still be talking to her after she'd finished. She didn't want to take her chances with the Dragons. It was hard imagining walking up to them and saying, *Excuse me but I chewed up one of your boys last night, so sorry. And oh yes, I may be back for seconds tonight.*

She reached the dojo, which was on the second floor over a trader's shop that carried an assortment of Japanese goods mixed in with the odd bit of elvin trade. The shop looked dusty and unvisited. Laura never did understand how the owner managed to make a living. She climbed the stairs, suddenly aware that she was nervous. Her palms were sweaty, and she wiped them on her jeans before she knocked at the red door to his flat.

"Chotto matte kudasai," his voice rang out. Laura blinked, ignorant of the foreign words, but waited quietly. After a moment he still hadn't come and she grew anxious, knocking again more loudly. Habit made her glance over her shoulder.

Koga threw open the door, and his face was flushed a rosy hue under his olive complexion. His black hair stuck up over the edge of a hachimaki tied around his forehead, and sweat beaded his face. He had on his gi, the faded black belt tied loosely and the jacket gaping open at the collar. He looked surprised at seeing her and opened the door wider to let her in.

"Laura, come in. I'm sorry I made you wait. Please, come in."

"What did you say when I knocked?" she asked curiously, trying not to pay attention to the fact that seeing him had brought back the giddy feelings she had experienced at the Dancing Ferret. But they were feelings that clashed now with the nightmare her life had become since last night. She felt self-conscious and touched her battered cheek with a shy hand.

"Hmm? Oh, nothing much, I just asked you to wait a minute. I don't get many visitors here who don't speak

Japanese, so I forget myself.'' He smiled at her, not saying anything more but looking very pleased to see her. She smiled back, uncertain what to say next.

She turned to look at his flat, which was hardly more than a long rectangular room. ''So,'' she started lamely, ''this is your place. I always wondered what it looked like.''

''Please,'' he said, gesturing with his arm, ''have a look around. Would you like tea? I can make some, it's no trouble.''

''Yeah, that would be nice. Thanks.'' Laura walked into the room while Koga turned his attention to a small counter that held a sink and a tiny magic fire. He banged a spell box with his fist to start it heating and put a pan of water on. Laura's attention was drawn to several large black and white paintings that hung across the windows. She stopped before them and studied them while Koga poked about, looking for cups. The paper was beautiful, a milky white with small flecks of pale grass and leaves scattered throughout. All the paintings carried the same image, a huge circle painted in a heavy black ink.

Koga saw her staring at them. ''They aren't very good. I am still learning.''

She looked back at him puzzled.

''It's calligraphy. Japanese characters painted with a brush. It's supposed to be a kind of meditation. But I am not very good. I rush too much.''

''They're neat. I like 'em,'' Laura answered, moving to look out a small door that led to the roof. There she saw makiwara boards, straw covering the striking surfaces. ''Were you working out up here?'' She nodded toward the roof.

''Yeah. It's nice working out outside, and up here I don't make a show of myself.'' He came toward her, his hands full with two cups and a small teapot which he held by its slim handle. She took the cups from him and looked for a place to sit down. There wasn't one. The room seemed

empty of furniture except for a bedroll and quilt that lay
in one corner of the wooden floor.

"Just a minute," he said quickly. He dove into a closet
and reemerged with two flat cushions that he sat on the
ground. He pulled out a low table that Laura hadn't seen
from under a stack of white paper and placed it between
the cushions. "Please." He motioned to the cushions, and
Laura sat down, placing the cups on the table and crossing
her legs.

Neither spoke as he poured the tea, and Koga found
himself wondering why she had come. It wasn't to be so-
ciable; he could tell that from the expression on her face.
It was bad enough to see the bruises, but it was the haunted
look in her eyes that tore his heart. He felt himself getting
angry, ready to go out and kill whoever had done this to
her. But he couldn't do that. She needed to be able to talk
about it in her own way and her own time and not have
him go berserk. The best thing he could for her right now,
he figured, was just to listen.

"You're not from Bordertown, are you?"

She startled him with her question. "No. I came from
the World about ten years ago."

"What brought you here?" she asked, her voice turning
harsh.

He shrugged. "I didn't want a life in a gray suit, going
to work with a hundred others wearing similar gray suits.
I came to Bordertown for a visit and found I couldn't
leave."

She grunted and stared in her teacup. "I'm Bordertown
born and bred, and sometimes I think the place stinks."
She fell silent, and he waited for her to continue. She
looked up at him again, and he caught a different pain that
lined her face and made it sad. "Oh sure, there's the elves.
We're supposed to be grateful for their magic. But what
good has it done for anybody? There are those that make
a living off it, the big Traders and the Gate Keepers. You
can see them wiggling their fat asses up on the Hill. But

what about the rest of us? Those of us born to the street? What's our life supposed to be like?'' She took a gulp of the tea and turned away. ''When I was a kid, growing up near here, if you didn't join a gang they beat the crap out of you until you did. Then when you joined the gang, you beat the crap out of somebody else. What a fucking life, heh? Half of my friends dead before they're grown and the other half flatbacking in the Scandal District just to support their babies.'' She stopped and examined the backs of her hands, turning them over slowly as if looking for something.

''I wanted out of that life, you know? When I came to the dojo the first time, I thought I'd found my answer. It was great. I could come with all my anger, all my hurt, and slug it out in a place that was safe. It was tough, but it was ordered, there were rules. And there was you, always making sure that nothing got out of hand. All that messy shit I faced on the street—suddenly it wasn't so scary. I could fight when I had to, better than I used to, but I could also chose not to fight. I thought I had it made. I thought I had escaped my old life, just like you're escaping a gray suit. But it's like they say: 'What goes around, comes around.' ''

She stopped speaking again, and Koga saw her swallow hard as if the words were too painful to speak. ''I killed somebody last night,'' she whispered to her hands. ''Bloods caught me and changed me with a spell, and they used me to kill a Dragon. They might do the same thing tonight, and the next night and the next night. They've turned me into a fucking monster, Koga, and there isn't a thing I can do about it.'' She looked at him, miserable and yet defiant, unwilling to cry the brimming tears.

Koga stared at her, shocked and silent, her words breaking like a wound on his skin. He ran his hand through his hair, the hachimaki slipping off in his hand. His face lost its rosy hue and became ashen. ''Laura, I don't know what to say.'' He wanted to hold her and comfort her, but she held herself rigid and apart from him.

''There isn't anything to say. There isn't anything to do. I can't afford some fancy elf mage to help me out and even if I could I doubt they'd be willing to cross Corwyn—the guy who's responsible. Not for a human. Look, I just want someone to warn the Dragons. They gotta know what's being planned and—'' She hesitated, her voice faltering. ''And I just want someone to tell the kid's family that I didn't mean it.'' She gave a harsh laugh. ''That's pretty meager. See, the truth is, I'm too stubborn to kill myself; someone else is gonna have to do it. I don't *want* to die— but I don't want to kill again either. I need your help.''

He stood up abruptly, frowning. ''Come on,'' he said brusquely. ''I can't help you, but I know someone who might be able to.''

Laura uncrossed her legs and rubbed feeling into them again before she stood up slowly. He was angry, she could see that, and she wondered how much he blamed her.

''Where are we going?'' she asked as he took off his gi jacket and drew on a gray sweat shirt over the gi pants.

''Her name is Fukumori Sensei,'' he said as he pulled on hi-top sneakers and tied up the laces. ''She is an exceptional person.''

Laura surprised him with a faint smile. ''Think I know the type,'' she said, fingering the hem of the blue T-shirt.

He lifted his eyebrows but said nothing. It relieved him to see her smile.

As they walked through Dragontown, Laura related everything to Koga that she could remember about the previous night. His jaw tightened when she told him about her fight with Keno and the other Bloods. He grew angry with himself, angry that his own arrogance had allowed him to take on gang members as students, believing that he could control them. Some were elves, for god sakes, and though he might have imagined himself as Bordertown's samurai, he was worthless fighting against magic. He stopped abruptly in midstride and turned to Laura, his face pale with rage and his black eyes narrowed with fury.

"I apologize, Laura. It's my fault that Keno used you. He was dangerous, I knew that. I should have kicked him out of the club a long time ago. But I thought I could handle him. I thought karate would change him."

She shook her head. "No, it's not your fault. There are dozens of creeps like Keno. Most of them you *can* handle. But it's hard when someone like Corwyn of Aldon House starts handing out instant power. That's just too big a gig to say no to. Look," she said matter-of-factly, "if I thought you were to blame, I wouldn't have come to you. But I trust you. Shit, I like you, Koga. I like you a lot and, well, I thought you were the only person who would listen to me and, maybe, not hate me." Laura flushed red, embarrassed by her confession.

"I like you too, Laura," he answered, and, with a self-deprecating grin, added, "What an asshole I am. I've been thinking about myself. Feeling guilty and angry. It's you I should be worrying about."

"Yeah well, for an asshole, you're all right." She smiled at him.

Now it was his turn to feel embarrassed. He covered it by taking her in his arms and holding her tightly. She hesitated, afraid of the touch and yet needing the comfort. Something stirred in her, a flicker of warmth against the cold spell, and she returned his embrace. They stood on the sidewalk holding each other silently while the passersby of Dragontown gawked.

Fukumori Sensei's house was set back from the street. It was a tall, narrow three-story house wedged between a noodle shop and a storefront offering acupuncture for a reasonable trade. It was one of the rare houses in the Asian district that had room for a small garden in the front yard.

"Why is she called Sensei? Does she do martial arts

too?'' Laura asked as they walked up the steps that led to the front landing. The railing was covered with a heavy vine that still held a few fragrant blossoms of purple clematis.

"She teaches koto, a Japanese instrument. 'Sensei' is the Japanese word for teacher."

Laura fell silent, wondering how a music teacher was going to be able to help her.

They didn't knock but slipped quietly through the unlocked door and into the front hall. It was dark, and it took Laura a few moments to adjust her eyes to the dim light. It had a salty smell like fish or pickles that tickled Laura's nose and made her strangely hungry. Koga motioned to her to follow him up the curving staircase. As they climbed she could hear the sounds of an instrument being played—a sweet lutelike sound. It stopped, and she could hear the murmur of voices, then the music started again. By the time they had climbed to the third landing, Laura had heard the same passage repeated several times and realized she was listening to a lesson.

At the top of the stairs Koga led her down a narrow hallway. Laura tripped over something stacked on the floor. It was a pile of books comprised of loose-leaf paper that spilled over the floor. She stopped to pick it up and noticed the odd marking on the pages, written in long columns.

"What is this?" she asked as Koga helped her to restack the pile.

"Sheet music for the koto."

"Why is it so dark in here?" Laura complained in a loud whisper.

"Shhh," Koga answered, and glanced quickly at the opened door at the end of the hallway. "Come on, but don't say anything."

Laura scowled but followed him, curious in spite of herself.

Outside the door Koga stopped and took off his shoes.

He motioned for Laura to do the same. She grimaced as she pulled off the boots and laid them alongside another pair of womens' shoes that were waiting by the door. They slipped inside. Koga sat down along the back wall, resting his weight on his haunches and sitting still as a stone. Laura copied him, but her gaze wandered everywhere, fascinated.

As in Koga's flat, there was almost no furniture in the room. The floor was covered with thickly woven straw mats, edged with strips of black fabric. In front of the large windows, screens made of translucent paper stretched on a frame blocked the direct sunlight and gave the room a warm, diffuse glow. At the far end of the room, opposite Laura, was an elaborate bookcase built into the wall. It was composed of many small shelves crammed with books and papers, drawers in various sizes with gleaming brass handles, and open niches that held small sculptures.

In front of it sat Fukumori Sensei, dressed in a tight black kimono, her back rigid and straight as she knelt on the floor by her koto. Her eyes were fixed on the pupil who knelt beside her, playing on a second koto. Fukumori Sensei was annoyed, her mouth pulled in a little frown. The student was nervous, playing the notes in a hurried fashion and skipping her finger picks too lightly over the strings.

"No!" Fukumori Sensei snapped. "Stop please."

The student stopped and leaned away from the instrument. Fukumori moved to her own koto and held her hand above the strings of the instrument. Laura could see the square-shaped picks like blunt claws that she wore on her playing hand.

"You are playing Godan Kinuta. The sound must be crisp and sharp. Each note must be clear," and she plucked a short, furious arpeggio on the strings.

"Shit!" whispered Laura, awed by the sudden vibrating sound. Koga looked over his shoulder at her and smiled in agreement.

Fukumori Sensei admonished her student: "The music is alive. Just as the samurai must seize the right moment to strike with the sword, so must the koto player strike the note. There must be no hesitation. One moment too late and the musician is defeated. Do you understand?" The student nodded, and Laura felt a pang of sympathy as the student screwed up her courage and tried the piece again. But for all her effort, it seemed to Laura that the music managed to give the student a good drubbing anyway.

The lesson over, student and teacher bowed politely to each other. The student then wrapped her koto in a cloth and set it upright on the wall. She bowed again at the Sensei and left the room, looking, to Laura, very tired—and relieved that it was over.

"Seems a lot like workout," Laura murmured to Koga.

"She's a tough teacher. But she's the best." He stood up and together they crossed the room to where Fukumori Sensei waited.

"Ah, Koga-san." She smiled and inclined her body in a small bow. "How nice of you to visit."

Koga bowed back. "Good morning, Sensei. I am pleased to see you."

He and Laura crossed the room together and then kneeled, sitting across from Fukumori and her koto.

Fukumori looked at Laura and smiled questioningly. Close up Laura saw that the Sensei was a much older woman, her head like a small dried apple on which someone had carved a slim face. Her hair, graying at the temples, was pulled back in a smooth, tight bun at the nape of her neck. But she had a presence that Laura found disquieting and intimidating. Her eyes were bright and the stare penetrating.

Koga introduced Laura, who bowed, feeling clumsy and awkward next to Fukumori, so tidy and restrained. Koga pulled a small square package wrapped in purple paper from the pocket of his sweat shirt.

"Please, Sensei, I hope you will enjoy this," he said, and pushed the package toward her.

Laura watched as Fukumori's face grew young with delight. "Ah, Koga-san, *domo arigato gozaimasu*. Thank you, thank you. You shouldn't have!" She unwrapped the paper, and even Laura gasped as she saw the two thick squares of dark chocolate, one of the most coveted and costly items in Bordertown. It was something that belonged to the World, tending to spoil when kept too long near the Border—no one knew why. In Bordertown, chocolate was an expensive habit. Laura's stomach rumbled at the sight, and she looked away. But the sweet smell caught up with her, and she imagined its taste on her tongue. She'd not eaten it often, but she remembered clearly the exceptional taste. Laura guessed Fukumori had much the same feeling for the sweet and admired her generosity when she offered to share it with her guests. Koga said no with a light shake of his head, and while Laura was dying to have a piece, intuition told her it would be better to refuse. Fukumori refolded the paper and placed the chocolate reverently to one side.

She returned her attention to Koga, waiting for him to speak. The pleasant smile vanished as he spoke quickly in rapid-fire Japanese. Fukumori's face grew serious. "So, so." She nodded her head every few words in response to his speech. Laura figured he was telling her about Keno, for she caught the mention of her name and his in the stream of foreign words. Laura's gaze strayed to a black, cast-iron teakettle that sat on a cushion near Fukumori. Just as she was thinking how strange to have a teakettle sitting on a cushion, the teakettle wriggled. From the spout a badgerlike head appeared, and four paws sprouted at the base, but the body remained that of a black teakettle. Laura watched amazed as the badger head looked at her and sniffed delicately. It licked it lips and then turned around slowly, like a dog looking for a comfortable spot, and then resettled itself. Once sitting, the head disappeared and the paws tucked themselves under the kettle. Laura shot a glance at Koga and Fukumori, wondering if they had seen it too, wondering if she should say anything. But they ignored her, continuing their conversation.

Koga finished speaking and Fukumori leaned back, pensive. They were quiet for a moment, staring into space, thinking. Laura's eyes did not stray from the teakettle.

"Laura, come here," Fukumori demanded.

Laura jumped at her voice and moved quickly around the koto to sit beside her.

"Please don't be afraid," Fukumori said. Laura gave a Koga a worried look. He nodded reassuringly, and Laura turned back to the woman. She took Laura's face between her dry palms and held her own face close to Laura's. It seemed to Laura that the black eyes changed color, becoming amber, and she found herself unable to look away. Laura tensed, feeling something tickle on her neck and edge its way across her scalp. It stopped and she relaxed. In that moment Fukumori hurled herself into Laura's mind.

Laura gasped with the sudden strike and arched her back. Strong hands held her face tightly but without pain. Laura's head ached and bulged, her breath was shallow and raspy. The room disappeared and all she could see was the amber glow from Fukumori's eyes. She focused on the color, and it held her in a soothing embrace. The pain lessened, the tightness in her chest relaxed.

Fukumori dropped her hands from Laura's face and slowly released her mind. Laura lurched forward, the brightness of the room painful after the subtle glow from Fukumori's eyes. Fukumori bowed her head and brought a hand to rest under her chin.

"*Ah so, so desu ka,*" she murmured to herself.

Laura was still blinking rapidly and her mouth was parched.

"*Ah gomenasai,*" Fukumori apologized. She reached behind her and brought down a tray that held a teapot and three round cups. She turned to her side and for a moment

Laura thought she was going to pick up the changeling teakettle. Instead she reached over it and brought out another pot that Laura now saw was sitting on an ordinary magic fire, though there was no spell box or cord leading from the plate. Fukumori poured hot water in the teapot.

"I am sorry, Laura. I hope I wasn't too rough. Some people are more difficult because their spirit resists and it requires me to be swift."

"I don't understand," Laura said. "What did you do?"

"I needed to know how the spell was cast on you. I had to search for the knowledge in your mind."

"What did you find out? Can the spell be undone?"

"Hmmm." Fukumori pursed her lips. "That depends on you. Let me explain.

"Fairy-dust is made with magic. It's harmless usually, used for decoration, illumination. But some people use it as a drug, ingesting the magic by swallowing it, or sniffing it. In elves this creates a sense of euphoria, mixing with the magic in their blood. In humans it creates an anxious, excitable state which some foolish children call 'high'—for magic is alien to most human souls."

She paused to pass a cup of tea to Koga and then one to Laura, balancing the cups gracefully on outstretched fingers.

"Even Keno has honor," she continued. "He would not make such a demon out of another elf. But you—you are merely human. Normally a spell such as Long Lankin gave to him would not work on one not of the Blood. But when you took—were forced to take," she corrected herself, "the fairy-dust, Keno literally poured magic into you, making you, for that moment, almost elvin. Thus the spell worked on you. Keno's music called the demon from the depths of your soul and bound it to his will. When he was done with the demon, he released you."

"Can he do it again?" Laura asked, afraid of the answer.

"Yes." She inclined her head toward Laura. "The demon is part of you. As you live, it will answer whenever Keno calls.''

Laura bent her head into her hands.

Koga spoke up ''What if she ran away to the World? The spell wouldn't work there. She'd be safe—or rather, others would be safe.''

''NO!'' Fukumori and Laura both said together.

''Bordertown may be a weird place, but it's where I live. It's all I know. I won't let some fucking elf drive me from my home,'' Laura answered vehemently.

''The demon is part of Laura,'' Fukumori added evenly. ''She can leave the Borderlands, but the demon can't leave her. It will eat at her heart, and in time it will destroy her—even in the World.''

''What about killing Keno?'' Koga asked coldly.

Again Fukumori shook her head. ''Keno holds the flute. But if you kill him, someone else may use the flute and Laura would still be bound.''

''What can I do?'' Laura asked quietly, fearing she knew the answer already. For the Japanese, there were times when suicide was honorable, and rituals governing the way it must be done. But this is not the answer Fukumori gave her.

''You must take control of the demon,'' she said. ''There is a moment when you are changing that everything is stretched to its weakest. That is the moment that you must fight Keno for control.''

Laura ran her hands over the shaved sides of her skull and shivered. ''How am I gonna fight them? That demon is one mean monster.''

''Laura, understand something that is very important.'' Fukumori held Laura's gaze steady until she was certain the frightened girl was listening. ''The demon is not evil. Everyone has a demon within them. And most times the demon is not a killing monster at all. The demon is a kind of power, energy drawn from your spirit that can be used to create or to destroy. When Keno called the demon from you, he stole power from your spirit and twisted it to destroy only."

Laura shook her head. "I don't get it."

Fukumori's hand lashed across the strings of her koto. Laura heard again the piece the student was trying so desperately to play. But in Fukumori's grip the notes struck the air like the crack of lightning. The music rippled and shimmered, each note precise and brilliant. Fukumori stopped abruptly, her hand poised above the instrument. Even in the sudden silence, the room hummed with the power of her playing.

Fukumori smiled at Laura's astonished face. "My demon." She shrugged. "It plays koto."

"Have you ever thought of going electric with that thing?" Laura asked, awed, thinking about the chaos Fukumori's playing would cause at the Dancing Ferret.

Fukumori laughed and hid her mouth behind the hand that still wore finger picks. "I have heard it done. But the sound is not as pure, though I admit it is exciting. Laura," she said, returning to the subject, "people have all sorts of demons. There is the mother with two children. She is a good mother, soft and loving. One day someone comes and threatens them. She doesn't think, just fights fiercely to save her children. She uses her demon to protect them. Some use the demon to paint, some to play music, some to teach," and she smiled at Koga. "The demon is like passion. But to control it, you must focus it and give it shape. When you have done that, it cannot be taken from you and shaped by others. Do you understand?"

Laura nodded slowly. It made a kind of sense to her, but it was still not quite an answer. "How do I focus it? And how do I do that while Keno's turning me into the demon?"

"Ah, that one I cannot answer for you. There must be something in your life into which you pour your spirit. Use that to channel the energy of the demon." Fukumori fell silent, studying Laura beneath half-closed lids.

Laura bent her head and looked at the tops of her thighs. Her head ached and her eyes itched with sand. She was tired and it seemed impossible to think. Fucking little bastard Keno, she thought bitterly. He should have just killed her. Instead he had reached into her soul and twisted it, turning her as cruel and evil as himself.

Fukumori turned to Koga and spoke with a low voice in Japanese: "Forgive me for speaking Japanese but I must speak with you and not upset your friend. Koga-san," she said carefully, "your friend has a very strong spirit. Very strong. The demon this elf has created is also strong. If Laura cannot regain control of her demon, you must kill her."

Koga forced his face to remain neutral, though Fukumori saw the dismay in his eyes.

"Please understand. This elf will not be able to hold the demon for long. He thinks his spell is powerful enough, but he is wrong. She must free herself—or be stopped. I can see you have a special feeling for her and I am sorry to ask this of you. But do you think that she would wish to be the cause of pain and violence? Would you ask the Dragons to go alone against such an enemy? But I have not given up yet. She does possess strength, strength enough, perhaps, to fight the demon. Keep her in Dragontown. If she is in Dragontown when the change occurs, I may be able to offer some assistance. But beyond the boundaries"—she shook her head—"I can do nothing."

"What can I do to help?"

Her shoulders lifted and dropped. "Help her find a way to focus her spirit."

"Hai—" Koga started to answer, but Laura interrupted him.

"Koga? What's that?"

Fukumori and Koga stopped talking and looked where Laura was pointing. The cast-iron teakettle was now undergoing a rapid transformation. A pink snout popped out of the spout followed by the badger head and tail. Head cocked, it examined them, black stripes across the eyes giving it a whimsical expression. It sniffed the air, searching for something, and then gave a high squeaky bark as it spotted the chocolate. With alarming speed it hefted itself on stubby legs and snatched the chocolate in its mouth.

Fukumori screamed at the creature and lunged to catch it as it sped past her. "Tanuki! My chocolate, give me back my chocolate!" It skittered out of the room, taking the curve too fast and nearly upsetting the round belly of its teakettle body. "Beast, thieving trickster!" Fukumori shrieked after the creature.

Laura stared, amazed, first at the disappearing teakettle and then back at Fukumori who had completely lost her composure. Her bun had come undone when she lunged for Tanuki, and now her hair hung down her back in a thin rope with a few straying hairs at her temples. Her kimono had become disarranged, and the neck gaped over the tight obi. Her face was a mixture of anger and extreme disappointment. She caught Laura's astonished expression and then sighed heavily.

"I am not without weakness, Laura-san." Something in Laura warmed at the use of the Japanese honorific. It seemed intimate and friendly, as if Fukumori had just taken her into a personal confidence. But then again, Laura thought with amusement, she had. Laura had just witnessed her come totally unglued for the sake of a bit of chocolate. Laura liked knowing that Fukumori had at least one small vice; it made her seem more human.

"Sensei?" Koga whispered as he leaned over to her. She was reknotting her hair and had a long tortoise-shell hairpin in her mouth.

"Hmm?" She turned to him, still distracted by the loss of her chocolate.

Koga pulled out of his pocket a second package wrapped

in purple paper. Her eyes widened with delight and hope bloomed in her face.

"I thought to give it to you later, when Tanuki was not here, so that you could decide if he deserved some or not. It seems he hasn't waited for his piece but taken his own. I hope this makes up for the theft of your piece."

Laura was flabbergasted. First Koga produces two big pieces of chocolate, then a thieving teakettle makes off with it, and then Koga produces two more pieces. Laura couldn't decide what was more astonishing, the escaping teakettle or the four pieces of chocolate.

"Koga-san, how kind," Fukumori was saying, smiling and looking very sheepishly at him. "You are so generous." She tucked the little package protectively in the front of her obi, which she had straightened, and stood up.

Koga and Laura followed her to the door. The sun was streaming in a narrow yellow band in the crack between the two screens. It dusted the floor with its bright light and caught the edge of Fukumori's body as she stood, bowing good-bye to them. Laura bowed back, and as she did so, she saw the shadow the koto teacher cast along the floor. She blinked at it, for it was all wrong. Laura looked back at the tiny woman and then again at the shadow. Instead of a round head, the shadow showed a profile of a dog—no, a fox, Laura corrected herself: a long nose and two pointed ears. Weirder than weird, she thought, but she said nothing, only watched secretly as the odd canine shadow bowed and nodded in perfect imitation of Fukumori Sensei. Laura chanced a look at Koga, but she was certain she saw him shake his head as a warning for her to be quiet.

"Please come again, Laura-san. I hope that I was of some help to you." She grasped Laura's hand firmly and spoke with a sudden intensity. "You have a good heart, Laura-san, and an even stronger spirit. Do not allow despair to make you weak."

"Thank you," Laura answered, moved by the words of encouragement. "I hope I can come back soon."

"Good, good." Fukumori patted her hand and then released her.

As they headed down the stairs again, Laura heard the sounds of the koto. The music was slow and stately, and something in the way the notes folded gracefully in a continuous stream of sound pulled at Laura's heart.

"I gotta ask," Laura blurted out as soon as they reached the street. "Where in the hell did you get so much chocolate, what in the hell was that teakettle thingy, and who is Fukumori Sensei really?" She looked at Koga, bursting with curiosity, and he chuckled at her bewilderment.

"First, I got the chocolate from my students."

"I don't believe it." Laura shot back scornfully.

"It's true," he insisted. "Some of the wealthy students from the Tooth pay me in chocolate. They think it will make me promote them faster."

Laura made a rude noise.

"I agree completely. Funny thing is I don't like the stuff. Never had a sweet tooth." Laura stared at him as if he were more peculiar than the runaway teakettle. "But Fukumori Sensei, well, you saw." He shrugged. "She has a fondness for it, so I am happy to bring it to her."

"What about the teakettle? I'd say it too had a 'fondness' for the stuff."

"Ah, well, that wasn't really a teakettle. That was Tanuki."

He stopped and Laura scowled. "Go on," she prodded. "Who's Tanuki?"

Koga hesitated and Laura thought him weighing whether or not he should share with her some secret of enormous importance. It only made her angrier and she poked him in the ribs to let him know.

"Okay, okay," he said hurriedly, and took a deep breath. "Elvin magic isn't the only magic there is, you know. Elfland doesn't have a monopoly. I think that being so close to the Border rekindled the magic that was already here, dormant, in Dragontown. It is one of the reasons elvin magic works so badly in the Asian district—too much magic in one place. It's like feedback in a microphone.

"Dragontown is very private, secretive in some ways. It wants to protect itself from all the crazy changes that have happened over the years. Asian magic is not a thing generally advertised around town."

"Wow!" Laura answered, shaking her head. "It never occurred to me that there might be other kinds of magic."

"Tanuki is a trickster," Koga continued. "Never to be trusted, but then not necessarily harmful either. In the right mood, he can be good luck. In a perverse mood, well, you saw what happened to the chocolate. Fukumori Sensei is a very rare creature indeed," Koga said softly. "She is Kitsune, a fox-woman. Kitsune is also something of a trickster, changing her shape into a human and sometimes playing dreadful pranks. But she has a compassionate side too, and can offer insight and wisdom."

"And what about you, Koga?" Laura asked. "What are you really?"

Koga's smile faded and Laura watched his expression suddenly turn grim. "Shoki, the Demon Queller."

Laura said nothing, but it seemed she heard the echo of Fukumori speaking in Japanese. That was it then, she thought, that's the job she laid on him. She swallowed, and it felt as if a hard pit cut into her stomach. "Shit!" she swore a few moments later, and kicked at a stone on the pavement.

They were a block from the dojo when Laura spoke up again.

"So, got any bright ideas on what I should do? I've been sorting it out and sorting it out, and I still come up with nothing." He didn't answer, just stared glumly at the pavement as they walked. "Fukumori Sensei said to find something that I have poured my spirit into, and to use it.'' Laura shrugged and looked up at the sky, ticking off items on her fingers. ''I don't play music, I don't dance like a banshee, I don't have kids. I guess the only thing you could say I have really worked at these last two years is karate. But I don't see how I can use that.''

Koga's head reared up and he slapped his forehead. ''That's it! What a fucking idiot I've been!''

Laura looked shocked. She had never heard him swear before.

''Come on.'' He grabbed her hand and began running for the dojo. ''I've got an idea that might work. We don't have much time so we've got to hurry.''

''Hey wait!'' she shouted, flying behind him as he dragged her along by the hand. ''Hey wait, what is it?''

''I'll tell you when we get there!'' Fukumori Sensei was right, he thought excitedly. Perhaps there was a way he could help her after all.

They arrived at the dojo breathless. Laura leaned against the doorknob, chest heaving, while Koga went into his flat and returned wearing his gi and belt. He pushed her gently but firmly through the door of the dojo.

''There is an extra gi hanging on the door to the changing room. Help yourself. There's also a belt. Hurry, get changed.''

''Hey Koga—'' she started to say, confused.

''No. It's not Koga in here. It's Sensei,'' he interrupted, and Laura heard the change in his voice and saw the subtle change in his stance. He was in complete command again, and she felt compelled by habit to obey. She didn't answer but went to the changing room to find the gi and put it on.

As she was dressing she thought about how abruptly Koga had disappeared and Sensei returned. His demon, she decided. And it wasn't a bad thing at all. As a student she relinquished her ego at the door of the dojo, gave herself over to the demands of the Sensei, allowed him to push and to drive her so that she might learn. He could be a bully at worst and a tyrant most of the time. Yet while he demanded complete trust and obedience, in return he gave back to Laura trust in herself and a growing confidence in her skill. It was a fair exchange, she decided, and when she returned to the dojo, she bowed to the Sensei and forgot about Koga.

"Hai, okay," he began after they had warmed up. "What is kata?" he asked.

"A series of attacks and defenses against an imaginary opponent arranged in a sequence," she answered dutifully like a student giving the date of a revolution or king's crowning.

"No," he replied sharply, and she looked at him, eyebrows lifted in surprise. But that was typical. Sensei always changed the answer depending on what lesson needed to be learned at the moment. "Kata is meditation in motion. It is not just against an imaginary opponent but yourself. Kata can show you your greatest strengths and your weaknesses. It is confronting the sum total of your spirit. Understand?"

"Hai," she answered.

"Good. Laura, use the kata to focus your spirit; use the kata to tame the demon."

She nodded more slowly this time, his idea sinking in and taking shape.

"Each move of the kata demands concentration and power. Take what you need from the power of your demon. Hai, we begin." He brought his hands together before him in a ready posture. "We will train kata so that when the time comes you will not have to think how to reach for the power that is in you. It will be as natural as opening your hand. We will practice one kata only. Bassai, a kata you should know, Laura, for rank examination."

Always a teacher, she thought dryly, thinking about exams. But it was a good kata for her and she liked doing it. The name meant "breaking the fortress," and it was a kata designed to teach the student how to change a disadvantageous situation into an advantageous one. Laura readied herself mentally and brought her hands together for the first move; an open palm pressed tightly against a closed fist.

"Hagemai!" Koga commanded, and they began.

Laura's arms came up and she slammed her fists forward into the air, the first strike breaking the opponent's sternum. She twisted around swiftly to block one attack, then a second behind her. Again she shifted to the side to meet another new attacker, blocking and flinging away an imaginary kick. Back to center again, she faced an opponent and swung her arm out in a slow arc to stop a punch, then followed with a series of rapid blocks and counterpunches. She reached for the body of her opponent, pulling him into a savage kick that would destroy the kneecap. She twirled again and fought two more behind her, driving a hardened palm into her opponent's groin. Beside her, Koga practiced the same kata, fighting his own opponents. His sharp exhale and the pounding of his feet on the wooden floor as he locked down with the punch made a rhythm that Laura tried to follow, catching up when she was too slow, slowing down when she rushed.

When she finished the final moves of the kata, she felt drained. There was too much to know in a kata. Too many things to concentrate on. It seemed impossible to her that she would be ready, that she could just do the kata and not panic. She felt afraid and her confidence slipped. Kata shows your weakness, she thought, discouraged. Yeah, but it will also show your strength, she argued stubbornly with herself, if you can stop feeling sorry for yourself long enough to concentrate. She squared her shoulders, took a deep breath, and prepared herself to do the kata again.

For the first ten katas Laura concentrated on every detail of her technique. She fumed when her timing was late, when a kick was rushed, when a stance was not low enough or strong enough. Each time Koga called the kata to begin again she renewed her efforts to be more precise, more in control of her body and the energy that was moving. After the second ten katas she began to tire, but her body relaxed and moved more swiftly and surely through the martial dance. Her face sweated freely and droplets stung her eyes, but she continued twisting and turning to meet the attacks of her opponents. During the third set of ten katas Laura thought only about her spirit, and she tried to invest each move with drive and determination. After the fourth and fifth set of ten katas, she stopped counting and just moved.

Training kata was like climbing a pyramid. Each kata brought her closer to the top, but instead of becoming harder, it grew more easy. At the apex Laura felt the pyramid turn upside down. She stood at a new point, one that stretched forever to an unseen base. Here her spirit was limitless and she knew that it was to this place she would bring the demon.

She lost track of time and space, and yet she was acutely aware of it. Though her body moved with agility and speed, it seemed to her she remained still, focused and seeing everything in the room. She knew how many boards lined the wood flooring, the depth of the cracks on the wall, and the path of every mote of dust as it danced and swirled about her. She could smell the ancient varnish mixed with the odor of age and their sweat.

And she could sense Koga almost as if they had become a single person. They moved as one with eerie precision. She could feel the tension of Koga's muscles flexing and relaxing through each attack as if they were her own. Her breath came and went as did his and about them the air was humid from the moisture of a thousand exhalations. There were no distinctions between Sensei and student, between male and female. Just the sensation of complete harmony as they moved in tandem through the deadly dance.

Laura knew at the same instant Koga did when they had done enough kata. They came to a halt at the end of the kata and bowed. The day had passed, the sky had become dark. They stood silently, basking for a moment in the peace and quiet of the room.

"Hai." Koga sighed deeply and released himself from the spell of the kata.

"Yeah," Laura answered, not feeling the need to say anything more.

Koga looked at her and smiled. She smiled back.

"Yeah," she repeated slowly, "I think I can make it work."

"Good." He nodded. "Let's eat."

Laura picked up her street clothes and followed Koga out of the dojo to his flat. Once inside he said, "Look, take a bath if you like and soak your muscles. I'll make dinner."

"Sounds good."

He showed her the bathroom and handed her a fairly clean towel. The bath was a small square wooden tub, big enough for one person to sit down in up to his neck. It was filled with hot water that was heated from a small unit below. "The water's hot," he warned, "so get in slowly, and don't stay too long or you'll melt."

He left and Laura stripped off the sweat-soaked gi and put a testing finger in the water. "Shit!" she exclaimed. "Hey," she called out to him in the other room, "I hope it's not me you're cooking for dinner." She heard him chuckle and then return to banging pots and pans in his tiny kitchen.

It took her ten minutes to submerge herself fully in the hot water, but once she had, she sighed, thinking she might never come out again. It was a peculiar sensation, Laura thought, this utter peace and calmness. All her life it seemed she had fought and scrapped to survive, from the mouthy comebacks that had earned her respect as a waitress to the fighting in the street that made up the life of the gangs. She thought about Koga too, how there had never been anyone willing to share with her something as needed as trust. The furious grapplings and heated sex she had experienced as part of **growing up** had not a tenth of the intimacy of the workout they had just completed. Laura grinned to herself in the bathtub. Sex. It would be something to look forward to, but not until after, if there was an after. She wanted to be with him, but she couldn't allow herself to become distracted now. It would take everything she had to face Keno—and to face the demon.

She came out of the tub reluctantly and toweled herself dry. She went to dress, but stopped when she held up Farrel Din's t-shirt. Bring it back in one piece, he had demanded, and Laura now hesitated. It might happen that the shirt would wind up the way of her other. She folded it and looked through Koga's clothes hanging on the peg of the bathroom door. She pulled out a faded black t-shirt with red letters that spelled "Tokyo." It had been worn already and she couldn't resist bringing it to her nose and inhaling. A man's smell. She smiled to herself as she put it on and felt her stomach curl and tighten with pleasure.

He was sitting at the low table spooning soup and noodles into bowls when Laura returned to the living room. She watched the steam curl up about his smiling face and couldn't decide which made her more hungry. She sat down beside him on the floor and took the bowl.

"Shirt looks better on you." He smiled appreciatively at her.

"Hope you don't mind my borrowing it. I wonder if I could ask you a favor? In case . . . something happens . . . would you please see that Farrel Din gets his t-shirt back? Just take it to the Dancing Ferret." Koga nodded solemnly and Laura could sense the concern for her that he was careful not to speak. "What is this stuff?" she asked, changing the subject and slurping up the noodles, broth splashing on her cheek.

"Soba, buckwheat noodles. And this is seaweed." He pointed to small black squares of paper thinness. "These yellow things are takuwan, Japanese pickled radish."

"How do you get all this stuff in Bordertown? I never knew it existed."

"You can buy them in Dragontown, but don't ask me how they get here. I can only tell you that no Japanese would ever consider doing without them."

"Sensei—Koga," she corrected herself, and they both smiled at what was becoming a joke between them. "You'd think I'd know the difference by now." She shrugged.

"And what is the difference?" he asked.

"One wants to do a million katas, the other wants to go to bed with me."

A noodle slipped from his spoon and landed with a noisy plop in his bowl.

"And which do you prefer?"

"Both, of course!" She laughed at him. "But only in the right place. No way am I gonna do those katas in bed!"

He laughed with her and she leaned over and kissed him lightly, her lips just brushing his. He drew her close and she nestled in the crook of his arm.

"But," she began, and she felt him stiffen slightly at the word. "But," she repeated, "I can't do that right now." She pulled away and regarded him seriously. "Koga, listen to me. If I can't get my demon back tonight, I want . . . I want you to kill me. I mean it. Fukumori already told you to, didn't she?"

He nodded, his face pale.

"Look, believe me," she said hurriedly, "it won't seem like it's me you're killing. It doesn't look like me at all. You gotta do it. You're the only demon queller we've got. Promise me?"

"All right," he said solemnly, "I promise you. But Laura, please know that I have confidence in you. I will hold off as long as I can give you the chance to fight."

"Yeah, well, just don't hold off too long," she replied huskily. "I don't want to add you to the list of those hacked."

"Hai, I promise." He kissed the open palm of her hand.

They continued eating, trying to hold on to the same peace they had shared in the dojo. But as time passed, both could feel themselves grow edgy with the waiting. Koga watched her, wondering if there would be a warning. Laura stretched her arms over head and tried to unkink the muscles that knotted down her back.

"What was it like in the World?" Laura asked, hoping to distract herself.

"Want to see a picture? I have one of me in my school uniform. It's sort of funny."

"Hey yeah," she said, "I can't imagine you as a kid."

He got up from the table and went to his closet. "Hang on a minute, I'll have to dig it out. Let's see," he muttered to himself, and tossed a few stacks of papers around in the dark closet. "One of these days I'm going to have to clean it out. I can't find a thing in it." He saw a postcard with the image of Mount Fujiyama and held it up. "Ah, Laura, look at this," and he peered around the closet door waving the postcard. He stopped short. She wasn't sitting at the table. He jerked his head around, searching the room for her. "Laura?" he called out in a loud voice. But there was no answer. He stepped out of the closet, refusing to panic. It was then that he noticed the front door was left open.

"Shit!" he swore in perfect imitation of Laura. He dove back into the closet and brought out two swords; both in dark scabbards, one was long and sleek, the other short. He threw down the long sword. It'll only get in the way as I run, he thought quickly. He clutched the shorter sword to his chest, praying with all his heart that he'd not need it, and bolted out the door.

Koga exploded from the doorway onto the street. "Laura," he called, hoping she still might answer. He saw no signs of her, just the evening mist as it collected around the lamplight. His mind raced ahead, trying to guess where Keno would lead her. Most likely out of the

Asian district. Keno wouldn't want any interference with the spell. And most likely away from Water Street and the other well-lit streets of Dragontown. He turned his head and looked up the street again. It would have to be the back way, and he started running in the direction of the alleys.

He ran down two alleys before he caught sight of her, moving swiftly toward her destination.

"Laura," he called again, and sprinted to catch up with her. She didn't stop or acknowledge his call. He watched as she passed beneath a stray street lamp—and his blood grew cold as he saw already the subtle changes taking place in her. Her Mohawk had grown into a shaggy crest, the quills glistening with deadly points in the silver light.

Keep her in Dragontown, Fukumori had said. Koga forced himself to run faster, his muscles screaming in protest as his feet pounded the pavement. He was a few feet behind her when he dropped his sword and threw himself at her back.

He had planned to tackle her around the waist, dropping her to the ground so that he could pin her down. She fell forward with his flying weight, but she braced her fall with her arms and rolled over to crush him beneath her back. He turned his face as quills threatened to gouge him. She scrambled up again and turned to him, her body crouched. Koga saw that her arms had lengthened and were covered with matted fur. Her fingers uncurled from a fist and she flexed claws. From the ground he swung out his leg and swept her at the ankles. She fell again to the pavement, landing with a hard thud. He heard her snarl and snap at the air. As she moved to pick herself up, he lunged for his sword, lying not too far from his hand on the ground. She loomed above him and Koga caught the silhouette of her horns against the night sky. He twisted his body away just as she brought her arm down in a furious arc, and her claws screeched against the concrete and drew a shower of blue sparks. He sprang up from his knees. With a hand at either end, he held the sword still encased in its scabbard as a short staff. She lunged for him, and he blocked her body with the sword, ramming it sideways into her chest. As she bent back from the blow, he used his foot to sweep her to the ground again.

Each moment that passed he saw her change and grow more powerful and frightening. He stepped back, panting hard and watching her, horrified. She rose slowly to her feet, weaving cautiously out of his reach. Her breath reeked like old meat, and she snapped her jaws, white with long fangs. Her eyes blazed, the orange glow hypnotic and terrifying. He forced himself to look away, and in that instant she grabbed him and tossed him like a child to the ground.

His body slammed into the hard concrete, and he felt a bone in his arm crack and splinter. Blood roared in his ears as the pain erupted in his arm. He rolled to one side, trying not to vomit, and cradled the broken arm. The sword lay just out of reach of his uninjured arm. Above him he saw the demon pull back her arm and prepare another strike. He tried again to reach the sword, the pain of failure a worse thought than the torment of his arm.

The sound of a flute chilled the air and stopped him. Its hollow tune wove an ugly despair about him, and he looked up, squinting with pain.

The demon was there, waiting, head weaving from side to side with the music. The music stopped, and standing around her, he saw the Bloods. Keno held the flute, the cruel face twisted with a triumphant sneer.

"Well, well, Koga Sensei," he spat. "It seems you are outclassed. How do you like my pet? I know she used to be your pet, but I have made her a better killer, don't you think?"

Koga didn't answer. He's gotten cocky, Koga thought, if he thinks he can work his spell in Dragontown. He moved his head a fraction and saw his sword out of the corner of his eye. Perhaps he could still reach the sword and take the demon by surprise. He watched Keno carefully, waiting for his chance.

"You'll be the first tonight, Sensei. I don't need your lessons anymore. I'll enjoy watching you die." Keno brought the flute to his lips and played a new tune.

In Laura's head the tune began to itch and sting. She swung her head madly, the music beating in her blood torturing her. She must kill, she must hunt to appease the music that burned along her skin. She moved toward the thing on the ground and dimly saw it roll and desperately reach for something lying near it. She raised her quills, ready to strike, when something stopped her—stopped her even as she foamed and clawed the air. It wrenched her neck and held her thrashing and snarling like a trapped wolf. Beneath her, the thing held out a naked sword ready to split her. She howled and snapped frantically as the sound of the flute flayed her body and drove her forward.

Amid her fury she heard another sound, a liquid thread of music that fell about her shoulders like cool water on the stinging flesh. The sound grew as each note was plucked from the air and vibrated with new power. The deathly sting of Keno's flute failed as the sound of Fukumori's koto resonated with electric fire. The tumbling notes beat against the coldness and forced an opening in the elvin spell. From within the demon, Laura's heart sparked and crackled with the awareness.

The demon's skin buckled as Laura stretched her arms and reached for control. It fought against her, struggling wildly as she tried to break free. The demon raged and Laura felt the fabric of her being begin to tear. "No," she cried to it, "we will be lost," and she clutched the demon tightly to her even as it clawed and tore the skin. She plunged deep within herself, taking the demon down with her as she sought the peaceful place that she had seen in the kata. It was there, just hovering out of reach. It only needed movement to set her on the path. She focused her concentration on a single act, willing the turbulent flesh of her demon body to obey. The clawed hands came together, open palm against the closed fist.

Laura stepped forward in the first move of Bassai, breaking the fortress. The quills of the demon rattled as she slammed her foot to the ground and struck the air with her furred arms. She felt the last of Keno's hold shatter into fragments. She turned and twisted with the moves, forcing the demon to follow. The clear and ringing music of the koto guided her, illuminating every step as she worked her way through each move of the kata. As Laura felt the thread of magic come undone, the demon ceased to struggle against her. "Come," she whispered to it, and it followed willingly. Laura opened herself to the spirit of the demon, absorbing its power in the flowing movements of the kata.

When she finished the final move, the demon was changed. No longer external, it formed a well of power within her, resilient and elastic, from which she had only to flex to feel its strength. My strength, she thought proudly, my demon.

She turned to Keno and saw the fear in his silver eyes. He was no more a threat to her than a wave that breaks itself against the rock.

"Get lost, Keno. Go back to Soho and take your Bloods with you. Within the hour every Dragon in Dragontown will know what you tried, and they're gonna come looking for you. Take off now and hide while you still have the chance."

Keno stared at her, his mouth agape. He licked at his lips uncertainly, afraid to turn his back to her. The Bloods next to him didn't wait but took off before she had even finished speaking. "Go," she hissed at him, "before I change my mind and do the job myself." He bolted at her words and ran, disappearing down an alley.

Laura turned and found Koga standing, his face streaked with sweat, his broken arm cradled against his body. He still held the sword, holding it rigidly before him, and stared at her face.

"Laura?" he asked slowly, his voice wary as two eyes still glowing a fiery orange fixed on his face.

Laura gazed at him and felt a wave of tenderness at his voice. She released the last motes of power and felt them slip into the sea and calm within her. The demon curled like a dog and slept, content. The color dimmed, and Koga saw her eyes sparkle with moonlight reflected on the dark surfaces.

Hands at her sides, she bowed a formal ending to her kata. He bowed back, acknowledging her victory. She came close and he handed her the sword.

"Your arm—" Laura started to say, but Koga shook his head and draped his other arm about her shoulders. She wrapped an arm around his waist, and as he leaned ever so slightly on her, they walked out of the dark alley and into the spell-lit streets of Dragontown.

BELLAMY BACH
Exile

She never talked about Elfland.

She had lost all but the echo of her accent, dressed pure Old City from the fairy dust in her hair to her boots' pointed toes—she should have fit right in with the street rabble down in Soho. But even if one did not immediately guess her origins, there was something noticeably odd about the girl (this in a city where oddity is the norm), a fey sort of wistfulness that had nothing to do with this world or life on the Border.

I first saw Dez on Chrystoble Street, my eyes caught by her halo of hair the color and texture of dandelions that have gone to seed. From that color, and the slanted eyes, the high cheekbones, the death-white skin, you did not need to see the ears hidden by the dandelion fluff to know of a certainty that they were pointed. I was startled to see her there, calmly eating a bagel on the steps of the Light-works. Trust Dez to never notice that she had stumbled into a human neighborhood, and was holding her picnic on the Pack's front stoop. There were a couple of Pack members watching her from the center courtyard, probably too surprised to find an elf on their turf to decide just what to do about it. I considered rescuing the girl, hustling her away before the Pack made their move. But I'm not prone to gallantry, not when I have to risk *my* ass to do it. I shrugged and went my way.

The second time I saw her she was also in trouble—squeezed between drunken toughs and a brick wall in a rowdy crowd milling around the Dancing Ferret. Dez, as you may have gathered, was often in trouble—that girl could get herself mugged in a room full of grandmothers. She attracted the unsavory element the way the Riverside Market attracts flies. It was terribly unsporting, two big humans against one slender elvin girl; but once again I did not feel compelled to play knight errant. You learn to take care of yourself first down in Soho. If you can't stand the heat, get out of the kitchen.

The third time I saw Dez, I was the one in trouble.

I'm one of the fastest lock-pickers south of Ho Street, a skill that earned me half a year in the Juvie Jail on Water Street before I made good my promise to my mother and went legit with my current job in the kitchen of the Hard Luck Cafe. But I was seriously contemplating returning to a life of crime when I spotted the sweetest, sleekest motorcycle I'd ever seen, a vintage 1989 Italian racer imported up from the World and modified for the Borderlands, locked only with a flimsy human lock and a chain. The chain was wrapped around a steel post in the alley behind Danceland. Anyone stupid enough or cheap enough to leave the bike alone without a proper spell-lock deserved to have it carted away.

I pulled my Swiss Army knife out of the pocket of my jeans, flipped open the pick and squatted down to examine the lock, muttering an apology to my mother under my breath. Well, after eighteen years of life with me she should know better than to trust one of my promises anyway. The alley was not empty. I was counting on the fact

that the evening was still young and the bike's owner was
probably getting drunk or trying to score in a dark corner
in Danceland, and that no one but the bike's owner was
likely to care.

A big, ugly Blood all decked out in red leather parked
beside me as I worked. He favored me with a slow and
speculative smile. His own cobbled-together machine
looked like a bad joke next to the Italian racer and he was
no doubt wondering if once I liberated it from the post he
could liberate the racer from me. I'm not tall, as humans
go; he was a lot bigger than I was. I casually snapped
open the blade of the pocket knife, looking the fellow
straight in the eyes to make sure he caught my drift. He
did. He locked up his own bike with a murmured spell
and sauntered out of the alley. I wondered if he'd be back,
with friends.

I snapped down the knife blade and pried up the pick
again, bending over the lock quickly in case the ugly dude
returned. My skills were rusty, but not gone; I listened
closely for the click of the lock's release. There was a loud
cracking sound. And then the pavement was in my face.

"What the fuck do you think you're doing?" asked a
curiously soft voice, too well-bred to match the words.

A pointed toe prodded at my ribs. I rolled over and
groaned and stared up at the evening sky.

"You were going to steal my bike, weren't you?" Dez
asked mildly. "I mean, I wouldn't have hit you otherwise." She sounded anxious about that, as if it were important to make that clear. What was I going to do, call
the coppers?

I could taste asphalt in my mouth, and the tang of blood.
Gingerly I touched my nose. She had flattened it—even
before I hit the ground. "My nose is broken," I announced to no one in particular.

"Shit," she said softly, the Elfland accent betrayed in
the single word. She squatted down on the pavement and
something soft was pushed against my face. I reached for

it and brought it into my line of vision: a glittering scarf of elvish weave from over the Border, covered now with my blood.

The elvin girl rocked back on her heels and regarded me with an expressionless stare. She was a dark shadow against the shadows of the alley, dressed in an old black leather jacket that was too big and new black jeans that were too tight; her halo of dandelion hair was the brightest thing in the waning light. I recognized her as the girl from Chrystoble Street. And wondered what game Fate was up to now.

Her hand grazed my cheek, then slid around to the back of my head. I wondered if it were true about elves—that they could heal a human with their touch if they chose—but all she was doing was pulling me upright, gently at first, more roughly when I tried to resist. I wanted to be left alone. I wanted to sleep in the alley forever. Or at least until the blood stopped, and the pain went away.

Dez brought me to my feet and made me stand—clutching her scarf to my nose and watching the ground tilt under my feet—as she kick-started the bike. Then she ordered me to climb on behind her, although I was dripping blood all over her racer's seat. "Where do you live?" she shouted over the roar of the engine. I couldn't think of any reason not to tell her. The bike slipped into gear with a kick that jolted right through me, and then we were weaving through the traffic on Ho, and down the dark streets toward Hell's Gate and home.

Home is a townhouse on the south side of Hell, a block of Georgian brick buildings badly ravaged by time. "Mine" is in the middle of the row. Only the ground floor is habitable, protected from the leaky roof by the two floors above it. The pipes are still intact, connected to the lower city water system, one fireplace still functions and the back bay window still has all its glass—luxurious living by SoHo standards. Beggars can't be choosers, but my squat isn't half bad.

Dez parked her bike beside the front stoop, chaining it to the railing with her worthless lock and chain. She was going to have to use a spell-lock if she wanted to keep the bike for long—she was an elf, after all, she didn't even have to pay for a spell like I did. I mumbled the spell that unlocked my front door while Dez hung politely back out of hearing distance. When the door swung open, she followed me in.

Perhaps it was nausea, or the loss of blood, or perhaps I was already caught up by that aura of unreality that clings to Dez like the smokey aftertaste of a spell, making the most peculiar circumstances or coincidences seem perfectly ordinary—but it didn't seem odd to me when she followed me through the door.

Or when she started a fire in my fireplace using human matches instead of a simple elvin spell.

Or when she put me to bed in my roll of blankets by the fire, and then nestled in beside me.

She wasn't like anyone else.

She wasn't like the other girls I knew. She didn't flirt. She didn't laugh at my jokes. She seldom even spoke, and sometimes I wondered why she hung around at all.

"She likes you, bro," Buddy said to me above the hiss and crackle of the deep fat fryer in the kitchen behind the Hard Luck Cafe. "Why else she come around all the time, now you tell me?"

I shrugged, and spooned fish-fingers out of the grease. I wasn't sure why she hung around. But it wasn't like Buddy thought it was; though she slept beside me I'd never touched her, at least not *that* way. I didn't want to. I didn't want to get that close to anybody—didn't want to worry about anyone's life but my own. Everybody who met Dez seemed to want something from her, whether it was the money in her pockets or the glamor that clung to her as an exile from the Elflands. I didn't want to take anything from her. I didn't want to take care *of* her. I just wanted to be a pal, so long as there were no strings attached. But that wasn't a thing Buddy would understand.

"You gotta tell me what they're like, elvin girls," Buddy said. "I heard say they're really hot, and then I heard say they're stone cold. I ain't never had one. So you gotta tell me, when you find out. Okay, bro?"

"Yeah sure. When I find out."

Liza thrust another handful of orders through the window into the kitchen. Everybody was hungry tonight; at this rate we'd have the grill fired up until dawn. I could hear the dull roar of conversation in the room beyond, and a mag tape of Wild Hunt played on the cafe's sound system. Usually the Hard Luck was a quiet sort of place, but on a Saturday night, with Danceland hopping across the street, it could get fairly rowdy. Rumor had it that Wild Hunt had put in an unexpected appearance at Danceland just the night before and the lines were unusually long in front of the club, kids hoping it would happen again.

The boss staggered up the cellar stairs with yet another keg of ale; we were going through the stuff like it was water. "Hector, give me a hand with this," he ordered. I took the load from him and backed through the swinging doors into the cafe. The room was jammed with people, the marble floor sticky with spilt ale. I looked around the cafe picking out the red leather—too many Bloods and there could be trouble. I caught a glimpse of Dez at a table in the corner. I could always spot her in a crowd. Her hair was a beacon that always drew my eye. She was looking soft and fragile tonight, wearing a long pink kimono over elvin tights and cowboy boots. She sat with a seedy looking halfie with lank yellow hair and crooked teeth; he was smiling at her with an expression that I wasn't sure I liked.

Liza followed me back into the kitchen. She perched on the counter's edge and lit up an herbal cigarette.

"What chew doin' girl?" the boss complained.

"Break. I'm on break," she said. "Leave me alone."

Scowling, he went into the cafe to cover for her; it was

too wild a night to leave little Peach on the floor alone. She'd get eaten alive. Liza glared at his broad back as he went. "I should have kept the job at the Ferret," she muttered. She pushed a long strand of fuchsia-dyed hair out of her eyes, and sighed. "Full moon tonight. Everyone's gone crazy."

"What's the moon got to do with anything?" I shouted over the noise of the deep fat fryer.

"Oh come on, Hector—the full moon. You know. That's when everyone goes looney. They've done studies on it and everything."

"That's when the werewolves come out," Buddy added with a grin. He threw back his head and howled.

"Yeah, sure," I said sarcastically—glad nonetheless that I knew exactly where Dez was tonight. "The only werewolf this town's got is tame as a pet poodle."

"But you don't see no Wolfboy out tonight, do you?" Buddy pointed out.

"Maybe Wolfboy does it in reverse," Liza speculated. "Maybe the full moon turns him human again."

She opened up the Scandal Sheet lying on the counter, one of those newspapers like my mother reads, filled with stories of U.F.O. visitations and the Bordertown fad diet of the week. Today's headline read:

MONSTER SIGHTED!!!

I was drawn to the paper in spite of myself and read the article over Liza's shoulder. It was the same old nonsense. Some drunk spots something at the edge of the city and the entire town gets all worked up that the monsters are going to start strolling in from the Borderlands, when everybody knows they avoid the city like we've got the plague, more afraid of us than we are of them. It's only when you go into the open Borderlands that you stand in any danger of the monsters—the beasties warped by magic leaking under the Border or created by elvin spells that have gone awry. This was just the same old shit: something spotted by the trailer park down past Hell's Gate and no two reports agree on what it was. It was a man, no it was an animal; it was covered with fur; it had spiral horns. Hell, it was probably just Wolfboy out to take a leak. It fled back into the shadows when a light was turned on it, and that didn't sound very vicious to me.

"Full moon, I'm telling you—that's what brings 'em out," Liza said, flicking her ashes onto the floor.

"If the full moon flushes 'em out, it's a good night to go hunting. . . ." Buddy mimed holding a rifle to his cheek, and made a sound like a burst of gunfire.

"Yeah, sure," I said. "You know how undependable rifles are around magic, even here in the city. How much use is one going to be out in the Borderlands? The fucking thing would probably explode in your hands." I turned back to the grill. "You've been watching too many old movies, my man. Now you want to be a cowboy and ride with the posse at dawn. Spare me."

"They *are* talking about forming a posse," Liza said. "I heard a couple of Packers talking about it. They want to go out and get this thing before it crawls through somebody's window at night." She shivered, and took a drag on her cigarette. You couldn't help but get nervous sometimes, as a human in the Borderlands. Elves had their magic. What did we have but guns that wouldn't fire and machines that wouldn't work without a goddamn spell? Most of these monster sightings were just hot air and hysteria. But every once in awhile some beast did come marauding—there was one hunted down when I was a kid. The sight of its bloody carcass on display at Traders' Heaven, those rows of gleaming, deadly white teeth, had given me nightmares for weeks.

"Hey, I'd like to get in on a hunt," Buddy said excitedly. "I'd like to go kill me a real monster! Wouldn't that be something to talk about, hey?"

I snorted. "Why go looking for trouble?"

And then I thought of the girl who trouble always seemed to find. Maybe finding it first, and doing it in, wasn't such a bad idea.

She's not your problem, she's not your responsibility, I reminded myself. Everyone's got to look out for themselves. It was none of my business where Dez went the nights she didn't tag along home with me, or the times she disappeared for days on end. It was none of my business where she picked up the bruises and scars that appeared from time to time. Not my life. Not my problem.

The next time I looked out into the cafe, Dez and the seedy looking halfie were gone. She did not reappear at the back kitchen door at the end of my shift, as had become her custom.

"Lose your girlfriend tonight, bro?" Buddy said with an unpleasant smile.

I shrugged, buttoned up my overcoat, and began the long walk toward home.

She hated the city.

Unlike most of us living in the abandoned buildings of Soho, she hadn't been lured there by the promise of magic, or independence, or drugs, or fast bikes, or rock'n'roll. She hadn't wanted to come to Bordertown at all; she'd been kicked out of Elfland. Or if not precisely kicked out, at least strongly encouraged to leave.

"Elves love perfection," she told me. It was one of the few times I ever heard her sound bitter. "They can't tolerate a cripple. They get rid of them, like drowning puppies. That's what they did with me."

"Why?" I asked. There didn't seem to be anything wrong with her, no physical defect that was obvious to me. But she was done making revealing statements for the evening. She fed a broken table leg into the fire and left my question hanging in the air. Just as well, I decided. If you knew too much about a person, you started to care, and if you started to care, you started to feel responsible

. . . my mother could have you feeling responsible for the whole sorry state of the human race if you gave her an inch. I didn't intend to be responsible for anybody but myself. That was hard enough sometimes.

The fire caught on the fresh wood and the flames danced high, pushing back the autumn chill. It wasn't really cold yet, but Dez sat as close to the fire as she dared. She was always cold. Whether it was warmer in the Elflands or she was just particularly thin-blooded I never knew. She wore two of my sweaters under her jacket, so large on her they hung down to her knees. I took the blanket I'd been sitting on and wrapped it around her thin shoulders. Then I rose to fetch more wood from the back yard. "Stay close to the fire," I said needlessly. Where else was she going to go? There was no furniture in my townhouse—just the blankets by the fireplace and big, empty rooms. I liked it that way. It was as though I didn't really live there, or anywhere, at all.

I unbolted the back door and stepped onto the rickety porch. A narrow, overgrown yard ran from the house to the southern side of the Old City Wall. Beyond the wall was the Borderlands, and beyond that the distant World. The evening was cold enough to make my breath frost but no colder. What would Dez do when real cold weather came?

In the distance was a sound like the howling of some strange beast. Alley cats probably—but my thoughts immediately turned to monsters. Prowling through the Borderlands. Coming to get Dez. Coming to get me. The monster I'd seen displayed at Traders' Heaven had looked like it was twelve feet tall; of course I'd been much smaller at the time, probably it hadn't been so huge at all. It had been covered with dark fur, with a great crimson hole where the spear had gored it. Yet in spite of the claws and fur, I remembered, the monster had walked upright like a man.

Through the branches of the sour-apple tree I could see

the silver disc of the moon. It was waning now, but it still looked full, a Wolf Moon, as Liza would say. I jumped when I heard a movement behind me, but it wasn't a wolf-man or a monster—just Dez, dragging the blanket with her. She too was looking up at the moon, her face turned silver, her hair glimmering with its own light. The wind caught the blanket and set the edges flapping. And then a curious thing happened—a trick of the light, as the moon passed behind a cloud. I saw Dez as she might have looked in the Elflands, standing in some wooded glen, elvin robes stirred by the wind, her eyes dark, her expression wild . . . and then the moment passed, and the moon reap-peared, and I saw Dez as she was, clutching a tattered blanket around an equally tattered leather jacket in a weedy city garden by a graffiti covered wall.

"Is it hard for you . . . to live in a city?" I asked. It had never occurred to me before. I've never lived any-where else.

She pulled the blanket tighter against the cold wind, "It's . . . different," she said. "A different kind of . . . rhythm. It took me awhile to understand. When I first came I was too wide open. That's how we are raised in the Elflands. Open to the sound of the earth moving, the messages in the wind, the voices of trees. . . . You can't be open like that in Bordertown."

"No." I laughed. "Our trees don't talk."

"Oh yes they do," she said quite seriously. "Only I don't like what they have to say."

She was always in the wrong place at the wrong time.

She had a proper home, a room in a House for Young Ladies at a respectable if not fashionable address at the foot of the Hill, paid for by some relative across the Bor-der—blood money, she sneered once, and I never inquired further. She'd never set foot in the House for Young La-dies—though it amused me to try to picture her there, in a sober velvet dress practicing the harp and sipping tea.

The first thing she'd done was pawn the family jewels, found herself the best bike her money could buy—a nice *up yours* gesture to the folks back home, for bikes aren't permitted in the lands beyond the Border—and headed down to Soho where, like so many runaways, she'd ended up at the Oberon Building until she'd gotten the good sense to get out of there and learned to make it all on her own.

She had a job as a messenger, delivering mail and parcels around the city. This took her into every corner of Bordertown on her fast Italian racer so that she, after six months, knew the city better than I, born and bred here—including the shadier quarters where a slender elvin girl just shouldn't go. It wasn't that Dez couldn't handle herself in a fair fight—the lump on my nose is proof that she could. But the nastier types of Bordertown can't always be counted on to fight fair.

This was something a girl raised in Elfland could not quite understand. She could not accept that there was any place in the city she should not go, and her simple innocence—the vulnerability of a foreigner in a strange, unfathomable land—drew the nastier types to her as inevitably as moths to the light of a flame. While the rest of the city joined the monster hysteria, my fears were of more common things: Dez beaten in some dark alley, Dez with her throat cut on the docks of Riverside, Dez walking blithely into some elf-baiter's den. . . .

Not my problem, I repeated over and over. Not my responsibility. In Bordertown, *you've got to take care of yourself.*

On Monday, on my way to the Hard Luck, I ran into a crowd packing Ho Street near Mock Avenue—unusual for this time of the week. I paused to find out what was going on. A tall black boy in the colors of the Pack was standing on the steps of the Oberon Building shouting something with his fist raised. Two Dragons stood beside him. What would make the gangs band together this way?

I saw a boy I knew at the edge of the crowd. "Hey Sammy," I said. "What's going on here?"

"Monsters," he said succinctly. "We saw one last night."

"Where?" I said, my stomach tightening. Sammy Tucker, the Pack's leader, wasn't prone to mass hysteria. If he said he saw a monster, you could believe he saw a monster.

"Down by you, Hector," Sammy answered cheerfully. "At Hell's Gate, trying to get into Soho. Riff-raff got a knife into the thing, but it got away from us before we could finish it off. We're talking about getting some muscle together to go out there and hunt it down."

I remembered again that bloody corpse at Traders' Heaven. I'd thrown up in the parking lot afterwards, and my mother had scolded me all the way home. . . .

I looked across the crowd, picking out the different colors: Dragons, Scorpions, Packs, Rats, Dragon's Fire . . . and no sign of red leather. I nudged Sammy. "Where are the Bloods?"

"Laying low," he snarled, "If they know what's good for them. Too many folks blame the elves for the monsters. Some people think the elves make them deliberately—send them to roam the Borderlands to keep humans out."

"Do you believe that?" I asked, startled. Sammy led the Pack, he was no friend to elves. But to believe the elves deliberately created the monsters. . . .

Sammy shrugged. "I figure maybe it's not intentional," he said slowly. "I figure maybe they have spells that go wrong, accidents they want to get rid of. . . . The monsters have to come from somewhere. They weren't here in the days before Elfland came."

I let out a slow breath. This was all Soho needed. The tension between elves and humans was already running high—we'd had more than the usual number of incidences in the Hard Luck Cafe. Instead of fighting monsters we'd be fighting each other, if the Pack had their way. At least the elves had the sense to stay away from this mob scene. Except, of course, for one.

"Goddammit!" I exploded. Sammy followed the direction of my gaze.

"Why there's a pretty little silver-haired darling looking to get her head bashed in," the boy drawled.

I cursed more creatively and began to shoulder my way through the crowd. Dez was strolling up Mock Avenue oblivious, as usual, to the world around her—to the hostile gazes of everyone she passed. As I pushed my way toward her, I could feel the crowd around me growing ugly. Go fight monsters, you dumb-ass jerks, I wanted to shout. What's the *point* of fighting each other?

Two big bruisers with the black bandanas of the Scorpions took up step behind Dez. I slipped past them and grabbed the girl by the arm. "For fuck's sake, Dez," I hissed in her ear, "get your ass out of here!"

She looked up at me as if waken from sleep, unable to place my face for a moment. "Hector? What's the matter?"

"Just shut up, Dez, and follow me."

Not exactly the most diplomatic way to put it, and Dez, as naturally stubborn as I am naturally surly, immediately pulled from my grasp and stood her ground. The thugs behind us were grinning with the anticipation of a good trashing.

"Come *on*!" I yelled, grabbing her wrist again, and this time I did not let go.

I hauled the girl up Ho Street, hearing laughter—thank the gods—rather than footsteps behind us. I wouldn't let her stop until we reached the cafe, then I pushed her through the doors ahead of me, breathing hard, my heart pounding like a hammer. The cafe was empty. I sunk weakly into a chair.

"Hector," she said, scratching her silver-blond hair, "what the hell was that all about?"

Relief made me giddy, and that in turn made me embarrassed. What the hell *had* that all been about? I could have gotten my own head bashed in trying to protect this elvin fool.

"When are you going to learn how to take care of yourself?" I exploded, my own confused emotions turning into anger. "You can't always expect me to be around, acting like some goddamn white knight come to save you. I should have just let them rough you up a bit, teach you to use a little sense and stay away from elf-baiters!"

She looked aghast. "I can take care of myself. I never asked you to take care of me."

"You walk around in your own goddamn fantasy world—well wake up, sweetie. This is Bordertown, not your precious Elfland. There are some b-a-d people hanging around this town, and I'm not always going to be around to save your sweet ass from them."

"Hector, damn you," she said, "what are you talking about? I've never expected you to watch out for me, honestly—"

But I was on a roll, I wasn't listening. It felt great to be mad. It felt great to sweep all those nights of worrying about her away. "I don't want to be responsible for you anymore," I went on; "you can bloody well look after yourself from now on. I don't care about you, I don't care what you do, I don't care about *anyone*. I just want to be left alone, you got that?"

"Yeah sure," she said quietly. "I got that loud and clear."

In contrast to that quiet voice she slammed the door loudly as she left. She was heading in the wrong direction, the idiot—headed back up Ho Street in the direction of the gangs. "I don't goddamn *care*," I said aloud.

I turned and saw the room was not quite empty after all. Liza was watching me coolly from behind the bar.

"If you don't *care*, Hector," she said, screwing an earring shaped like a crescent moon into one ear, "then why

are you crying?'' I ignored her as I walked past her into
the kitchen of the Hard Luck Cafe.

Buddy was animated with talk of monster hunts; he
droned on and on until I thought I was going to throttle
him. Liza kept giving me the knowing eye, and even little
Peach was getting on my nerves until I snapped at her
once too often and the girl burst into tears. I don't care, I
repeated to myself all evening long. As the long night
dragged through the hours until dawn I almost convinced
myself that it was true.

At the end of the shift I put on my long overcoat, wound
a scarf around my neck, slung my hat low over my eyes.
The night was very cold. I wondered briefly where Dez
would sleep, and then I forcefully pushed the thought away.
Ho Street was quiet, the crowd long gone. Even the drag-
racers on Gateway had all gone home. My sneakers made
a soft slap-slap against the pavement as I headed down to
Hell; my fingers were frozen by the time I reached my
house, muttered the elvin spell and turned the human key
in the lock. Warmth greeted me as I opened the door.

A fire blazed in the fireplace. Dez's pale hair was turned
red by its light. She looked up as I came in, her eyes two
dark shadows. Was she bruised again, or was that a trick
of the light?

"I'm not staying," she said quickly. "I just came . . .
to say I'm sorry. For causing you any trouble.''

I couldn't think of anything to say. So I didn't say anything.

"I, uh, brought you a present," she said, nodding toward a jar filled with pale violet blossoms.

I looked at the flowers on the mantel above the fire. I
thought, idiotically, *no one's ever given me flowers before*.
They were exotic looking, wild, like nothing I'd ever seen
in the shops of Bordertown.

"Well, see you around Hector."

"Look," I said, finding my voice at last, "if you need
a place to stay tonight. . . ."

"Thanks. I'm okay. Really. I just came for a moment. To say I'm sorry. And also, um, thanks—for what you did today. Helping me out and all. I'm . . . not used to that." She reached out and touched my face with her cold hand, delicately tracing the bump where she'd broken my nose. Her eyes were on a level with mine, which surprised me. For some reason I always think of her as small. "Still pals?" she said, biting her lip as she waited for my answer.

I smiled. "Still pals."

I settled down before the fire she had made, and heard the roar of her bike as she took off for god only knows where.

She never said anything about the Borderlands.

Everyone else could talk of nothing else, of the monster who'd been wounded by members of the Pack and the other monsters that might be out there, waiting to steal into Soho by the dark of night. Posses were gathering to go hunting in the Borderlands—Packers who wanted to finish the job, Bloods who wanted to strike a blow for the honor of Elfland, kids like Buddy who just wanted a thrill.

"It's been spotted again, by the river above the Troll Bridge," Buddy told me. "They say you can't kill a monster with a gun—but I'd sure like to get me one and see for myself! You remembered that monster got one of them River Folk some years back? They shot that one dead with a gun. Used silver bullets and it worked just fine."

"What's this thing supposed to look like?" Liza asked him.

"Hairy. Big and hairy, Sammy Tucker says."

"It's the boss," Liza wisecracked.

Little Peach giggled.

I tied on the waiter's apron, my turn to do the floor. Thank god it was quiet tonight. This monster scare was keeping kids off the street.

"What about you, Hector?" Liza said as I turned toward the door. "You going on this monster hunt too?"

"Me?" I asked. "You've got to be kidding."

"Oh excuse me, Mr. I-don't-give-a-shit-about-anything. I forgot you don't do anything unless there's something in it for you. If there was cash money offered up as a reward, you'd be the first one out there, Uzi in hand."

"And Buddy here is doing this out of the goodness of his heart? Give me a break. He just wants to kill something."

"Damn straight," Buddy said cheerfully.

"It's his hormones," Liza muttered.

"What about you—are you going on the hunt?"

Liza looked at a torn fingernail painted with fairy-dust, and grimaced. "I'm more than happy," she said, "to leave this to the gangs. Let them make themselves useful for once."

"Has anybody," Peach spoke up, "figured out whether the monster is *dangerous*?"

Liza looked up from her fingernails and raised an eyebrow at the younger girl. "Honey, at this point, I don't think anyone *cares*."

This was the night chosen for the hunt. The moon was full in the sky once again, lighting the open hills with a clear, silvery light. The boss let Buddy off early, to join the caravan. I almost laughed to watch them go—with such a crowd they'd scare any monster within ten miles away— but there was something sobering about the sight of all those fresh young faces, eager to kill. I kept seeing that gaping wound in the monster at Trader's Heaven. The hairy face, contorted like a man in pain.

The town seemed oddly subdued as I trudged home by moonlight. Without Buddy, the shift had been long and tiring. My feet were aching as I turned down Gateway. I wished I had a fast bike to carry me home; two more months and I'd finally have enough money. Two whole more months . . . no wonder I'd turned to crime in my madder, badder days.

I turned onto Hell Street, my steps dragging. And suddenly realized the dark trail I was following was blood. Fresh blood. Leading up the sidewalk in the direction of my squat.

Godammit, Dez, what have you gotten into now? I thought as I sprinted up the walk, my breath a tight fist in my chest. Sure enough, the trail led right up my stairs. Dez's racer was parked in the rose bushes by the porch. I fumbled with the key, had a moment of panic trying to remember the lock spell. The door opened after an eternity; I slammed it closed behind me as I ran through the front hall. "Dez!" I shouted. "Dez, where are you? Are you all right?"

She appeared in the doorway, even paler than usual. She was wearing one of my shirts, and it was stained with crimson. I grabbed her by the shoulders. "What happened?"

She pushed me away with more strength than I'd expected her to have. "I'm okay, Hector. Stop shouting. It's not me . . . it's my friend."

I looked over her shoulder into the room beyond, and froze in horror. The nightmare of my childhood lay sleeping before my fire. It was covered all over with a pelt of red-brown fur. Its side, like the day I'd seen it at Traders' Heaven, was a crimson hole. But no—I shook myself out of memory. This wasn't the same one. That one was dead and this one—

I turned to Dez. She shrank from my expression.

"Hector, please . . . He's my *friend*."

"Dez," I whispered, "He's a monster." You goddamn innocent idiot, I wanted to shout. Wake up, dammit girl. You're not in Elfland anymore.

"He's my friend," she repeated. "He came from the Borderlands looking for me. He was worried about me."

She knelt down beside the beast and looked up at me,

looking pathetically young beneath the tangled halo of dandelion hair. "I go there sometimes," she tried to explain. "I hate the city, Hector. I can't breathe here. The trees say horrible things. I just have to get away . . . so I go out into the Borderlands. On my bike. I grew up on the land—it was cruel of them to send me to a city. They must have known. . . ." She shuddered.

The monster groaned softly, and she put a hand on its gruesome brow, stilling it. I shuddered too, then, watching that tender gesture. The monster's wound did not seem so bad at second glance, but there was a great deal of blood, and its breath came out in tortured gasps.

She looked up and met my eyes. "I'm just like he is," she said, her hand smoothing the fur of his head, "a reject from the Elflands. A mage's daughter born without magic. Not the littlest bit. No better than a human. Can you imagine what that's like in Faerie? Like being blind, deaf, and dumb . . ."

"That doesn't make you a *monster*, Dez."

She laughed bitterly. "Tell that to my parents."

She rose, wiped her hands on her jeans. The shirt she wore had been my favorite, ruined now. I didn't care. The creature at her feet was barely conscious; if he was anything like elvinkind, his body was busy healing itself. He was frightening to look at—not because he was so different from mankind but because, but for the fur, he was so much the same.

"Is he dying?"

"I don't know." Her voice caught. "I don't think so. But I have to take him home. Before anyone finds us here."

"Home?"

"The Borderlands."

"But it's dangerous out there!" I shouted. "Dez, are you totally out of your mind?"

She just laughed again. "I've been hurt by my own family in the Elflands. I've been hurt by complete strangers here. I've never been hurt in the Borderlands, Hector. They like me out there. Please, will you help me? I can't take him on the bike, you see—it frightens him. . . ."

"To the Borderlands?"

Not your problem. Not your responsibility, the voice in my head reminded me. Shut up, I told it. I took a deep breath. "Okay," I said.

She loved the Borderlands.

It was strange to see her there—to see how obviously she belonged to those barren hills, as obviously as she had never belonged in Soho. We'd used the bike to carry her "friend" home—we'd had no choice in the end, it was too far to go any other way. Then I'd driven the racer back to Bordertown alone. She said she'd come and visit me, but I told her I knew she never would. She'd grow wild like the land and then she'd avoid the city like the others do.

Well, I was wrong. She still turns up in front of my fire from time to time.

Monster fever died down some time ago. The hunt was unsuccessful and even Buddy grew bored with the whole sorry business. Sammy Tucker would still like to know whose blood it is that leads to my door.

I still live alone. I still like to mind my own business. Like Liza said, I don't do anything unless there's something in it for me. Nothing's changed, really.

Except that now I have the sweetest little Italian racer to get me back and forth to the Hard Luck Cafe.

ELLEN KUSHNER & BELLAMY BACH
Mockery

The room looks as though it has been ransacked. Papers, books, hardware, ale bottles are strewn across every surface; piles of miscellaneous debris litter the floor where drawers have been upended in Hale's search for a number-two lead or a newspaper clipping he could have sworn he put there once. . . . Draped over one canvas is a pair of dirty socks.

Hale kicks papers out of his way, clearing a path to the other end of the room. Tall, narrow windows let in gray light and a breeze to disturb the dustballs in the corners. A cat with pale pink striping, one of the elfish breeds, is asleep on a pile of laundry on top of a priceless Stickley chair. "Sorry," Hale mumbles around the stem of his pipe, gesturing vaguely around him. "Ought to clean up around here . . . one of these days . . . ''

The student looks around the room with an expression of equal parts horror and awe. "This is where . . . you paint?'' he breathes.

"Well, like I said earlier, I don't paint so much now—

or at least not the kind of paintings you're interested in.
Those were done years ago, of course—at the Mock Avenue Studio.''

The student nods gravely. It is all a history lesson to
him. He picks his way carefully to the long, windowless
wall where Hale has tacked up a random collection of
pencil drawings, etchings, oil studies, and takeout-restaurant menus, stopping in front of the single piece on
the wall from the Mock Avenue period. Naturally. No one
is interested in what Hale is doing now. Hale glances toward the unfinished canvas on his easel, painted in the
abstract elvin style, and sighs. There are days when even
he isn't much interested in it.

The Mock Avenue painting is of a halfling girl, hunched
over and smoking a cigarette. Linny had posed for it. It
is a preliminary study for a much larger painting that also
includes Bear, standing behind her, holding that old shotgun of Billy Buttons' that never did actually shoot. Now
the larger painting hangs in a famous collection somewhere out in the World, where Hale has never been. The
price he received for the canvas completed the renovations
on his house. The study the student is admiring isn't very
good, in Hale's opinion; he keeps it up on the wall because
. . . well, because it is Linny.

The storage room behind the studio is filled with such
work—thirty-year-old drawings and paintings and cartoons, gathering dust. It drives Hale's dealer to distraction
that he hoards this old work, when it is so much in demand
beyond the Borderlands. Hale parts with a piece only when
he needs the cash. It seems somehow indecent that Worlders take seriously work that he has never taken seriously
himself—or that he can make so much money off the faces
of old friends.

The boy gasps as he steps into the storage room. Just
like a Worlder, soft, every emotion written right across his
face. He reminds Hale, embarrassingly, of himself—when

he'd first come from the suburbs across the Mad River to take Soho by storm.

"Like I said," Hale mutters, "It would be a tedious task to catalogue all this junk. . . ."

"I don't mind." The boy reverently fingers a sketch scribbled on the back of a poster announcing a gig at the Dancing Ferret. "Mr. Hale, I've planned and saved for two years to come up here," he says as though the Borderlands are Outer Mongolia—which perhaps, to a Worlder, they are, "and it would be an honor to—"

"It's your funeral," Hale interrupts, silently cursing his dealer for persuading him to do this. The boy ought to be out painting himself, raising hell like he and Ash and Bear had at that age—not here burying himself in Hale's vanished youth. Yet he'd wanted so much to come, had written all those goddamn earnest letters. "Look," Hale says, taking pity on the kid, "I'll be in the next room if you need any help. At least it's all labeled. If you look on the back of the canvases, you'll find the dates they were painted, the places, the names of the people in them—if I knew them. This was kind of diary for me, you understand. Like you Worlders keep snapshots in photo albums, just to remember things by. I never thought of it as, well, *art*."

The kid—now what *is* his name?—is pulling canvases out of the racks, oblivious to the dust smudging what is probably his best suit. His dark face is flushed with excitement as he kneels before a large canvas and peers closely at it, pushing the dreadlocks out of his eyes. Hale pauses in the doorway. He remembers painting this one as if it were yesterday. Ho Street, by daylight, looking derelict and dangerous, a couple of runaways lounging on the stoop of an ancient, graffiti-covered building. The kids, who couldn't have been more than nine or ten, had been happy to pose for the picture while eating the remains of Hale's lunch, and had written their names on the back of the canvas-board in childish block print. The gods only knew what had become of these two, how they had survived. Or *if* they had.

The student pulls out a second canvas, and a third, paintings filled with thirty-year-old memories staring out at Hale with oil-painted eyes, the old Soho street scene brought back to life. Perhaps that is why the Worlders like them, calling Hale a punk Norman Rockwell. They are the only visual record anyone has, in this half-elvin city where cameras do not work, of a time and place long gone.

Oh, Soho is still here; still, oddly enough, considered the underbelly of Bordertown. The clubs are still here: old Farrel Din books the best bands at the Dancing Ferret, the bouncers at the Factory still discourage the silver-haired from entering. The Mock Avenue Bell Tower clock still chimes the time, incorrectly. Some things never change. But Soho has. When Hale first wandered its streets, the buildings had been long abandoned and ignored by the rest of Bordertown, left to squatters and runaways and junkies and gang members both elvin and human—in the days when those distinctions really mattered. Back then, the coppers rarely journeyed south of the Old Wall. Back then the kids and crazies claimed the Old City as their own. When you walked down Ho Street, you felt like anything could happen. And more often than not, it did.

When Hale started making money, when the first unbelievable voucher had come from his first dealer, the crooked one, he'd been told he was crazy to use it to reconstruct a sagging, roofless townhouse on a decrepit Soho street with a third-floor view of the river. He didn't care. He loved these streets, the crumbling brick, the graffiti, the glitter, the flash. Now the entire block is restored, the neighborhood around it turned fashionable with "artistic" little shops and trendy boutiques painted in that nauseating fashion that is supposed to make them look quaintly 20th Century. Now the artists and musicians and street punks that had brought him to Soho, had been his friends, are gone as real estate investors claim the last of the abandoned buildings they used to call home. Now the Mock Avenue Church is a goddamn elvin hair-braiding salon.

"The Mock Avenue Church," the student reads aloud, *"Ash Bieucannon, on the roof.* Ash Bieucannon! He looks . . . like he's about my age," he adds wonderingly.

"Younger, I expect. We all were," Hale comments, feeling very much just then like the Old Man.

The student stares at the painting of Ash: a pretty elvin boy leaning against a rooftop gargoyle, a nine-pack of bitter ale beside him, a distant view of the Mad River behind him. "I must have known that. But it's just . . . *facts*, you know? I mean, you're *famous*, Mr. Hale. It's weird to think of you as ever being young." He blushes then. "I mean—"

Hale winces but waves away the *faux pas.* "I know what you mean. But I *was* young then—just a kid, just having fun and painting pictures of all my pals. You see this boy?"

Hale points out another canvas, Ash and Bear and Robbin and Billy Buttons lazing in the sun on the stoop in front of Gutierrez's "store."

"That's Robbin Pearl. Oh yes, he was part of our Studio too. And the others—Ash again, and Billy Buttons, you wouldn't have heard of him. And Bear, Mat Bear—you wouldn't have heard of him either, but you *should* have. He was the best of us, I think."

Hale grows silent. It still hurts to think of Bear—as though Hale were silent partner to an elaborate Cosmic Hoax that has allowed the rest of them fame when Bear achieved none.

The boy hauls another stack of canvases into the light. Here is a painting of José Gutierrez, the amazing tattooed José; and one of the ugly bloke who ran the Bloods for a while, after Steel died—Hale can't remember the name. And that little human girl Ash picked up—Charis was it?

Years later she'd become some kind of power up in the
City Council and the Bordertown bourgeoisie had been
appalled when Hale's nude drawings of her had surfaced
in a Chrystoble Street gallery. . . . The old streets, the
bikes, the Bloods festooned in scraps of leather and the
Horn Dancers in their motley rags, the kids elvin and human trying to make a life for themselves in an abandoned
slum on the Border of Elfland . . . too many memories
crowded onto these canvases. No wonder he'd locked them
away. Too many familiar faces staring back at him. And
too many of them are Linny's.

"Linnea Garnett," the boy reads aloud. *"Early morning, down by the river."* He turns, excited, to Hale. "This
isn't . . . is this *the* Linnea Garnett? Linnea Dark Garnett?
All these paintings you've labeled 'Linny'?"

Linny. Bordertown's claim to fame.

Hale nods, his eyes caught by the cornflower-blue eyes
of the painting, half obscured by a thatch of hennaed hair,
and that familiar expression that had exasperated him so
thirty years ago.

"I had no idea *she* was ever a punk. My god. Wasn't
her father some sort of elvin lord?"

Was she still using that line?

"Did you really know Linnea Dark Garnett?" the boy
is asking.

"Yes. I knew her," he says shortly.

Hale takes the canvas from the boy's hands and stacks
it against the others, turning the blue eyes to the wall.

The Mock Avenue Church was not imposing. Sandwiched between shopfronts with peeling paint and broken
glass, it had a single wooden door arched to a sharp point,
nailed shut. From the street the building looked sturdy, its
massive, age-blackened stones solid—but this front was
like the false façade of a Worlder's movie set, with open
air behind where the roof had caved in, exposing the central chambers to vandals and the weather. Grass grew be-

tween the mosaic tiles of the floor and over the tumbled gravestones of the inner courtyard. Only the Bell Tower still stood intact, and the small chapel beneath it. The bells still rang to announce the hour—except when Bear forgot to recharge the spell.

Hale climbed Gutierrez's fire escape up to the existing portion of the parsonage roof, where he could enter the tower through a third-story window reserved for this purpose. The sun was unseasonably warm, beating down on the asphalt of the rooftop, but the wind was brisk with a warning of winter approaching. The smell of the river was strong, the wind coming from the east. Were it blowing from the north or the west, it would carry the smell of the realm beyond the Border, a smell like wildflowers and brandy, to hover teasingly above the garbage-strewn streets of the Old City.

As Hale climbed through the window, there was another smell, of something burning. Smoke billowed from the central stairs.

Hale dropped his package, thinking of Ash or Bear caught in the flames, of precious canvases burning. In the chapel below he found Robbin stirring something in a frying pan, unconcerned as smoke filled the room up to the second-floor balcony.

"What the hell are you doing?" Hale threw open the portals beneath stained-glass windows, and the ginger cat squeezed through to escape out to the alley. The wind carried in the smell of the river, blew papers across the floor, and chased smoke up to the rafters. Robbin lifted the smoke-blackened pan off the flames, stirring its crackling contents like an old witch crouched over her brew. *Double, double, toil and trouble, fire burn and cauldron bubble.*

As the smoke began to clear and his heartbeat to return to normal, Hale realized there were others in the studio. Bear had rolled himself into a blanket and was asleep beneath a trestle table, snoring. The little elvin girl Ash had been growing bored with was stretched out on the model's platform near his easel, wrapped in the overlarge folds of his brocade robe, playing solitaire with a deck of those baffling elfish cards.

Ash was across the room with Robbin, sitting cross-legged like a potentate on the ancient army footlocker they'd bought off of José, and at his feet was what must be his latest: a tall elvin girl, her silver hair dyed red, eating chunks of a sour-apple off the tip of a switchblade.

"Now we grind it into a powder," Robbin lectured Ash and the tall girl. He tilted the contents of the pan into a mortar—another find from José's "store"—and began to grind it with precise movements, elegant twists of a pale elvin wrist. He had carefully rolled back the sleeves of his immaculate antique Oxford shirt. A silver band held silver hair, streaked with black, out of his eyes.

Hale stalked over to the Magic Fire, boot heels loud on the tiled floor. "What the hell are you doing?" he repeated.

"Wait and see," Ash answered mysteriously; but Robin, always ready to pontificate, explained.

"It's *abed peca'aryn*," he said, savoring the elvin word. "Dragon's Milk to you."

Hale whistled. The drug, which was traditionally mixed with whiskey and cream, was once a staple in aristocratic elvin homes; now highly illegal, it was also highly expensive, and difficult to come by this side of the Border.

"What High Council lord did you roll for this?" he asked, only half joking.

"We traded with José for it," Robbin said smugly. "Silly little human . . . he didn't realize what he had."

"Aw, he did so," Ash said. "He just didn't want the stuff on his hands. As if the coppers give a shit what kind of drugs float around down here—"

"What exactly," Hale interrupted, "did you trade José?"

Hale didn't have to wait for Robbin's answer; the sudden

flush on Ash's face told all. Cursing, he brushed past Ash
to the ladder they'd built up to the balcony that run along
three sides of the chapel. Here, beneath a huge round window depicting the Quest for the Holy Grail, he'd set up a
worktable, a couch, and a couple of easels. The unsuccessful abstract he'd been wrestling with for weeks glimmered against the window's rosy light. The little sketch
he'd drawn the other night—of the lead singer for the Guttertramps on stage at the Factory—was laid out on his
worktable, its corners held flat with push-pins. The painting he'd made from that sketch was gone.

"You swine!" he shouted down to the floor below. "You
goddamn pointy-eared swine! Leave my goddamn paintings alone!"

"Calm down, young Romeo," Ash drawled. "Or was
it Juliet up on the balcony? Never mind. Stop flapping your
arms and spitting fire and come down here. It was only
one painting. No harm done."

"No harm done? What do you mean no harm done?"
Hale shouted, rounding the balcony toward Ash.

"Look, it was just that picture of the Guttertramps
chick—José has a crush on her. I didn't give him any of
your *good* paintings, the abstract ones. José wouldn't know
what to do with a real work of art if an elvin masterpiece
was handed to him on a silver platter."

"That's not the point! First you trade my clothes, my
goddamn favorite jacket! Then you hock my spell box and
I have to pay a goddamn wizard whenever I need my bike
revved up. Now every time I turn around something else
is goddamn gone!"

Hale took the last steps of the ladder in a leap that landed
him behind the other boy and, in a sudden move, twisted
Ash's arms behind him, hauling him to his feet.

"You cut this out," Hale said pleasantly, "or I'll shave
off all that pretty silver hair while you sleep and sell it to
the hair-braiders up in Traders' Heaven."

Ash shifted his weight, and Hale allowed himself to be

thrown over the boy's hip, bringing Ash crashing to the ground with him. The two rolled, grappling, laughing, across the floor, knocking hard into the trestle table and sending a porcelain cup flying. Bear woke with a grunt as it smashed inches from his face.

Ash was taller, but Hale had the advantage of solid human weight, making it an even match. Bear, however, combined elvin height with a burly, muscular physique—and was cranky when he woke. He grabbed two fistfuls of clothing and hauled both boys to their feet.

"Decorum, gentlemen, decorum. There are ladies present."

The little elvin model giggled at this, but the red-haired girl merely glanced disdainfully at the lot of them, and then returned to her sour-apple.

Breathing hard, Ash shook plaster dust from the billowing sleeves of his white linen shirt and out of the long silver hair of which he was inordinately vain. He extended a hand, encased in the black fingerless gloves he habitually wore, toward Hale. "Aw shit, Hale," he said. "Forgive?"

Hale licked his lower lip and tasted blood. He smiled at his friend. "No."

"But I promise: I'll never do it again, Blood's Oath."

"Liar. You just remember, Ash-me-boy-o . . ." Hale tugged at a lock of his own hair, an undistinguished human brown, and made cutting motions with his fingers.

Ash laughed, but there was a flash of uneasy speculation in his eyes.

Bear yawned and shrugged into the paint-stained shirt he'd been using as a pillow, rolling up the sleeves to expose the heart tattooed on his left forearm. His hair, dyed black, stood up in sleep-tangled spikes about his face, and his chin was covered with silver stubble. He looked more like a Scandal District thug than an artist; when he spoke, his soft voice contrasted oddly with his bulk. "What's going on around here? What day is this? Is this Tuesday?"

"Thursday," Robbin informed him. Bear shook his head and sighed. "We were going to wake you anyway, albeit a little more gently. I've found a recipe for Dragon's Milk and it's almost ready." Robbin stirred the brownish powder at the bottom of the mortar.

"No," the red-haired girl spoke up. Her voice was low and husky, startling Hale with its unusualness. "It's still too coarse. It won't dissolve."

Robbin looked down his nose at the girl, arching an eyebrow.

"I've seen it before," she said, answering the look.

"You have?" Ash asked her. "Where?"

But the girl cut another slice of sour-apple and did not volunteer any more information.

With a sniff, Robbin went back to grinding. Hale regarded the girl curiously. Either she was an aristocrat or a liar; young girls from the streets of Elftown, where Ash usually picked up his feminine company, weren't likely to be familiar with the properties of "the drink of lords."

Yet this girl wasn't the Elftown type. In bikers' leathers and a black Danceland t-shirt identical to Hale's—the sleeves torn off to reveal slim, muscular white shoulders—she looked like a young boy, sprawled comfortably on the floor and handling the switchblade with familiar ease. Her henna-dyed hair was cut short as Bear's, exposing the arch of elvin ears; the bangs, worn longer than the rest, fell over one eye like an eye patch. No, not Ash's usual type at all.

When the powder passed the girl's inspection, Robbin stirred it into a jug of cream, turning the liquid an unattractive shade of gray. "You sure you got this right?" Hale asked him. "What is this stuff anyway?"

"Herbs. Wormwood. The seeds of the *peca* plant—which only grows in the Elflands—roasted and burned. Catnip. Ginger—"

"*Catnip?*"

"Well, yes—elves are susceptible to it too. Ginger.

Sugar. And the shavings of a peony root. I'm not making this up, Hale; I found the recipe in an old cookbook, printed before the peca trade was banned. It's addictive you know—worse than river water on humans. It rots the brain.''

Hale glanced warily at the gray stuff in the pitcher.

''Then why are you making it?'' he wanted to know.

''Don't worry, Romeo,'' Ash answered for Robbin, ''we're not likely to lay our hands on this stuff again. How could we possibly become addicted? I've always wanted to try Dragon's Milk, just once. It's so . . . romantic. All the great elvin poets lived on the stuff; that's why they all died young. My teachers used to say their muse burned so brightly that it burned them right out—but actually they were junkies, like half the lords and ladies on Dragon's Tooth Hill.''

''You don't have to try it, Hale,'' Robbin added with that superior smile that grated on Hale's nerves. What had Robbin got to feel so superior about? When in his entire life had this Tooth-bred snob ever done anything dangerous?

''I didn't say I wouldn't try,'' Hale said quickly. ''As long as you're sure you're not going to get it wrong and poison us all.''

''Now that's my boy-o,'' Ash said approvingly; ''I told Robbin you would want to try it too. Druienna, get us some cups, will you?''

The girl in the robe pouted at being ordered about, but she fetched the cups from the table and brought them to Ash, who had spread a shawl of elvin-red silk over the footlocker like a tablecloth.

''Are you going to paint anymore today Ash?'' she asked, putting her hand on his sleeve. ''I'm getting cold. And I'm, like, not into drugs, you know? I ought to get home. My mom would kill me if she knew I was here.''

Ash patted her hand like she was a small child or a puppy. ''That's okay, kid. Run along then.''

She darted a glance at the new girl, then smiled up at Ash uncertainly. "I have these free passes to the Wheat Sheaf tonight," she began, but he shook his head, cutting her off.

"Not tonight, Drui."

She shrugged. As she collected her clothes, her unhappiness was evident in the stoop of her shoulders, the bowed head of silver curls. Hale found himself feeling sorry for her, although he thought she was a silly little twit and had found her presence over the last weeks annoying. But she was no worse that any of Ash's other ladies. Someone ought to have warned her about Ash. Someone ought to warn this new girl too. But as Hale glanced her way, saw her watching Druienna with a similar pitying gaze, Hale realized that the new girl could probably take care of herself just fine.

"Come back tomorrow," Ash called as Druienna slipped through the doorway toward the stairs. "I'll need you to pose again." Then he turned to the others, the elvin girl forgotten, and produced a bottle of good Worldly brandy. Hale sighed, wondering which of his belongings went to pay for that. His cowboy boots, maybe? His paint-brushes?

Robbin poured each cup half full of brandy, then topped them off with the doctored cream, measuring fussily. The little porcelain cups felt too delicate to handle and looked absurd in Bear's huge, paint-stained hands. Ash lifted his up and pronounced a toast.

"To fame and fortune!" he said, as he always did. "Or vice versa."

"To *art*," Bear corrected him.

"And poetry," the new girl added.

Hale sniffed at the concoction. It had an acrid smell. He took a cautious sip—and it was all he could do not to spit it out again. For god's sake, Robbin *was* going to poison them.

"I think you fucked something up," he muttered, wiping the taste from his mouth with the back of his hand; but Ash and Robbin were making appreciative murmurs and Bear had downed his in a single gulp and the girl was sipping delicately, an unreadable expression on her face. Was this some kind of joke? Let's put one over on the human kid? He wouldn't put it past them.

Hale tried another taste. No. The stuff was definitely foul.

"Don't you like it?" Robbin asked smoothly, watching Hale's reaction. "Hmm, I suspected as much. Doesn't work on humans," and the mildly contemptuous way he said the word made Hale's eyes narrow.

"No," Hale spat out, "but it probably works just fine on cats, proving, of course, that they are a superior race. Why don't you just call Frodo in and give him my share, rather than wasting it on me?"

And he was up and out of the room, something tight twisting in his chest. Damn, damn, damn. Hale climbed the stairs two at a time and the litany echoed the climb. Damn. He knew he was overreacting. But this always happened. Just when he started feeling good, like maybe he belonged somewhere, something came along to make it clear he didn't. It didn't matter how good a painter he was, or could become; it didn't matter that the boisterous male camaraderie of the Studio felt like the thing he'd been looking for practically since the day he was born. It didn't matter that he'd saved Ash's goddamn life or brought most of the groceries that kept the other boys—including rich-kid Robbin—alive. What really mattered, when you came right down to it, was that he was not an elf. And at times like these, even a girl, even a goddamn stranger, belonged more than he did—because he didn't have goddamn silver hair.

He pushed open the door to the roof in a shower of crumbling plaster. The wind raised goosebumps on his arms—but he was not going back downstairs to fetch his jacket. He crossed the roof to its southeastern edge and sat, his feet dangling high above Mock Avenue. The sun warmed him and a leering gargoyle sheltered him from the wind. Hale wiped tears from his eyes, feeling like an asshole, and scowled at the distant river. Somewhere out there was the magicless World, a place he had absolutely no desire to go. This was where he belonged. On these streets, in this place. So why did he feel he still had to prove it?

The ginger cat climbed over the crest of the roof, avoiding the patches where the shingles had caved in. He sidled over to Hale, taking a proprietary interest in Hale's sunwarmed lap, and with a great deal of kneading, pricking Hale's flesh with alley-cat claws, he made a nest of the boy's army fatigues and settled down for a nap. Hale ran his fingers through Frodo's bristly fur, over the lumps and scars of old cat fights. He felt the rumble of Frodo's motor low and steady beneath his palm.

"Catnip," Hale muttered. Then he shook his head and began to laugh.

"Are you stoned, Romeo?"

Hale jumped, and Frodo protested the sudden movement with a well-placed claw. He hadn't heard Ash coming up behind him. The boy was alone. "No," Hale answered him, shielding his eyes from the sun as he squinted up at Ash.

Hale wasn't stoned, but Ash was. His eyes were dark, his steps unsteady, and he had a foolish grin spread across his alabaster face. As he lurched toward the roof edge, Hale took hold of his shirttail and ordered him to sit, worried that Ash would stumble right over. Ash's bones popped as he sat down; he leaned against Hale's bent knee with a sigh. He had brought half a cup of Dragon's Milk with him.

On the street below, José was arguing with members of the Pack over a pile of elvin junk stacked on the sidewalk—stolen probably. Sammy Tucker, the Pack's leader, was ignoring the dispute entirely, sitting astride his modified Yamaha, reading a book. The argument grew heated, voices drifting up to the roof, and a Packer with feathers braided into her long dark hair began loading the junk back into a sack. She flipped a finger at Gutierrez as the Pack roared away on bikes so stripped down it was a wonder spells held them together at all. José shook his head and then climbed the stairs of his stoop. He was wearing Hale's faded denim jacket, embroidered with the words "Hell's Angels" on the back, which Ash had traded for the brocade robe. Hale thought that was a terrific name for a band—but if they'd every played Soho, it must have been before his time.

Ash reached over to pat the ginger cat, singing what lyrics he could remember of an elfish pop song, offkey, humming the parts he couldn't. He must have been really high; Ash knew he couldn't sing.

"So where's your girlfriend?" Hale asked him, and Ash stopped the serenade to take a hit of Dragon's Milk. He sipped it slowly and sighed with pleasure.

"My girlfriend? You mean Linny. Told her to go," he said and he took another sip. "She didn't though," he added. "She's still down there, with Robbin and Bear."

"Who is she?"

"Just some girl; thinks she's a poet. Picked her up at . . . hell, I don't remember. Somewhere. She gave me a ride home on her bike; she's got this sleek, mean motherfucking machine. Nice kid. *Real* nice bike. What'd I say her name was? Linny."

Hale relaxed, pleased that this girl was no more important than any of the others, pleased that Ash would still rather spend time with him—though until that moment he hadn't realized this had worried him. Perhaps because this girl seemed different from the others. The kind of girl, Hale mused, you could get all wrapped up in. He shook his head, dismissing the thought. A gust of wind blew silver hair across his cheek, and he pushed it out of his eyes.

Ash was so loose and relaxed from the drug he was practically oozing into the asphalt. He couldn't remember the third verse to the song he was trying to sing.

"I thought this catnip concoction was supposed to inspire you to write great poetry or paint some masterpiece," Hale commented snidely. "All that fuss over the stuff, and all it seems to inspire you to do is sing pop tunes. Terrific."

"I *am* inspired," Ash said dreamily. "I think I'll be a rock star. Free booze at the Ferret, little girls from the Tooth . . . ah, that's the life for me."

"You're not exactly slaving it now, boy-o."

"But I want fame and fortune. What's the point of painting all day if nobody outside the Studio except crazy José ever sees it? Or writing poetry that nobody reads, or playing music in rat-infested clubs for a bunch of headbangers and junkies and runaways? Have you ever been to the galleries on the Promenade near Dragon's Claw Bridge? Where they serve champagne to the patrons and treat elvin artists like royalty? Man, I'm sick of day-old donuts and a john that doesn't flush."

"Come off it, Ash. Nobody forced you to leave the Elflands. Your problems is you've read too many books about artists starving in garrets; you thought it would be *fun* to live in a slum. It never occurred to you that you might get hungry, or cold, or have your throat torn out for the silver on your wrists. Admit it—you left your parents' fancy house because you thought poverty would be *romantic*, didn't you?"

"Hell no; I left my parents' house to get laid! Becoming an artist was an afterthought. Girls love it. Just you wait and see, Hale."

Yeah, sometimes it worked that way. Hale spent a lot of time on the streets and in the clubs, sketching compulsively as he had done since he was a child—as if by pinning it down, he could keep time from slipping away. And sometimes some girl would be intrigued and follow him back to Mock Avenue. Where invariably she'd fall for Ash. Every goddamn time.

Hale dipped his finger into Ash's teacup, then held it under Frodo's nose. Frodo opened his eyes, sniffed then licked the milk off the boy's finger with a sandpaper tongue. Ash lay back flat on the asphalt, eyes closed, the sun raising a flush on his pale cheeks.

Down below, a motorcycle circled the block, slowed, and stopped by the steps of the Mock Avenue Church. The girl with the feathers had come back, alone. She carried a lumpy bundle cradled in one arm. She glanced around cautiously, locked her bike with a two-penny spell, and disappeared behind the doorway of Gutierrez's place.

When she was gone, the alley kids came out—pint-sized punks with painted faces and oiled, spiky hair. They clustered around the solitary bike, admiring the paint job and surreptitiously testing the spell lock and chains. Hale rattled asphalt pebbles onto the street below and the children scattered, melting back into the cracks and shadows from which they came.

Hale didn't like the alley kids. They looked too young to be really dangerous—but looks were deceiving, particularly in Bordertown. It was children who had gotten Ash the night Hale found him in a Ho Street alley, fresh from the Elflands, his white throat cut from ear to ear. Only a True Blood could have survived such an attack—and not even then, had much more of that blood seeped away between the cobblestones. Yet it was not just because it was Hale who found him that the bond was so tight between elf and human. It was because Hale upheld the fiction that it was Rats that got hold of Ash that night, or maybe some renegade members of the Pack. Not little kids, barely nine or ten years old.

Beside Hale, Ash smiled, lost in drug-induced dreams. Behind them the Bell Tower clock chimed the time, two o'clock—which meant it was a quarter to noon. Fifteen minutes, not enough. Not even if he broke every speed limit in the city. He hadn't intended to stop at the Studio; he certainly hadn't intended to stay. But he couldn't just leave Ash on the roof all alone. And the others down below were probably just as stoned.

"Ash, Ash," he said, nudging the older boy, pulling him upright. "Get up now. Let's go back down. I have to go away now. Stop smiling, you fool, and get up. Get up!"

Ash looked at Hale through crossed, dilated eyes. He allowed Hale to help him to stand, but the moment Hale let go, he sank down again. "Twenty thousand volts is not enough, to . . . to . . ." He looked up. "Shit Hale, how does the song go? Twenty thousand volts . . . aw . . ." He began to rise, clutching at the gargoyle, perilously close to the roof's edge.

Hale put a steadying arm around Ash's waist. The boy felt curiously light, insubstantial, as if the drug was making a ghost out of him. "Come on, Ash," Hale muttered as he coaxed the boy to the stairs. "Think art, not rock'n'roll. I don't think your elvin poets would approve."

"No, it *is* poetry," Ash insisted. "I just never realized it before. Listen, Hale: 'Once I burned for your touch, now every look is too much . . .' "

"Yeah, yeah. Everything sounds profound when you're stoned, Ash. Come on, now, take a step. Careful down the stairs—there's the missing one. Thadda-boy. Watch out for the cat . . . aw shit, Ash." Hale sighed. "Come on, man. I've got to get going."

"Why? Where do you go, my Romeo? When you disappear. A cold-water flat in the Scandal District? An alcoholic mother hidden in the tenements of Water Street? The trailer parks down past Hell's Gate—is that where you go? Why such a secret? There's nothing wrong with a tragic past. It's so . . . romantic."

"And you're so . . . disgusting. Ash, I'm going to put you to bed. Come on, unlace your shoes, there you go. Now the other one. Phew. Christ. Don't you ever wash these sneaks? Now lie down. Stop grinning. Just lie down there; here, take the pillow. By the time you sleep this off. I'll be back.'' Hale pushed the pillow under the silver head.

At the far end of the chapel Robbin was staring off into space. Bear was back beneath the trestle table, snoring with his mouth open. The tall girl sat on top of it, writing something in a leather-bound book. Feeling Hale's gaze, she looked up and met his eyes. She put her pen down and crossed over to the mattress where Ash lay.

Ash was humming softly to himself, mixing the New Blood Review tune with a Bach Brandenburg Concerto. Linny squatted down on her heels, placed her hand against Ash's flushed cheek. The scar was vivid across the white skin of his throat. The elvin boy moved suddenly, taking her wrist in his gloved hand, pulling her down beside him. Hale crossed his arms over his chest, staring down at the two of them.

"Catnip," he muttered, and stalked out of the room.

Hale ate his dinner in silence. He didn't want it. The Mad River Mix-quick stuck in his throat and the potatoes sat in his stomach like a lump of clay. But to refuse it would add insult to injury, considering he'd nearly missed the meal altogether, arriving home as his mother began to clear the leftovers from the table. Too bad he couldn't just save this stuff for Ash. Ash was always hungry. Hale snuck what groceries he could out of the house and down to Soho, but it was never enough.

Hale's father sat at the end of the table, silent now himself after the explosion that could probably have been heard halfway across the flatlands. He was buried behind yesterday's edition of the *Church Times*, smoking a cigarette and stretching out the last minutes of the meal before he went back to his beat across the river. The jacket of his Silver Suit hung on the back of his chair, the copper card pinned above the left breast. Hale's mother was bustling about the kitchen, whistling cheerfully, oblivious to the tension, doing five things at once—as usual. She was washing up the dinner dishes, whipping up a batch of Troll Bridge cookies, jotting perky reminders to herself on the chalkboard next to the sink: "Note: less salt in the Mix-quick mix!!!" "Note: Sissy's piano lesson two P.M. *sharp*!!!" "Note: Inspirational message for the *Church Times* due Friday. Message of Hope? Feed the Little Children? Discuss with the Group!!!" The dishes made a loud clatter as she scrubbed them and stacked them on the drainboard to dry. Hale chewed and chewed the overly salty stew. He concentrated on each bite, on chewing and swallowing. He thought that if he didn't concentrate real hard, he would probably scream.

When he had finished everything on his plate and dutifully eaten three of the cookies his mother insisted were his favorites although he had not liked them since he was three, he was excused from the table. He escaped through the back door, feeling like a prisoner receiving a pardon. His father did not speak to him, or even look up as he left, slamming the door behind him.

The house was large and pink. Behind it and to either side were identical stucco houses, painted turquoise and mauve and lime green. The hedges masking the foundation had been clipped into precise rectangular shapes; the flowerbeds that edged the walk were symmetrically planted with alternating pink and white puffball blooms. In the yard next door, a boy who had been Hale's classmate before he'd been booted out of his third and final school was playing fetch with a pink French poodle. The boy was wearing his school sweater, the class insignia embroidered on the breast pocket, over a pair of spotless white trousers; his broad, pleasant face was marred by the black eye that had earned Hale his latest expulsion. Hale looked down at his dirty fatigues, his ripped, skintight t-shirt, his scuffed jackboots, and sighed.

The door opened behind him. He tensed; but it was only Sissy; he could smell her distinctive scent: *eau de bubble gum*. She stood behind him for a moment, her shadow covering him; then she sat down on the step beside him, chin in her hands, elbows on her knees. "Good going, asshole."

Hale grinned. For a ten-year-old, she had a hell of a mouth. "It wasn't intentional, you know," Hale said conversationally.

She snorted. "It's an accident you come to Sunday dinner dressed like Old City scum and give Ma a heart attack? She had two ladies from the church group here, Hale; you missed them by, like, two seconds." She sounded like she was pissed, but Hale knew her better than that. She loved it when he got into trouble; at ten, she already found life dull in the 'burbs. Sissy narrowed her eyes and poked him in the ribs. "Where d'ya get the clothes?" she wanted to know.

Hale shrugged. He'd had his other clothes in the package he'd dropped when he thought the Studio was burning down; he'd been halfway home again, stalled in traffic on the Riverside Bridge, before he remembered.

Sissy slid her hand into his pants' pocket—nosy little brat—and pulled out the elvin bracelets and studs he'd taken off in a vain attempt to look less disreputable. She slid the bracelets onto one thin wrist, snapped the studs around the other. In her soccer-uniform shirt and her jeans with the holes in the knees, her bony, scabbed kneecaps peeking through and Ash's studs heavy on her wrist, she looked so damn cute Hale had a sudden mad urge to scoop her up and run away with her—to raise her right, before the 'burbs hammered all of the juice out of her. But what the hell would he do with her at the Mock Avenue Studio?

Lost in his thoughts, he didn't realize she was speaking to him until she smacked him, hard, a left punch to his bare shoulder. Her expression was her usual scowl, but her eyes were wide with concern—and fear?

"What's going to happen now?" she was asking. "With you and Daddy, Hale? He's pretty mad."

Hale ran his fingers through his carefully slicked-back hair, making it all stand on end again. "I dunno, squirt."

"You'll tell me when you do know? Do you *promise* Hale?" Her small hand was at the back of his knee, gripping him tight.

"Yeah, sure, Sissy. Look, it's no big deal. This'll blow over too," he said, but she wasn't buying it. She scowled at him even more fiercely, snapped her gum, and punched him again for no apparent reason before she disappeared back into the house.

The ultimatum was simple enough. His parents didn't want to throw good money after bad buying him a spot in another school where he'd just get into yet another fight . . . and that was a relief, because he wouldn't have gone away. They wanted him to get a job. They had it all worked out; they had probably made a list on his Ma's chalkboard: "Note: decide what to do with Hale!!!"

They had graciously offered him a choice of what his future was to be. His father could pull some strings, send him for training as a Silver Suit. Or he could work with his mother on the Church Council paper, "put his god-given talent to use" illustrating inspirational articles and Ma's recipe column and editorials debating whether elves have Christian souls . . . wouldn't that make him real popular down in Soho?

Hell. He liked his family; he never meant to disappoint them. So why, when he was home for more than an hour at a time, did he feel like he was going to puke, or scream?

Sissy was asleep when he tapped on her door. It was late, near midnight. He'd been pacing for hours in the room right above hers and it was amazing he hadn't kept her up with the noise, jackboots thumping on the shaggy carpeting of the floor. Maybe he had. Maybe this pose of childhood innocence, arms curled around her stuffed cat, Mr. Potato-head, was feigned. She woke suspiciously quickly when Hale called her name.

She sat up, brushing tangled brown hair out of her eyes.

She was wearing a flannel nightgown—and Ash's studded bracelet.

"What's up, asshole?"

"I promised I'd let you know what's gonna happen . . ."

How was he going to tell the kid he was leaving?

"You're leaving," she said. It was not a question. Was he this quick when he was ten? She was always a step ahead of him. He ran a hand through her baby-soft hair.

She pushed his hand away and slid out of the bed. Beneath the nightgown she wore her jeans and sneakers. From the depths of her closet she produced a backpack, already packed; she slung it over her shoulder, carrying Mr. Potato-head in her arms. "I'm coming too," she announced matter-of-factly.

Hale stared at her. "Sissy . . . Squirt . . . You can't . . ." he fumbled. What the hell would Ash say, or Robin, if he brought his baby sister to Soho?

She put the backpack down on the floor, looked up at him gravely through raggedly cut bangs. "Hale, are you in some kind of trouble?"

"Trouble?"

"Dad thinks you've gone and joined one of the gangs. He says you've been seen down in Soho. Are you a Packer, Hale?" she asked solemnly, pronouncing the word carefully like she'd read it in a book.

Hale laughed, and shook his head. He patted the mattress beside him and she sat warily on its edge. "It's worse than that, Squirt." She looked at him, her eyes troubled. "Don't tell anybody, but"—he shifted his eyes right and left, then lowered his voice theatrically—"I'm an artist."

She gave him another one of her left hooks; he was developing quite a bruise on that arm. "Cut it out, asshole. I'm serious."

"So am I, Squirt. Honest to god. I'm going down to Soho to learn to be a painter. Look, I'll still visit you—"

"Is that what you're doing? *Painting?* Why haven't you told Dad? He's worried sick, Hale. He thinks you're taking drugs, or gonna get yourself killed by some big, mean Blood.''

Hale poked a finger into the hole in Sissy's jeans. ''I can't tell Dad, Squirt. He'd *rather* think I ran with a gang. *He* did, when he was young. Sure, what did you think Dragon's Fire was—a soccer team? Lots of coppers did. It's a hell of a lot easier for him to tell his copper friends that I've run off to the Old City to bash in elvin heads than to tell them the truth—that I've run off to be an artist, for crissake. That I share a painting studio with a bunch of elvin guys.''

''You *do*?'' Sissy was taken aback for once. ''Oh *Hale* . . . Mother says they don't even have *souls*.''

''Sis, if you ever saw the way they paint, you'd know they have souls—maybe even finer than you and me. I want to learn to paint like that, even if it takes me a million years.''

Sissy was silent for a long time. Her teeth nibbled at her lower lip and she held on tightly to Mr. Potato-head. Finally, she turned to him and said, ''Will they like me, Hale? Your elvin friends? Even though I'm human?''

He stood then, his arms crossed over his chest, regarding her sternly. ''Of course they would. But I can't take you with me, Squirt. For god's sake, you're only ten years old!''

''I'm as tough as you.''

''Huh. I don't doubt it. But I can't show up with my kid sister in tow! You're a goddamn child! You're a girl,'' he added, exasperated—like maybe she hadn't noticed.

Sissy looked like she'd been slapped. Her cheeks flushed bright red, hurt covered over with anger. ''Fine, swell,'' she hissed. ''Just go away and leave me behind. Go on, Hale. I'll probably die of boredom . . . but don't you worry about me. Just go off and have fun with your new friends.''

''Sissy.'' He tried to touch her, but she flinched away. ''Look, kid, it would just be impossible—''

"Shut up!" she cried.

Down the hallway, a light was snapped on. He heard voices coming from his parents' room. Shit. Oh shit. He had to go. Now.

"Sissy . . ."

"Go away, Hale. Just leave me alone."

He heard footsteps in the hall.

"Sissy?" his mother called. Are you all right?"

Sissy glared at him. "Go out the window, asshole. Can't you do anything right?" She pushed him in that direction and turned to the door. "Everything's fine, Ma."

He glanced back at her as he slid out the window, trampling the begonias. She was sitting in her bed, sneakers covered by the quilt, elvin bracelets covered by her nightgown's sleeve. "Asshole," she muttered, clutching Mr. Potato-head and scowling at the walls of the empty room.

—And then it was night in Soho. That was the next thing Linny knew. Black night, without any comforting home lights. And she was lying half on, half off a mattress on the floor, sprawled across another sleeping body that seemed to glow white in the dark.

She tensed, the way she always did when people came too close. *This* was too damn close by half. Slowly and stiffly she eased her body off and away from the other's. And, rising groggily to her feet, she remembered where she was, and why.

The Mock Avenue Studio. Where Ash Bieucannon had brought her to show her his art, after that wild conversation they'd had in the cafe. They'd found some *peca*, made Dragon's Milk, just the way she'd always read about it. More talk; she'd looked at the work of his studio mates, felt as the drug kicked in that she was seeing through to their souls. Then Ash had come back and she had discovered some profound truth lurking in the scar on his neck, which now made no sense at all. Then she fell asleep.

But wait—she must still be stoned. The universe, or her

particular corner of it, was arranging a cosmic metaphor, just for the pleasure of Linnea Garnett, poet: at the moment her own memories came clear to her, the entire room burst into light. Every crack and filthy corner of the chapel was mercilessly illuminated; but so was its intricate stone carving and jewel-like canvases, glowing with color and half-formed life.

Ash, the elf on the mattress with the scar, rolled over and groaned. Up in the rafters, a newcomer gave a triumphant cackle.

"Arise and shine, my beauties!" he called, the bringer of elvin light. "It is I, Billy Buttons, the artists' friend"— he began shimmying down a side ladder—"although you wouldn't know it from the way you shits treat me. Dragon's Milk, I hear, and guzzled it all like the swine you truly are. Some for Ash, and some for Bear, and some for Bonny Robbin; and even some for Human Hale, But never a drop for me." He prodded Ash with a booted toe. "How 'bout it, how's that for poetry?"

"You *bastard*!" Ash sprang up. His eyes were blazing with fury. Buttons stood his ground, although Linny was not sure she would have. "I've *lost* it!" Ash cried, his hands reaching to nothing. "I was there—I had it—and now I've lost it. Oh, for the love of blood, somebody give me some paper!"

Buttons took Ash's thin shoulders in his broad hands. "Easy, guy. Bear!" he called. "Robbin-a-Bobbin! Are you all just as lost as your buddy here?"

There was no answer. Billy Buttons seemed to notice her for the first time, although Linny had a feeling he never missed anything. "What about you?" he leered. "Ash must have drawn your tits from seventeen different angles already; what are you sticking around for?"

Linny met his silver eyes. "Gang bang. I want Bear to immortalize my hands, and Robbin to do a little study of my ears. As for my face . . . we'll save it for that human guy who hangs around: humans are good at eyes, they say they're the windows of the soul. What's your specialty?''

Billy Buttons just grinned at her. His pale hair hung long and stringy, white with a buttercup tint. His long nose had been broken so many times it almost looked human, and his teeth were amazingly crooked.

Linny knew what that grin meant. She'd passed the test, defended herself with her words against his. Still she didn't want to stop. The words kept coming: ''As for my tits, if you think Ash could find his own *dick* in that state . . .''

Billy Buttons chuckled; and that was another victory. She couldn't believe how good it felt. The words were power. They flowed in her like blood, like mother's milk, like desire. All those years of pretending they weren't there, because the other girls might call you an elfie bitch, even though you tried to hide your ears with your hair and darken your skin with makeup to look the same as all the others . . . Well, she could do something about her looks, but not about her thoughts. And her thoughts were full of words. But the words that hurt people, words that made them laugh and words that called attention to you and your wit and mastery; those words were for the boys alone. Girls used their bodies and their eyes, and their loud, high-pitched laughter. The only power words they had were ''yes'' and ''no.'' She'd tried hanging out with the boys in school, because they at least felt right to her with their insults and their wisecracks. They weren't too thrilled, though. They knew that girls were supposed to be beautiful, or ''cute,'' whatever that meant. Girls were there to admire *their* words. Even when the boys put up with her for her cleverness, Linny knew she stood out like a pig in a church. And standing out, as her mother told her over and over, was not good here at the fancy school in the nice human suburb we worked so hard to get you into.

But now Billy Buttons chuckled and Ash put his arm around her neck and said, ''Well, if I can't find it, let's say you find it for me—''

And the words kept coming to her: "Yeah, sure, Ash; then what would I do with it?"

Billy Buttons drew back in mock surprise. "Don't you *know*?"

"Nah, Billy Boy," Ash said, delighted to be the center of attention, "she don't know. Why don't you tell her?"

Billy guffawed, and flung one arm around Ash and one around Linny, so that they made a circle, all linked together by arms around necks. "Hey, Ash, I like this chick. What's she do? Another artiste?"

Even now—*Don't ask HIM, ask ME*—"I'm a poet," Linny said.

"Whew!" Billy drew his arm away as though she were too hot to touch. She liked that. "What kind of poet?"

Linny looked Billy Buttons in the face again. Their eyes were on a level. She knew he was seeing the deep blue in hers, a little too dark for elvinkind. But so what? These days, in these lands, not everybody was pure, pure, pure. He didn't have to know from where, or how much.

"An elvin poet," she said.

Later Robbin and Bear wandered in together. They wouldn't say where they'd been, but Robbin draped himself in a picturesque pose on the old footlocker, and stayed there, smiling smugly at nothing, and Bear took an old canvas and began painting over it with ferocious sweeping strokes.

Ash got out the rest of the brandy, and Billy produced some coltsfoot cigarettes from one of his numerous pockets; and they all got to talking about where they'd come from and where they were going.

Linny wondered how much of what they said was really true. She had a feeling that the ones who said the least had the most to tell. Ash made a big deal about how useless he'd felt growing up in Elfland, without getting specific. None of the emigrés ever gave out details. It was as though Elfland itself wouldn't translate, as if the language for it didn't make sense on this side of the Border. But he went on at great length about the gang of toughs who'd cut his throat for him his first night in Soho.

"Humans," he said, "maybe even the Pack, out to do a little elf bashing. And too stupid to realize they'd dealt me a wound I'd recover from." He absently traced the line of his scar. "I don't know, it was too dark to see."

"Elves," Linny suggested. If he didn't like her disagreeing with him, it was too damn bad. "Elves who knew what they were doing: wanted to rough someone up without murdering them."

"Not the Bloods," stated Billy Buttons with authority. "That's not their way." Something about the way everyone was quiet for a moment after he made this simple declaration told Linny all she needed to know about Billy Buttons' background.

"Could have died," Bear grunted from his corner easel. No one had thought he was listening, but he was. "Hale saved you."

"He did. A fine man, Hale."

"Your pet human," Robbin sneered. "Did he really help you, Ash, *peca'aryni*, or do you just keep him around to be eccentric?"

Billy laughed. "A little of both, huh, Ash?"

"Hale's all right," Bear said laconically; but Linny heard more warmth in that than in Ash's heated defense.

"Can it, Rob, you fucking Dragon's Tooth snob! You're beginning to sound like my purebred Elfland mother, you know that?"

So, Linny thought, that put young Robbin in his place. He was a True Blood, all right; but Ash's Elfland origins outclassed him. She filed it away with the rest of her survival tips for the Studio—supposing they let her stick around, supposing they didn't turn next minute and politely ask when she was leaving.

She didn't want to go. Ever since she'd come in the door—well, the window—the Studio had been humming in her blood a song of welcome. She felt as if the building recognized her. It was almost too perfect to be real: the art, the clutter, the books and brushes and bleached animal skulls, the piles of dirty, paint-stained rags that would have given her parents fits, the gorgeous collection of old chipped jars full of more kinds of weird tea than she'd ever seen in her life. . . . The old church was a nest for the only people she'd ever met who saw things the way she did, who cared about what she cared about with the same terrible passion. She didn't expect them to see that, really: they probably met people like her every day. And just because they didn't treat her like a girl didn't mean they had to treat her like a friend. Which was too bad; because she knew she belonged there. They lived art, breathed art, ate art, slept art, just like she did. They were pictures, she was words. She realized now how little difference it made, why it was all called "The Arts." She wanted to stay here forever, making messes and drinking and arguing. . . .

Besides, she had nowhere to go.

Robbin drew stiffly away from Ash, fussed with his silver cuff links. Even Linny could tell he was furious, trying to hide it the way elves do. "So, I'm a snob? And I suppose you grew up eating the dirt of Elfland."

Ash had the grace to smile. It was an extraordinary moment. Linny wondered if he could pull it off every time he got someone mad at him. She suspected he could. It was a concept not entirely foreign to elvin philosophy—victory through yielding—although it was not a popular one.

"A hit." Ash was still smiling sunnily at Robbin. "Game, and match." He put his hands on Robbin's shoulders. "Oh, Rob . . . two noble gentlemen who have drunk Dragon's Milk together shouldn't quarrel over something so trivial." Trivial like Hale, Linny thought, amused. Robbin shrugged, smiled dismissively; it was clear peace had been made. She admired Ash's game of manipulation;

but some imp in her that was full of power tonight made her call it.

"And Bear and I, not being noble gentlemen, are exempt from the general comradeship?" If she was going to lose them all, she wanted to do it in a big way, on her own terms.

But Ash rose to the occasion. "Bear is Bear. He needs no title. And he never quarrels." Ash considered his moon-white fingernails. "Although he occasionally decks someone. On provocation. As for you . . . we know nothing about you, besides the fact that you own a great bike, have strong opinions on epic poetry, and write in a notebook you won't let anyone else see." He started walking around her, examining her like a specimen. Linny tried to look bored. "Good clothes," Ash observed. "Healthy skin, elfin-pale; elfin-eared. Red hair, probably dyed. Educated. The wrong accent for Elfland, though. Therefore, unless you were stolen by humans as a baby and brought up in the World, a Bordertown elf from an affluent family."

Linny shrugged. "Amazing, Holmes," she muttered.

"Huh?" said Ash.

"Nothing. You forgot to point out that I read too much. The bike was a Name Day present from my father. He doesn't cross over much, but when he does he likes to make a splash."

"Tragic." Billy Buttons wiped imaginary tears from his eyes. "The child of a broken home."

But the others were trying to hide the fact that they were impressed. And why not? She'd practically come out and told them that her father was a very important resident of Elfland, either a trader or a lord, someone who could cross back and forth with ease. She could practically see the wheels turning in Ash's head: a noble with a wife in Elfland, sneaking off to visit his mistress and illegitimate daughter in Bordertown. . . .

"Yeah," she said, "real tragic. But it's like you were

saying before, Ash, you know? None of it seems real. I mean, you can't write great poetry sitting in a pretty bedroom with framed Lillet prints in it. You know: *The Horns of Elfland, The Lovers' Farewell* . . ."

"Message from Home," Robbin finished in disgust. "*I* couldn't write a *laundry* list in a room with a Lillet in it. All that sticky sentiment, those tired images. . . . Did you know Lillet designed unicorn t-shirts before he became famous?"

"Oh, come on, Robbin," Ash said. "Your parents are collectors. You know what an original Lillet is worth these days; don't tell me you didn't have one hanging on the wall when you were a kid. Or was it bold new statements of Bordertown chic like those Fern collages? Frodo the cat could barf up more meaningful work! Come on, Rob," Ash urged winningly, "what were your earliest inspirations? What makes even this dump look better than Dragon's Tooth Hill?"

Proud Robbin was actually laughing. "It was the dining room," he groaned. "They actually got him to paint the walls. Pure Lillet, the whole thing. It was like eating dinner inside a dog's stomach." He buried his face in his delicate fingers in mock horror.

"Hey . . ." Ash turned a comforting caress into a yank of Robbin's braid. "It's okay, lad. All that's behind you now. You never have to look at another Lillet again. No more Lillet . . . no more Lillet . . ."

"No more Lillet . . ." Robbin took up the chant like a spell. Billy Buttons was rapping out a drumbeat on a pile of boxes, and Bear's bass rumbling voice joined them against the sweep of his brushstrokes.

"No more Lillet," Linny joined in. "No more Lillet . . . There never was a Lillet . . . We are the knaves of Elfland, We are the fools of Bordertown. Where we pass, Carnival riots. Where we stand, Soho shakes. Nothing we set our hand to is not achieved, and what we curse is nine times blighted. We ravish the old, we are the new. We are born tonight, we are with you now!''

Linny found that her hands were clenched in fists on her knees, and her body swayed to the beat of her chant. She stopped, opened her hands.

''Ha!'' Billy and Ash and Robbin chorused. Their shout rang with approval. Linny looked at them, trying to pretend she knew what had happened.

''A rant!'' cried Ash, slapping his knee. ''I haven't heard one of those since . . . since my tutor . . .'' His eyes misted over with memory of Elfland.

''I didn't know anyone still wrote those,'' Robbin said. ''One of the classic elvin poetry forms; we had it crammed down our throats at school.'' He looked hard at Linny, as though reassessing her to discover if she were an old classmate in disguise. ''Not bad. Do you write a lot of them?''

''I told you I was a poet,'' she said primly.

She had never written a rant before. Because, she thought, she'd never had anything to rant about. She'd never belonged anywhere: not with the boys, not with the girls, not with the nice people her parents wanted her to associate with, not with the toughs who were so stupid you could drive trucks between their ears.

Ash was standing over her, beaming with delight. ''But this, this is your greatest work! 'The Mock Avenue Rant.' *''Where we pass, Carnival riots. Where we stand, Soho shakes. . . .''*

''We are the fools of Bordertown,'' Bear came forward, wiping paint off his hands with a rag. ''I like that.''

Ash picked up Linny's leather notebook from the table where she'd left it. She would have killed anyone else who touched it, but now she felt that it was time. No one else had ever seen the contents of that notebook. It wasn't so much that she was afraid of being judged as she was afraid of being misunderstood. But if she hadn't been saving it for this precise moment, what had she been saving it for?

Ash was leafing through her notebook, looking at her

poems. From time to time he nodded. Linny took her switchblade out and began shaving little bits of wood off the end of a bench. Ash's criticism became audible. "Yes," he murmured. "Yes, good. Oh, good!" Unbidden came the thought that it was as though her book were making love to him. She quashed it.

"Yes!" Ash looked up at her, his finger still holding a place in the book. "This is fantastic. You've really got something here."

"I thought you hated epics," Linny said, remembering the conversation between them at Taco Hell that had started all this.

"Yeah." Ash shook his head with a crooked smile. "I thought so too. Because they seemed so dead to me. But what you've got here"—he waved the notebook—"is real, this is alive—"

"It's the old elvin forms," she said, made suddenly shy by his praise. "I just wanted to see what I could do with them. . . ."

And no mention of the hours she'd spent reading the old romances, dreaming of life beyond the Border and the prince who would carry her off to it . . . until she realized one day that he just wasn't coming.

No elvin prince was on his way to 299 Middleton Street to carry Linnea Dark Garnett off to the moonlit country; and so she'd stood in front of the mirror one afternoon, hacking off the long, flowing hair that had always hidden her ears, revealing now her strong, boyish jawline, high forehead . . . she even gave herself sideburns.

And when she'd done, someone stared back from the mirror who could have been anyone, anything. Tall, raw-boned, with broad shoulders and heavy, capable hands . . . and on the face in the mirror now there was an amused, sardonic smile that had never been seen there before.

Linny pulled together a few things, and left her parents' house on her brother's motorcycle. . . .

"Well, you've done it!" Ash pulled her back to the

present. He sounded so positive. Must be nice to always be sure of yourself, no room for doubt.

Robbin was reading over Ash's shoulder now, his fine eyebrows raised. He nodded. "Impressive."

Bear seemed content to take their word for it.

"You know"—Ash tapped the leather notebook—"there are some very powerful images in here. I could do something with this . . . that one about the battle at the end of time, for instance." He went to the canvas he'd been working on. Druienna wrapped in a shawl that looked at once like a cocoon and a spider's web. Linny thought it was a nasty image: all you could see was the girl's head, her face half obscured by hair. The rest of her was just curves and bones jutting against the enveloping cloth.

Ash looked at the painting on the easel for a moment, and shrugged. He took out a jar of gesso and began painting over the canvas. Stroke by stroke, Drui and her shawl disappeared, until the artist had before him a plain field of snow; the white sheet of a bed that hadn't been slept in.

"Don't look over my shoulder now." He gestured fussily at Linny with his brush. "Wait until it's further along."

"Well," she said, standing there feeling helpless. They were all busy now: Ash painting, Robbin scraping at the pot he'd roasted the *peca* in, Bear cleaning his brushes; even Billy Buttons was investigating a broken window.

"You gotta go?" Ash asked her.

"Yeah, I guess."

"Where you staying?"

She risked it. "Nowhere particular."

"Oh." For much too long, Ash seemed to be thinking, the tip of his paintbrush between his teeth. "Hey, Bear!" Ash called across the studio. "You still got that old sleeping bag Charis left here?"

"Sure. Why?"

"Lin needs someplace to crash. That okay with you, Robbin?"

"I don't see why not."

Was it really that simple? Linny let out the breath she hadn't known she'd been holding. "I'll get the bag," she said casually; "just tell me where it is."

"Hey, hold on!" Ash said. Her breath stopped again. "What's your hurry to go to bed? We've got hours of work ahead of us!"

Relief made her strong. "What do you want me to do," she asked cockily, "pose for one of the warriors?"

"Aw, no. You just finish that poem about the bike rider. I have another great idea for that one."

"What's the rush?" she demanded, picking up her notebook anyway.

"New stuff for the Ferret show!" Ash said enigmatically. She waited for him to explain. Mistaking her silence for disinterest, he said nonchalantly, "It's nothing special, really. We thought it was time Mock Avenue Studio got a chance to show our work, so Rob talked Farrel Din into letting us hang some paintings in one of his side rooms. It'll be open to the public, so to speak, in the afternoons when the club isn't being used anyway."

"Hey!" Bear shouted from his side of the room. "What do you mean, it's nothing special? This is *it*, our first show as a group."

"Oh, yeah!" Ash scowled. "And who's going to come and see it? The cognoscenti of Soho: a bunch of derelicts and drugged-out kids, and maybe if we're lucky, a few of the Bloods: big art collectors."

"That"—Robbin drifted over with an air of infinite weariness—"is why we're holding it at the Ferret, Ash. Remember? I seem to recall someone who looked a lot like you saying that the Dancing Ferret already had a lot of credibility around the Tooth: it's the hot club for kids to dance in, even rich kids, and their parents know about it. You happened to be right. And what about all your emigré friends, the ones who weren't crazy enough to slum it in Soho? Some of them are doing all right in B-town. You said they'd come to the opening.''

"Sure." Ash looked more cheerful. "And Hale is doing us a great poster. Humans are good at design. That, at least, will be a collector's item.''

"Sounds great," Linny said. "When is it?"

"Couple of months," said Ash. "So get to work!"

She ensconced herself cross-legged on the table. All around her work was going on. Now she was working too. She felt like something inside her was breaking, and it made her want to cry. Except that what was breaking up was a great sheet of ice, an entire river that had been frozen all her life. She'd never believed there was such a thing as crying for joy. Now she found it was because tears were the quickest and easiest way her body had of releasing all the tension of sudden happiness.

But she wouldn't cry. She would write; and later she would go somewhere dark that had a loud band, and dance it all out.

She didn't know what time it was when a loud thump above their heads heralded a new arrival at the window entrance.

"Who's that?" Bear called up loudly. Linny realized with a chill that it could be anyone.

"Me. Hale."

Linny recognized the human boy from the afternoon, the one who'd hated the Dragon's Milk as much as she did, but not had the sense to hide it. He was carrying a pack. In the arbitrary light of the studio, he looked gawky and angular and drawn, as though he hadn't slept in a long time.

Ash rushed forward to see him. "Hale! It's not like you to honor us at this hour. Did you have a fight with your rich mistress, or did your drunken mother kick you out?"

Hale smiled faintly. "Women. They're nothing but trouble." Then his eye fell on Linny. Yeah, she thought, and up yours too, fella. "Who's this?" he asked bluntly, as though her being there at night made her a different person from the one he'd met that morning.

"This is Linny," Robbin said. "She's a poet, like Ash, only better. She's staying in the Studio for a while. Bear, where did you say that sleeping bag was?"

"Hale, are you sure you're okay?" Ash looked at the boy with concern. "You're not hurt or anything, are you? Hale, are you *stoned*?"

"Ash, are you an *asshole*?" Hale parodied. "Nah, I'm fine. It's just that . . . I thought maybe . . . I was wondering if it'd be okay if I moved in here."

"You mean for *good*?" Robbin demanded.

"No, I mean until my herpes clears up!" Hale snapped. He passed a grimy hand across his face. "No, I mean . . . look, if you guys think there's a problem . . ."

Bear said, "What kind of problem? There's plenty of room."

"Sure, no problem," Ash agreed. "Unless you're planning on bringing chicks in here at strange hours." Linny looked sharply at him, but Ash seemed oblivious to the implications of what he'd just said. "Or unless you snore."

"He can't snore louder than Bear," Robbin said. "It isn't physically possible."

"I keep telling you," Bear answered him, "it's the acoustics of this place. Picks up sound. If we just laid down some cheap carpeting—"

"Not on my gorgeous antique Christian tile floor!" Ash squawked.

Linny sat back and considered Hale. She remembered the tender way he'd laid Ash down on the mattress only that afternoon, like a kid with a pet, a girl with her favorite doll. Hale thought Ash was his personal property. She saw the way he was looking at the tall elf even now; as if he were a hungry dog, and Ash held all the biscuits. She looked away.

One by one the members of the Mock Avenue Studio settled down to work, to sleep, to play. Billy and Bear went out to check out some new music. Linny sat on the trestle table, a cigarette in one hand, a pen in the other, writing about the motorbike that ran faster than elvin steeds, that carried its rider through perils undreamt of on the other side of the Border. At last, the room was quiet. Linny could feel the presence of the others. It enfolded her like a warm, comfortable blanket, the kind of blanket you read under with a will-o'-wisp when your parents have put out the lamp.

When eventually she looked up, there was one other light left in the enormous room. His back to the wall across from her, Hale was sitting sketching her.

Hale never spoke to her if he could help it. As the days passed and it became clear that she wasn't going away, he kept on pretending that she didn't exist. If he wanted to know something, like whether it was her jacket on the chair, he'd ask someone else, even if she was in the room.

At first it made Linny mad. Then she decided there was no point in both of them being pissed off. So she started paying attention to Hale—a lot. She'd ask him what he thought of an article in *Nightlife*. She'd ask him where he got his canvas. It made him wildly uncomfortable. He'd answer as briefly as he could. She thought that was funny as hell.

None of the others in the Studio had any trouble dealing with her. But then, she thought if Ash brought home a three-fanged demon and said it tap-danced, they'd play soft-shoe for it. When they were all together, drinking or planning the show at the Ferret, she took a nasty pleasure in directing most of her remarks to Hale. Let him try to pretend she didn't exist!

She stood behind him one day, watching him paint a landscape. It was abstract, didn't look like anywhere she'd ever been or Hale'd ever seen. It was something Robbin did superlatively well; from Hale it was . . . unconvincing.

"Get out of my light," Hale said. "You're in my fucking light."

Linny swung herself up on the railing of the balcony next to him and lit a cigarette. "Hale," she said, "what do you do all those other sketches for, if you're not going to put them in the show?

He frowned at his palette. "What sketches?"

"You know what sketches. The ones you do in the clubs. The ones you do by the river. Of the kids, the artists, the punks." *Of me*.

"That's not art," he said with a fine scorn borrowed from Robbin. "That's craft work. It's picture-taking. It doesn't say anything."

"Oh, yeah? And what does *this* say?" She gestured at the blobs of blue and green.

He whirled around, and she saw how white his knuckles were on the palette. "I don't know, Linny," he said furiously. "You tell me. What does it say to you? Lay a few of those precious words on me."

For the first time, he was looking her straight in the eyes. His eyes were green, with bright gold flecks. Then she saw that they were bright with pain, not with anger at all. *Windows of the soul*. What had she been trying to do all this time—get him to notice her? By making him angry? Linny felt a gut-wrenching surge of self-disgust. She was no better than those girls at school, trailing after boys and giggling. . . . They wanted attention too. Wasn't it enough for her that she had the friendship of the others? Hale wasn't even elvin. Why waste her time?

"Hey," she said, "I'm sorry. It's a great painting, Hale, really."

But he threw down his brush, spattering the floor and his boots with misty green. "It's a shit painting! Give me a break, Linny, don't dish that crap out to me. This painting doesn't say anything to you except 'Poor bastard.' " He mixed a blob of paint into a tin cup of oily stuff and began painting with rough, angry strokes across the canvas. With amazement, she saw a face taking shape there. He added shadows, hollowing the cheeks, tracing the curve of bone with a tint of white . . . it was her own face, gazing out from a fantasy background of misty hills . . . but the face was transparent, as if the viewer were being allowed to look behind her eyes to see what she was imagining.

The frightening thing was that it was true. It was what she saw, when she was dreaming her dreams of Elfland.

Linny sat frozen, her cigarette burning down to ash. If she moved, she felt she would crack. He shouldn't know her that well. No one should. How had she given it away?

Hale didn't even notice her. All his attention was on his work; it was as though she didn't exist again. This time she was grateful. She stubbed out the cigarette, slipped off the railing and climbed out of the Studio. Her bike was nearly out of power, and she didn't have the money to recharge the spell box. She got on it anyway, and took it as far as it would go, out along the river, past the trailer parks and into the dangerous Borderland.

She had to walk it home in the dark from the Troll Bridge.

It was barely a month until the show. There were enough paintings and drawings lying in the corners of the chapel, stacked in careless piles in the unused portion of the balcony, to fill the walls of the Dancing Ferret three times over, but this, Robbin explained disdainfully, was old work—at least several months old, not good enough now. So in the weeks before the opening, the show was created from scratch, brand-new works that would contain the soul of Bordertown within the magic-tinged, ever-shifting colorfield paintings that were the tradition of the Elflands: Ash's canvases dripping with romance, hinting at the contours of the little Elftown girls who had posed for them; Robbin's landscape-inspired abstracts of the open Borderlands; Bear's huge paintings that suggested no imagery at all, just bursts of color with a driving energy like rock'n'roll. Even Hale painted several new canvases in traditional High-Elvin style—or tried to. Hard as he worked, his paintings simply didn't resonate as the others' did. Perhaps it just wasn't in his blood. His landscape portrait of Linny had disappeared; painted over, she hoped.

Billy Buttons did not paint. He flattered and criticized, posed and pouted, scavenged props, found mysterious tubes of free paint, cheese sandwiches, glass for the frames, always hustling, always on the move, always in the way. He did not live at the studio as the others did, but had a squat of his own somewhere in the west end, with a girl no one was ever allowed to meet.

They lived catch-as-catch-can. They took items scavenged from garbage cans on the Tooth to trade in José's store for old canvases to scrape the paint off and paint over. Hale made a little money designing posters for the clubs; got them free passes, free beers—there were days when dinner was the popcorn at Danceland. Bear pulled down a gig every so often—once known from Ho Street to Hell as the hottest bass player to hit the clubs, he'd given up that little bit of fame to concentrate on a more lasting art. When money came in, they'd blow it on extravagant meals, expensive coffee and cheap champagne; the next day they'd be back to day-old pastries from the back door of the bakery on Water Street, rationing tea like it was holy water, inventing outrageous recipes for Ginger Cat Soup.

"I'm hungry," Ash said suddenly one afternoon, tossing his brush up in the air and catching it with a flourish. "I wish we had more of that *peca*. That was good shit."

"Ha," said Hale. "All you did was try to sing and fall asleep."

"You think," Ash retorted. "You wouldn't believe what I saw on that stuff. If BB hadn't snapped me out of it—I had a whole poem perfectly formed, meter and verse—"

"Try catnip," Hale snapped.

Linny, sitting silent on her table, raised her eyebrows. It wasn't like Hale to lash out at Ash that way.

"Here." Robbin tossed a bundle of newsprint to Ash. "Eat this."

Ash stared at the paper. "It'll give me the shits."

Billy Buttons came over to look. "Fuckin' *Nightlife*. Turner's thirtieth annual review of the bright young artists . . ."

". . . who are the same bright young artists he was raving about thirty years ago," Robbin finished. "Lord. I used to read this when I was a kid. Same names then as now. I always thought I'd be in there someday."

"No way," said Hale. "Not while you paint and show in Soho."

"Well how the hell are we supposed to get our paintings into the Promenade galleries when we can't even get reviewed in fucking *Nightlife*?" Ash demanded.

"That's not the point," Linny said. She too had grown up on *Nightlife*, and remembered when it represented all that was avant-garde, daring, and artistic, all that she now knew to be old and tired. "Everything that's happening in art these days is happening in Soho, not uptown, right? It's not just us, it's music and theater and comics and dance . . . And nobody knows about it. There's kids out there—"

Hale suddenly looked as if he'd been struck. "Yeah," he said. "Kids. Not the slummers; kids whose parents keep them at home, nice kids with nice parents who don't know—"

"—who don't know anything about what's going on," Robbin continued. Finishing each other's sentences was something the Studio did when it was really clicking.

Ash stood there looking like he'd just received a divine revelation. Before he even said anything, Linny knew what it would be: "Let's found our own paper!"

"No," Linny said. "Same problem: who'd read it? Just more Soho people."

"So what?" Ash turned on her. "At least it's a start! And who's to say that in a few years—"

"No," Linny repeated. "That's not the point." Something about the way she said it alerted Billy Buttons, who was looking at her with a fixed, vulpine intensity. "Go on, Linnet," he said.

"We infiltrate," she announced.

She came forward and took Ash's copy of the paper. "Look." She rattled the pages. "Type. Drawings. Cheap paper. They can do it. We can do it. And who's to know the difference—until they read the reviews of Squatter's Theater, of *Stick Wizard* comics . . . and Alf Turner's rave preview of the Mock Avenue Studio show at the Dancing Ferret?"

"You . . . fiend!" Ash's fair faced glowed with delight.

"Let me get this straight," said Robbin, fiddling with his silver hairclasp. "We do an exact copy of *Nightlife* but with Soho arts reviews—including a big plug for our show—and somehow we manage to substitute our paper for the real thing all over the city?"

"Oh, yes." Billy Buttons chuckled richly. "Oh yes we do. Who do you think distributes *Nightlife*?"

They thought about it. Ragamuffins did: the alley kids of Soho, those fierce little children with their war paint and spiky hair.

"The Bloods have an 'arrangement' with those kids," Buttons said, smiling evilly. "I think we can work something out there . . . I definitely think so."

"There's one thing no one's bothered to consider," Hale said pugnaciously, "and that's the small matter of how you're going to get this thing actually printed. Or do the Bloods have an 'arrangement' with the Third Street Printers' Guild too?"

Ash laid one finger along the side of his nose. "Now, now; you just let your own Nuncle Ash take care of that. I happen to know where there's a printing press lying unused not one hundred yards away from where we sit!"

It caused the sensation Ash intended.

"Yeah," Hale said sourly; "but does it work?"

Ash brushed his objections away with butterfly hands in the air. "Don't be a doubter, Hale! It'll work by the time we need it to."

"Then we can do it," Linny said blissfully. "We can really do it."

"Sure," said Ash with finality. "Linny, you and I will write the articles—and anyone else who wants to, of course. Bear can copy the picture style—he's good at doing that realistic crap when he has to—and you too, Hale, of course: you're great at that, you can copy all the ads."

Linny watched Hale stiffen. Ash could be so dumb, sometimes. "And what," the human boy asked carefully, "makes you think I want to waste my time on a dip-shit project like this?"

"Are you kidding?!" Ash demanded. "This is going to make our fortune! It's the one thing I can think of that'll get our show publicity all over B-town! By the time people realize it's a hoax, *Mock Avenue Studio* will be burned in their brains. They won't be able to go on ignoring us after this. Linny's a genius." Hale shrugged. Ash came up to him, put a slender hand on his muscular shoulder. "Anyhow, it's going to be fun. Those ads don't have to be *exact* copies. Don't you want to draw the Fairfield Soap Girl in a garter belt and push-up bra?" Hale tried and failed to repress a smirk.

And somehow large sheets of paper appeared, and all over the floor people were spreading them out and sketching mock-*Nightlife* layouts, page by page; and Linny was compiling the list of articles in her notebook, and she and Bear were arguing about whether the Ferret or Danceland ought to have been voted best dance club in the Annual Poll. . . .

And in the years after, when she had gotten all the fame that Ash ever wanted, all the worship Robbin craved and the recognition that Bear never had, Linnea Dark Garnett was to remember that as the best afternoon of her life.

Hale smelled the armpit of his favorite shirt with the mutating fish on it. No way. But his t-shirts were almost as bad. What did people do when they didn't have a mom to make the dirty clothes magically disappear? He put on the least offensive shirt and tried not to inhale. Maybe he could find something new at José's.

He stumbled down from the balcony, barking his shin on the ladder again. The room was cold and drafty, the tiles chilly beneath the boy's bare feet. There was a thin, rusty trickle of water from the tap of what used to be the Ladies' Room beneath the chapel; Hale splashed water on his face and over his head, slicked back his hair. He dried himself on the single grimy towel, and scowled at himself in the mirror above the sink, startled by how much the expression resembled Sissy's. He'd gotten thinner, developing shadows beneath his cheekbones and under the scar from the fight at his last private school. He fingered his beardless chin and sighed. When the hell was he going to stop looking like a kid?

Hale brushed his teeth with his finger, sourly remembering all the things he hadn't thought to bring with him from home. Sissy was right; he couldn't do anything without screwing it up. But he couldn't go back there; not now, perhaps not ever. His dad was a copper—if he'd wanted Hale to come home, he would have tracked him down before now.

Upstairs in the chapel, pale morning light set the stained-glass windows glowing, casting rainbow colors on age-stained white walls, falling on the dust and soot thick on the windowsills. Top Cat, the scrawny tom with the seven-fingered left paw, sat in a sunny patch cleaning plaster dust from his black fur while above him a benevolent angel smiled placidly. Robbin sat before his easel, pulled close to the heat of the Magic Fire, mixing turpentine into a tub of green-gray paint. Whether he'd gotten up early or been up since the night before was impossible to tell; he was immaculately dressed, as always, as though for afternoon tea on Dragon's Tooth Hill. He glanced up at Hale with disinterest, and then away again. Hale had seen him look at girls that way, dismissing them. Unimportant.

The jars of coffee and black tea were empty. The pot on the Magic Fire contained one of those elvin herbal brews that Hale had never grown used to. He poured some into a paint-spattered mug anyway, letting the warmth of the pottery thaw his frozen fingers. They had only been squatting in the church since spring; what were they going to do when winter came?

Yet he'd rather wake up cold and hungry here than to the breakfast table at home—his father angry, Sissy trying to disappear into her chair, his mother somewhere far off in the ozone. In the 'burbs the commuters would be hustling now and the traffic would be loud on the Riverside Bridge. In Soho the days started quietly, revving up slowly for the nights to come.

Hale gazed around the vast, empty room. Ash's mattress was piled with clothing and blankets; the bogus newspaper was all laid out on the floor. At the far end of the chapel wet clothes were hanging over a rafter beam. He could hear the water dripping onto the tiles below. The corner Linny had claimed was the only part of the studio besides Robbin's that was tidy. She kept her books in a little pile, her meager wardrobe in a little pile—if she'd owned anything else, she'd probably keep that in a goddamn little pile too.

"Where is everybody?" Hale asked Robbin, though what he really meant was: where is Ash?

"Upstairs. In the tower," the other boy answered without looking up. Beneath his paintbrush, shifting colors echoed the shimmer of the Elfland Border. A blotch of color indicated the city, nestled beside it in the Hills. Hale looked over his shoulder and suppressed a sigh, envying

Robbin his smooth technique. The trick to elvin art was for the painter to put his own perceptions into the shifting imagery, and this was Robbin all over: beautiful, precise, and a little cold.

Hale borrowed a pair of socks left draped over a pile of books, laced up his jackboots, stole Ash's overcoat from the hook on the balcony post. As he climbed the treacherous, circular stairs up the Bell Tower he was careful to avoid the missing steps and the places where the treads were in danger of giving in. The walls of the stairwell were covered with Ash's poetry, Billy's cartoons, and old graffiti. THE BELL TOWER GHOST WAS HERE. DANTE LOVES BEATRICE. BEWARE THE BLOODS—crossed out and emended to BEWARE THE JABBERWOCK, MY SON. Hale was breathing hard and had a kink behind his bad knee by the time he reached the top.

At the head of the stairs was a circular room, with ropes in the center leading to the bells above. Open windows were cut into the stone on three sides; on the fourth side, looking north to Elfland, they'd been bricked up, protecting good churchgoers from the unholy view. Ash sat on an eastern window ledge facing the rising sun and the Mad River valley. Bear leaned against the other side of the windowsill, a mug of the herbal concoction cradled in his broad hands. Between them was the elvin girl. Hale froze halfway through the door. Then, before they noticed him, he turned and went back down the stairs.

Dammit, the girl was always there. At night, when he went to his bed on the balcony, laughing with Ash and Robbin below. In the morning when he awoke, when a guy needed a quiet moment alone with his friends. She was always there, with that exasperating smile, with the cornflower-blue eyes that caught his own and challenged them every time.

Frodo accosted him coming back down the stairs, appearing through the gap of a missing tread to dance at his feet and demand breakfast. Hale draped the cat over his shoulder, wincing as the claws dug through the wool into his flesh. As they reached the third-story window, he saw a grinning face peering through the glass.

"Hale, my man!" Billy Buttons said, squatting on the parsonage roof outside. "Just the person I was looking for! Come with me and I'll buy you a cup of tea—hell, a cup of coffee! Got some business to attend to down at the Hard Luck Cafe."

Normally Hale would be suspicious of Billy's generosity, but right now all he wanted to do was to get out of Mock Avenue. "Yeah, sure," he said, climbing onto the roof, bringing Frodo with him attached to his coat like a fur collar. He'd go anywhere this hour of the morning on the promise of a cup of good human coffee.

Buttons was looking even seedier than usual. His raincoat was too large for him, rolled up at the sleeves and hanging below his knees, wrinkled as though he'd just pulled it from some laundry bin. His eyes were rimmed with red, his hair hung in yellow tangles beneath an old broad-brimmed hat, and he held a toothpick between his clenched teeth. He extended a hand in a peeling red leather glove, helping Hale make the jump between the fire escape and the sidewalk. Frodo scrambled down the back of Hale's coat, disappeared through a busted window leading into José's store.

Mock Avenue, like the rest of Soho, was quiet at this time of day. José's place was chained and spell-locked up while he slept off the effects of yesterday's profits. Madame Sydni, the card reader, sat in her parlor window, smiling at the boys as they passed by. A bum lay on the porch of a gutted townhouse—elvin or human, it was impossible to tell through the mass of gray-white hair. Elvin, probably, for this was Blood territory—the east end of Soho, over to the river wall.

Mock Avenue followed a winding course that cut across the streets of Soho, past Carnival south of the Dancing Ferret; past Gateway, the drag-racing strip; north and west until it ran into Ho. On the corner of Ho was the Oberon Building, an immense structure, boarded up, that took up an entire city block. Once it was a ballroom or some such thing; now it was runaway central, the place they all ended up, sooner or later.

On Ho Street there was a little more early-morning action: a couple of kids trying to bum some change, some Packers cruising on low-slung bikes, eyeing the two of them suspiciously. Hale was clearly human, his brown hair slicked back behind round ears; but with his yellow hair, his hat slouched low, there was no telling what Billy Buttons might be.

The Hard Luck Café was clear on the other end of Ho, across the street from Danceland near the turf ruled by the human Pack. Ho Street was neutral territory, where the gangs held to a truce. But Hale wouldn't care to be caught south of it this far down if he was wearing red leather or had silver in his hair.

The building had once been a bank, its history evident in the stamped tin ceiling and the marble of its walls and floor. Someone had taken it over before vandals could strip and ruin it; the café had been operating out of the ground floor for as long as anyone could remember. It was a place you could come on a cold winter's night, nursing a penny's worth of tea from dusk until dawn. Danceland, across the street, had been around almost as long.

Buttons chose a table in a back corner, positioning himself so that he could keep an eye on the door. He ordered coffee for them both from a little human girl, her fuchsia-colored ponytail bobbing above her shoulders. She chewed her gum with her mouth wide open, popping it loudly as she turned back to the bar. The smell reminded Hale painfully of Sissy. He scowled at the girl as she put his coffee down in front of him.

"So what's going on?" he asked Billy Buttons, but all Billy would say was, "Wait and see." Hale pulled out his ubiquitous sketchbook to pass the time. They didn't have to wait for long.

A tall, ugly Blood came in through the double doors, drawing attention with his height and the conspicuous red leather he wore from head to toe. He sauntered back to their corner, shook a cigarette out of a crumpled pack, and lit it, staring down at Billy, without sparing even a glance for Hale. He had a scar like lightning across his forearm and wore three ruby studs on the lobe of a pointed ear.

"Nice you could come," said Billy with a crooked smile. "Coffee? Tea? A draft of bitter ale?"

The elf waved away the offer, dragged another chair over, scraping it across the marble floor. "Let's get down to business, Buttons. You have something we want. I want to know what *you* want."

"Well now, it's simple, really—"

"Money? Drugs? Chocolate? Protection?"

"Cooperation. What we're proposing is a little joint venture, between the lads I represent"—he nodded toward Hale—"and the Bloods."

The elf looked at Hale finally, and down at the sketch he'd made on his white pad. "Humans?" he said, as if the word was sour.

Billy leaned back in his chair, playing with his toothpick, enjoying himself. "Don't be too quick to throw around insults, my fine buck. Some of my best friends are human. Including my mother."

The Blood's pale eyes narrowed. He scratched his shaved silver skull. "Buttons, we got no feud with you. Just tell us what you want. Give me a straight answer for once in your goddamn life."

Billy outlined his plan, explaining the bogus edition of *Nightlife* to a thug who had never read an arts review in his life. "Distribution, that's where you come in. You get the papers to the alley brats, and they'll hawk it all over the city. They'll never know it's not the real one; never met an alley kid yet who could read."

The elf looked skeptical. He tapped his ashes onto the floor. "Why us? Why not do this yourselves?" He looked back and forth between Buttons and Hale. Hale continued sketching and tried to look cool, as though it was every day he sat making deals with gang leaders in Ho Street cafes. Lordy lord, what would his father think? Hale pushed the thought away.

"You've got the manpower," Billy explained. "And the alley brats come from your turf. Besides, I thought the Bloods would want to have a piece of this—tweak the noses of all them rich True Bloods looking down at us from the Hill. . . ."

A slow smile spread across the big Blood's face. He was not a smart man, Hale realized with surprise. Little Sissy could run circles around this guy.

"All right," the fellow said. "Now I know what you want. When do we get what we want?"

"When the job is done. Blood's Oath."

"Blood's Oath," the other repeated. "Buttons, you have a deal." The big elf rose, drew lazily on his cigarette. "I don't know what an elvin oath is worth to a halfie. But if you fuck with us, remember: you're dead meat in Bordertown."

All of the humor left Billy's face then. "I ran with the Bloods once," he said softly, and the way he said it made the coffee in Hale's stomach roll. "My dear young man, don't question my honor again."

The Blood stared at him for a moment, then inclined his head—a rare gesture of respect from full blood to halfie. The color returned slowly to Billy Buttons' cheeks as the ugly elf turned and walked out the door.

"Well, well, me deario, wasn't that entertaining? Drink up now, Hale, mustn't let good coffee get cold."

Hale had a thousand questions, but as he put his pad away he only asked one.

"What is it the Bloods want, anyway?"

Buttons paused. "Something that I haven't got," he said.

José's store had once been a pharmacy. Some of the fixtures were still there: the Formica-topped counter, yellowed with age, tall cabinets from which the glass had been scavanged long ago, empty display cases for toothpaste, condoms, deodorant soaps. The sign outside still said REXALL DRUGS, and every once in a while some semiconscious kid would wander in looking for fairy-dust.

The shelves lining the walls of the front room were crammed with odds and ends of junk both elvin and human: dishes, books, broken appliances, mismatched shoes, odd bits of carving from over the Border, strange elvin gadgets whose uses were near impossible to determine. The second room was filled with old clothes and draperies—the velvets, the sequins, the lace and vintage spandex that were all the rage for nights out on the town. Kids came to find fashions from times past to wear into the clubs, and to trade goods they'd found in trash bins or stolen from the fancy houses on the Hill. José had started the store when he and his old lady first came to Bordertown, cutting a deal with the Bloods for this tiny piece of their turf. Then his old lady ran off with a True Blood, and now José ruled over his kingdom of junk alone.

José was a small man, even for a human, and compact, the muscles of his arms covered from shoulder to wrist with intricate tattoos. For each one he had a different story about life beyond the Borderlands, in cities that sounded imaginary, far away in the human World.

The store was open when Hale and Billy turned back down Mock Avenue. José was reading the latest issue of *Stick Wizard*; Frodo and T.C. were sleeping off breakfast, having made a nest in a pile of Elfland brocades. There was a nine-pack of bitter ale on the counter beside them— José's hangover recipe.

"Mr. Gutierrez, how are you this fine autumn morning?" Billy began.

"Get out, get out," José interrupted him, bristling. "I know that tone of voice—it always means trouble. Hale, do me a favor, will you, and remove this personage from my store?"

"Now José, don't be too hasty," Billy protested. "I have a perfectly legitimate business proposition here."

"Legitimate, my ass. I might as well make a deal with Frodo the cat as deal with you; he'll pay me just as fast. Get out of here, Buttons, before I forget I'm a man with high blood pressure and throw you out myself!"

"Hey, okay, my man. If that's the way you want it. But I came here to do *you* a favor. If you don't want it, hey, no skin off my—"

"What favor?" José asked suspiciously.

Billy pulled out a silver knife and began to clean his fingernails. "Oh, concerning a little hot item you just might want to get rid of. A red-hot item; 'explosive' you could even say."

José crossed his arms over his chest, chewing on the ends of his black mustache. "What exactly do you know about this, kid?" he asked.

Buttons smiled, crooked teeth showing. "That you've got it. That the Bloods want it. And that the Pack wants it back."

"Dammit, Buttons," Gutierrez exploded. "Where do you get your information? How do you always know exactly what's going on?" He sighed. "Sometimes," he said, "I think you know what I had for breakfast two hours before I wake up and decide." Gutierrez pulled a quilted bundle from under his Formica counter. Beneath the wrappings lay a sawed-off shotgun—deadly, too unpredictable to be truly useful in a place like Bordertown. The last time the Bloods had gotten hold of a gun it had worked, surprisingly, just fine—worked so well it killed one of their own.

"A woman running with the Pack brought it over to me. She was desperate for bucks, wanted to go back home to the World. Stole it right from under Sammy Tucker's nose—and like a prize ass I bought it, just to get it off her hands. What am I going to do with it? The Pack and the Bloods are gonna know I got it. No matter who I trade it to, somebody's gonna be sorely pissed at old José."

"You could give it to the coppers," Hale suggested. He didn't much care for the thought of some thug like the one from this morning being out on the streets with a gun.

"And have them on my tail? They've got ways of tracing things that makes my head spin. . . ."

"You could give it to me," Buttons said, staring at his nails. "Give it to me, your problem is solved, simple as that. One, two, three."

José snorted. "Buttons, I trust you even less than I trust the gangs. Why the hell should I turn this over to you? What do you want it for, that's what I want to know."

"I want to give it to the Bloods. I promised them they could have it."

"*You* promised," José sputtered.

"Perhaps I was just a little hasty," Billy admitted. With a movement quick as lightning, he plucked the shotgun from the counter. "But I *did* give my word. So I think you really ought to reconsider, my deario. I'll give you fair trade for it. I suggest you name your price." He lowered the gun until it was aimed at José's stomach. He smiled cheerfully at the smaller man.

"Buttons . . ." Jose said warningly.

"You won't sell?" Billy said. "Then I'll lose my honor in front of all the Bloods. Guess there's only one thing left to do."

Billy reversed the gun's aim so that it pointed at himself. "Billy!" Hale shouted as he squeezed the trigger.

"It's not loaded, you asshole; calm down," José said, grabbing the gun back from the halfie boy. "But you couldn't have known that for sure, you young fool."

"No," said Billy, "but I did know that the firing pin is soldered shut. Yes, my dear; the Pack's famous gun is completely, utterly useless. They just want it back before the Bloods find out."

"It is?" José picked up the gun warily and examined it more closely. "I'll be goddamned. I'd barely touched the thing—these little mamas are a risky business so close to the Border. Only bought it off the girl so it wouldn't fall into worse hands . . ."

"So what do you say, *mi amigo* José, that we give this piece to the local Bloods and let Sammy Tucker know that his little gig is up?"

"Sure, sure. Take it, Buttons. I don't give a shit. This thing is goddamn useless—and I can't tell you how many nights I've lost sleep over it. Take it, with my blessings. Only remember . . . you just promised fair trade."

"And *you* just said it was useless, my man!"

"Useless is not the same as worthless, as you well know."

"Look, I just spent my last pennies buying Hale here a cup of coffee and—"

"Take this," Hale said, taking off Ash's overcoat. "It's warm; it's wool or something. Ash'll never miss it. And if he does, well, hey, no harm done."

"You're an evil man, Hale," Buttons said approvingly.

José took hold of the coat, inspected it with a critical eye. "It will do," he said finally, and hung it up in the second room. "Ash is down in the basement, by the way. He's looking over that old printing press of mine, the one I traded the car seats for."

Buttons led Hale through the store to the basement stairs, the shotgun riding across his slim shoulders. Below they found Ash and the elvin girl on their hands and knees on the concrete floor.

"Is this a new party game?" Buttons asked the two of them.

Ash sat back on his heels and pushed silver hair out of

his eyes. His white cheeks and the knees of his black jeans were covered with dust. He clutched something like the pieces of a puzzle in the palm of his gloved hand.

"We're skunked, man," Ash said with a dejected sigh. "*Nightlife* is off. After all that work."

"What the hell do you mean it's off?" Billy Buttons asked irritably. After a morning of successful wheeling and dealing, he clearly felt he deserved more than this.

Ash rapped his knuckles against a decrepit piece of sagging machinery. "This is the letter press," he explained. "And this is the type, all over the floor. So far as we can tell, a good third of it is missing—carried off by literate mice, I guess. Or else it was never here to begin with. How the fuck can we print the thing up if we can't even find all the vowels?"

Linny was searching the corners of the room by the dull light of a will-o'-wisp hovering above her palm. She was wearing an old elvin velvet dress over her leather boots; probably something she'd found upstairs in the store. Hale had never seen her dressed halfway like a girl before; neither had Billy Buttons, from the way he was staring. The plain dark green set off the paleness of her skin, brought out the lights in her red hair. The skirt of the dress was getting covered with soot as she crawled across the floor collecting tiny metallic letters.

"This is it, Ash," she said. She looked over at their little pile. "We'll have to rewrite all the reviews so that they only use the letters T and S and R. We've got lots of R's—at least four or five. What do you think of the Rock Avenue Studio?"

She was trying to jolly Ash out of his sudden depression, but Hale could have told her it wasn't going to work. Ash's downs were as extravagant as his highs. The elvin boy drooped on the cold concrete floor, as though he had just lost all will to live.

Linny came over to him, put a hand on his shoulder. "Listen, Ash," she said, her voice low and husky, "we'll figure something else out. Don't give up yet." But even she looked doubtful, with shadows of disappointment beneath her blue eyes. Ash smiled up at her, and Hale felt his stomach tighten.

"Look, Ash," Hale said suddenly. "I can get it printed up. I know a press . . . Only thing is, it's not in Soho."

"Where is it then?" Billy Buttons wanted to know,

"It's, umm, across the river."

Ash brightened at this new plan, but Billy was regarding Hale curiously.

"Your mysterious past reveals itself at last, eh Hale?"

"This has nothing to do with my past," Hale answered quickly. "You're not the only one with connections in this town."

"Connections . . ." Linny interrupted, looked comically from one boy to the other. "Who cares, as long as it works! He's got connections, and we've got a press! Come on, guys, let's get back to work! We've got a paper to put out: deadlines to meet, shows to review . . ."

Her arm was around Ash's shoulder. Hale caught himself staring at it, at them. He looked quickly away. But he could not block out the sound of Linny's laughter as she and Ash climbed the stairs. He never wanted to do her goddamn paper anyway. So why was he suddenly volunteering to do it now?

At the top of the stairs Linny stripped off the elvin dress; underneath it were her usual baggy trousers and a man's undershirt bleached as white as her skin. She handed the velvet dress to Gutierrez. "No thanks. I guess it's just not me after all." He gave Linny her leather jacket and she shrugged back into it with familiar ease. The jacket transformed her into a young boy again. She pulled her leather gloves from the pockets, and a pack of cigarettes.

Outside the day was cold and bright. Hale shivered in his thin fish shirt and quickly climbed the fire escape to the roof. In the chapel Bear was running paint through a spray gun onto a piece of masonite. When he saw them, he mumbled the spell to shut off the air pump and nodded toward the other end of the room. Drui was there, curled up on Ash's bed, reading the half-penny Scandal Sheet they sold on he streets in Elftown.

She wore nothing beneath Ash's brocade robe, waiting to pose. She jumped up and ran to the elvin boy as he came in the door behind Hale. "Ash!" Her eyes clouded as she spotted Linny behind him. "Ash?" she asked uncertainly. "Did you forget you told me to come back soon as I could? My mother found out, see . . . I'm sorry it's been so long."

"Oh, look kid," Ash said with no embarrassment. "I meant to send a message up to Traders' Heaven. I'm finished with that painting. You don't have to come down to sit for me anymore."

"Oh." Her mouth drooped just a little. "Well, can I see it, Ash—now that it's finished? Will it be in the show at the Ferret?"

"No. It didn't exactly turn out. So I painted over the canvas. It just wasn't what I wanted. Some paintings are like that—you try and try, but you just never get anything worth keeping."

"It looked pretty good to me," Druienna said quietly. "But hey, what would I know? I'm not an artist, am I?" She tossed back her silver curls, tried not to look hurt, almost succeeding.

Ash steered Linny over to the warmth of the Magic Fire, poured her a cup of the overbrewed herbal potion. She looked uncomfortable as he fussed over her, effectively dismissing little Druienna, suddenly turning Linny into his girl. For once, Linny seemed as if she didn't quite know what to say.

Drui stood with Ash's robe clutched tightly around her. Then she began to gather her clothes, the frilly shirt, the spangled trousers, the high-heeled shoes that Hale could not imagine how she walked in. She'd come all the way down from Elftown for Ash in those goddamn stupid shoes.

"Wait, Drui," Hale said to her suddenly. "Don't go yet. Do you want to come up to the balcony and sit awhile for me? I'd like to do some sketches, maybe even try a painting . . . if you've the time, that is," he added, smiling encouragingly. Druienna lifted her head and looked at Hale with the puppy-dog gaze she had previously reserved for Ash.

"Sure, I've got loads of time," she said to Hale, her gaze flickering across the room to Ash and Linny. She tossed back her curls and smiled brightly at the boy, his interest animating her, making her pretty once again.

"That's swell, Drui. Terrific," he found himself babbling, all too aware of blue eyes following him as he crossed the chapel and up the balcony ladder behind the tiny elvin girl. He glanced down once, and Linny was indeed looking up at him. But this time, when he caught her eye, she smiled.

Bear was an expert lock-picker. No one cared to ask the burly, quiet elf how he had come by such a disreputable talent, but Hale was grateful for it now as they clustered shivering around the backdoor of the Church of Saintliness on Middletown Road, across the corner from his parents' house in the suburb of Pleasant Gardens. The night was cold, the air clear; overhead the stars of Elfland wheeled in patterns that would have mystified the astronomers of the World. From the open Borderlands beyond the housing tracts came the occasional howling of creatures with no names.

Billy Buttons had set the entire plan into motion; between Ash's enthusiasm and Billy's plots and deals the whole mad scheme had turned into reality. Somehow, from the seed of Linny's whimsy had grown this moment: fingers frozen into shards of ice, breaths held against the fear of sudden voices in the dark: *Hey you kids—what are you doing there?*

Around the bend, two blocks away, his parents lay sleeping, encased in pink stucco. He'd passed the house riding on the back of Bear's Harley and seen the light on in Sissy's room. It had given him a queasy feeling to have his two worlds collide—as though Sissy and Dad and Linny and Ash and Bear could not exist in the same world, side by side.

With a grunt, Bear jimmied the lock into opening, and the double doors swung into the dark of the church's back hall. Inside, there were no windows to let in starlight or moon. Hale prayed he'd remember the way to the press; he prayed at this hour there would be no one there. He wondered if the patron saint of the church still had any interest in listening to his prayers.

They left Ash guarding the door—watching for Bloods, coppers, watching over Bear and Linny's bikes parked behind the trash bins. Robbin and Billy were back in the city, making sure the real edition of *Nightlife* never reached its destination. Linny—the only one of the lot of them who could spell—would oversee the setting of type. Hale would run the press. Bear would break through any door that stood in their way.

Dressed in black, creeping down the darkened hallway, Hale felt like a terrorist on assignment, with copperplates in the pack on his back instead of international secrets or high-tech explosives. If it weren't for the tension eating at the pit of his stomach he might almost find this fun, like the spy games he used to play with the neighborhood kids when he was young. Bear worked on the lock of the inner office door; Hale found himself holding his breath, listening for footsteps in the dark, and then the door clicked open and they passed through into the back rooms of the *Church Times*. All they needed now was to find the basement room that housed the *Times'* own press.

Hale had been in these back rooms more times than he

cared to remember, running off his mother's popular cookbooks filled with bible quotes and bad recipes masked with aggressively perky names: "Turkey Delight," "Rumless Rumcake," "Dragon's Tooth Filling" . . . for god's sake. Empty, the dark, ugly warren of modern rooms—so different from the old church on Mock Avenue—was unfamiliar and disorienting. Hale had the sudden sick feeling he had never been here before. That it was someone else's life.

"This way," Linny said, tugging at his arm. "I've got a hunch. Let's try these doors."

Elvin hunches must be magic, for the doors she chose led to the room with the press—a huge, gleaming monster machine that Hale had come to love. Nothing like the pathetic letterpress Ash had thought they could run a whole paper on. Like so much in Bordertown, the press was a haphazard mishmash of elvin spells and human technology, designed to override the problem that the principles of photography worked no better in Bordertown than the principles of firearms.

Hale flicked on the spell-lights, his nervousness forgotten. As he started up the machinery he felt happiness run jolting through his veins, like when a painting began to take shape under his brush—a better high than any fucking elf drug. He patted the machine's plate cylinder like he was greeting a friendly dog, put down his heavy pack, and turned to the others to explain what they were about to do. *Nightlife*, still affecting to be an "underground" paper after all these years, was produced on a press little better than this. Their edition would be crude, but not instantly recognizable as a counterfeit. Bear's eyes began to glaze over in the way typical to elves trying to cope with alien technology—but the elvin girl caught on surprisingly quickly, Hale's enthusiasm the spark that set fire to her own.

The clock was ticking off the hours until the time set for their rendezvous with the Bloods in the hour before dawn.

Hale and Linny set quickly to work. Bear—mystified by, and perhaps even a little frightened of, the loud machinery—retreated to scouting the hallways and watching the street for signs of coppers. By the time Hale realized he'd been left alone with Linny, he was too caught up in the rhythm of their work to care. It was as if the girl could read his mind; like Sissy, she was always a half-step ahead of him, always knew what he was going to need next—not only anticipated him, but offered up suggestions of her own. This was the way work should always be, a syncopated dance—not a fight and a struggle. Step by step the paper came together. They stood silent, tensed, as the machine fed newsprint between the cylinders, gobbling up the *Church Times'* supply of paper like some big hungry beast. Then the first pages rolled wet and gorgeous from the press.

Linny let out a whoop she couldn't contain. Hale grinned from ear to ear, hugging himself as though to hold in the overflow of delight. They leaned over the sheet together, reading the headline that jumped from the page:

SOHO: WHERE ART MEETS LIFE

"Saturday nights are a carnival all over Bordertown," Linny read aloud, *"but especially in Soho. The streets boil with kids looking their best and wildest. The gangs live for this, and Soho owes a lot of its dazzle to their weapons of war: clothes, hair, bands, bikes. Each gang wants to sport the best, the hottest, the newest of all of these, and that arms race makes the Soho streets blaze with eye candy.*

"Not, of course, that a few kids don't get stupid on occasion, tune each other up, and break some heads. When you find that some tall elvin Blood looks better in one of the new ribbon coats than you do—well, the temptation to take it out on his aristocratic nose can be tough to resist. . . . Ha! I think Ash is right—we can't pretend the

gangs don't exist or aren't a nuisance, but we can make them fashionable as hell!''

Above the article was one of Hale's engravings, the street scene on Ho at night, only a bit romanticized. The Page One Table of Contents listed a complete Soho tour guide: An overview of Squatters' Theater, staged at unpredictable intervals in the gutted ruins of Carnival Street. A rundown of the bars and cafes tucked in hidden corners of the Old City. A lesson in Soho fashion—how to avoid looking like you've just come down from the Hill. A guide to Soho nightlife, rating the dance clubs, the bands, even the gangs according to the spectacle they put on as they cruised Ho Street on a Saturday night. And, of course, a preview of the Mock Avenue Studio show, opening this week at the Dancing Ferret, touted with Ash's distinctive hyperbole as only the most brilliant grouping this side of the Border.

"What's this?" Linny asked, pointing to a line of type at the bottom of the page. It read: *Squirt, Life gets better when you get older, I promise. Love, Asshole.* "I thought we put the personals on page three. Is this some kind of a joke?"

"Yeah," Hale said, "just some kind of a joke." He hoped the kid would see it. But what were the chances of *Nightlife*—even this edition—getting into Sissy's hands?

Her head bent close to his, Linny looked at him sideways out of those extraordinary eyes, catching him with his mask of indifference down. "You're nicer when you're doing something you care about Hale." She was probably comparing this to his black moods when he painted, wrestling with those elvin abstracts that never did come out quite right. He scowled.

"And you're nicer when you're not sucking up to Ash," he retorted. The smile left her face. Instantly he regretted it. Words, they were her weapon; he would always be outdone by them. What had possessed him to ruin that flow of iron-hot energy that had passed between them over the last few hours? He didn't want that to go away. He didn't know how to make that stay. Now she was going to let him have it.

Surprisingly, Linny's smile returned. "Yeah," she said, "Ash takes a lot of stroking to keep him happy. Would you rather I sucked up to *you*?" She laughed, not nastily, but as if they were sharing a private joke.

Hale felt the sudden tension in him drain as suddenly away. He grinned uncertainly and turned back to the press.

Half an hour before the scheduled rendezvous the press run was done. All that remained was for the papers to be collated and bundled into stacks for distribution in the city. Hale went into the hallway to search for Bear to help with this task—and ran straight into Ash, white-faced and a little shrill.

"Coppers!" the boy said. "Driving slow past the back of the church!"

"Shee-it," Bear said softly, emerging from the shadows. "Just a little longer and Billy'll be here with his Bloods."

"Yeah . . . just a little longer and the coppers will find this place crawling with elves," Ash echoed.

Hale's stomach heaved. Why was it bad news always went straight to his stomach? Maybe it was just that thinking of coppers, of his father's face if they hauled him in, reminded him too painfully of all the arguments over the dinner table. Coppers. Dinners. It all made him want to puke.

As the three boys stared dumbfounded at each other, Linny took over.

"Okay you guys, pull up your flys and let's get cracking. Move the papers out the back door so when the Bloods come you can load up and take off. Don't worry about putting the pages together until you're safely back across the river. Ash, you take my bike when you go—but mind the gears, it sticks between first and second. Hale, you can ride with Bear again."

"But what about Silver Suits?" Ash said.

"What about *you*?" Hale wanted to know.

"I'm going to lead the coppers a merry little chase," she said jauntily, with more confidence than she could possibly feel. "An elvin girl, an elvin rant, a bit of hide and seek by the river-o." Linny grinned, her smile almost feral. "Not that I intend to get caught, you understand. I'll just lead them away while you get your asses out of here—*and* the paper. Don't you dare lose our beautiful paper!"

"I know the neighborhood," Hale pointed out. "I'll come with you."

"I can make it back to Soho by myself, Hale."

"Through *human* suburbs?"

" 'You're not the only one with connections in this city,' " she quoted back at him. "I know what I'm doing."

Bear said mildly, "If you argue about this much longer, children, the coppers are going to come up the walk and knock at the door. Here's a cop-mobile coming up the street now."

"Go get the papers!" Linny pushed Hale and Ash in that direction. She sprinted down the hall, and climbed out a first floor window. As she crossed the broad front lawn, the sweep of a spell-light caught her. There was a startled cry, a moment of confusion, and then the coppers gave chase.

Hale bounded out the window after her, falling flat into the calla lily bed. A spell-light caught him full in the face. What if it was his father behind that bright beam?

"Hale, you asshole! If you're coming, come!"

Linny ran back to the window, hauled the dazed boy to his feet. "Goddammit, Hale, you never get anything right, do you?"

"I've been told that before," he gasped, and the two of them sprinted off into the night.

* * *

It was hard not to love the night. The damp earth, the smell of late blooming flowers, even the gutter mulch of dead leaves made a wonderful change from the constant stale stink of the old city's streets.

And Hale, running beside her, his feet pounding the pavement in the same rhythm as hers, like the steady beat of the printing press when they'd finally gotten it going together . . . Linny laughed with pure pleasure of the night.

"Christ!" Hale panted. "Suits coming right up the street!" It was true. The cop-mobile had circled the block and was heading straight for the two of them. In a moment, they'd have to freeze in the light of the beam or be mown down. Hale froze.

"Don't be such a rabbit, Hale!" she said jovially. "We may be the hunted, but never the hare: we are foxes for cunning, stags for speed—"

"You are out of your mind," he accused, following her nevertheless across the suburban lawns—where the cop-mobiles, of course, couldn't follow them. The Suits would have to get out and run after them.

They did. Shouts of, "Hey, you kids!" and "Stop, in the name of the law!" Feet pounding behind them.

" 'Do as thou wilt shall be thine only law,' " Linny crooned the arcane quotation, running. She forgot where she'd dug that one up. She couldn't even remember if it was elvin or human. Maybe she *was* out of her mind. She felt out of her mind. It was great.

"In here!" Hale dragged her by the wrist into an alley-way of shrubbery: the division between two backyards made by neighbors who loathed each other so much that they couldn't even share a hedge. The fleeing pair dived headfirst into the gap between the carefully manicured bushes.

"Hey!" a man's voice squawked under them.

"Eee!" a woman shrieked. "It's my husband! He's found us!"

"My wife!"

"Sorry, sorry," Hale muttered, disentangling himself from the amorous couple. Linny was laughing so hard she could barely stand up. But she led the way out of the hedge.

The neighborhood was waking up with all the noise. Lights were going on all over. Behind them the coppers were running for the hedge, following the racket. It would buy Hale and her a few moments to gain some space. But it was important not to let the coppers lose them—not until she heard the roar of bikes and vans that meant *Nightlife* was safely on its way.

Hale hesitated for a moment in the shadows between houses. Then he whispered, "This way! I know somewhere we—"

"Wrong again, Hale," she said. "We go *this* way."

He didn't argue. "Where are we going?"

"Why, to school, where all good children go!"

The coppers finally caught sight of them again as they crossed the parking lot of an old shopping mall. It was filled with junk, now that cars were such a luxury. Some old holocaustic movement of the earth had set the entire ground tilting away from the building behind the lot. Linny took them up against the building wall, letting the coppers across the lot play their lights on her. Suckers. She ran forward and set a pile of defunct rubber ties in motion. They bounced and rolled down toward the coppers, who were trying to weave their way through piles of junk to get their quarry. Hale stared at her. His face was elvin-silver in the moonlight, and his eyes were wild. He was really scared, Linny realized. Something awful was going to happen if he got caught.

Didn't he realize that she was the hero tonight? They were going to win through adversity to triumph over the enemies of fun and art. Soho was running wild in Pleasant Gardens.

"Here." She shoved a tire into Hale's hands. "Roll

'em!'' To his credit, he did. He put more force into it than she did, and his aim was better. "Yow!" she shrieked with glee. "Knockout in one round!"

The coppers finally had the sense to shelter behind a pile of junk until their antagonists ran out of ammunition, which they shortly did.

"Our backs are to the wall," Hale said, literally, with gallant desperation. "Tell me, O Queen of the Night, how's a poor boy to get to school?"

"Hale." She clapped a hand on his shoulder. "To get anywhere in this world, you have to *climb*."

"That's what my dad says," he growled, boosting her up onto the first rung of the old fire escape above their heads.

"Your dad—uh—" she grunted as she lifted him after her, "is, in this case, right."

They made it to the roof. The shopping center was still in use, but hardly busy at this hour. Linny thought with regret of the chaos they could make with all the merchandise passing under their feet as they ran across the store roofs. No time. She had stopped listening for the roar of motors. The elves must have gotten well away by now. And there was something she had promised herself she would do before she went back to Mock Avenue. She hadn't known Hale would be with her . . . but what the hell.

The coppers rattled after them across the roofs of the shopping complex. "Whoopsey!" Linny jumped down from a high roof to a lower one. Hale followed, skidded on the tiles, yelled "Shit!" but righted himself and kept on.

They were coming to the end of the row of stores. The coppers had both skidded where Hale skidded, but it took them longer to get up.

Hale grinned ruefully at her. He thought they were trapped again.

"Having fun, Hale?" she asked cheerfully.

He grabbed her hand, drew it to his chest. "Linny, I—"

"Not now, Hale. Now we disappear." She took him forward one more step.

And they disappeared.

"What the hell?" Hale's voice was muffled by the gray fog all around them.

"Antiburglary spell," she answered. "Set on the jewelery store beneath us.—Well, not anymore."

Now they found themselves standing on a street of regulation Pleasant Gardens stucco houses. It was dark, and there was no sign of the coppers.

"It's a very expensive spell—and very illegal in this part of town," she explained. "That's why the Suits don't know about it. The jeweler carries emeralds and elphinstones direct from the Elflands, and the merchant's suppliers want to protect their client; so they do him a favor and let him have the spell cheap. Good thing it's working tonight."

"How do you know all that?"

He would ask her that. She chose to misinterpret. "I'm an elf, remember? We know these things."

But he was persistent. "No, I mean how did you know that spell was set on that store?"

She raised her left eyebrow, a trick she'd perfected years ago after weeks in front of a mirror. "That's for me to know and you to find out."

"What if the coppers step on the same spot?"

"Doesn't matter. The spell is completely random: it dumps you anywhere in a five-block radius, the theory being that you won't try that store again. Hale?" She surveyed the tidy rows of houses. "Do you have any idea where we are?"

He looked up and down the street. There was nothing to distinguish it from miles of others. "No. Wait—yes, I do. See that birdbath? We're on Remson Street, off Pierce."

She didn't question his answer, or its source. "Right."

Linny began walking again. Hale followed her. "We're

not all that far from the church," he said. "Do you want to go see if everything's all right?"

"No," she said, walking, her hand in her pocket. "I have an act of petty vandalism to commit."

The sign over the gate said, "Willowcrest Academy."

"Oh, shit," said Hale. "Do we hafta?"

"Come on, Hale."

They climbed the old brick wall, left there by the academy more for show than for defense; as Linny had always said, no one would want to get in there who didn't have to.

The school was a beautiful red-brick building that had probably always been a school. A shallow flight of stone steps led up to a wide door, painted pristine white. Its polished brass handle shone in the moonlight.

Linny took her hand out of her pocket. In it was a tube of fairy-dust. She raised her arm, like a wizard casting a spell. A fine spray of glittering dust shot out of the tube. In enormous curlicue graffiti letters, she scrawled across the front door of Willowcrest Academy:

THE MOCKERS

She stepped back a pace, two paces. It looked just great.

"Tell *me* I can't write poetry!" she muttered. She put the tube back in her pocket.

Hale had watched the whole performance with quiet intensity. "I know you," he said when she was done. "You're the girl who won the essay contest. 'My Hopes for the Future' or something."

"And you're the guy who got kicked out of school. Two bloody noses and a fractured wrist or something."

They stood looking at each other. The moon was growing pale in the sky; dawn was coming up over the Borderlands.

Hale smiled crookedly. "My, how you've grown."

"Yeah," she said. "Hard not to. You were a punk even

then, Hale. You're lucky you didn't have to stay here. Some of us it takes a little longer to figure things out.''

''I wish I'd known. . . .'' he said.

She wished he had too. She wished *someone* had. But it was all right now. No one else could have made the press work, then run that chase with her through the flats—not Bear, not Robbin, not even Ash.

Hale took her face in his hands, running his fingers over the planes and curves he'd traced so often on paper. She could feel his fingertips revelling in the texture of her skin. She closed her eyes, felt his light touch on her eyelids, his breath on her face . . .

''Hale,'' she said. ''You kiss better than you paint.''

He murmured into her cheek, ''If that's an insult, I'm not listening. You should be more careful with those words, girl; they'll get you in trouble someday.''

''All right,'' Linny said, resting her chin in his soft brown hair. ''No more words.''

Before they left the school, Hale wrestled the dust tube out of Linny's pocket.

                    he wrote on the door.

Hale felt so high it was a wonder to him that his body was still earthbound; any second now he would go soaring over the rooftops of Soho. High from work, high from joy, high from a night without food or sleep, high from running, high from Linny. Everything felt strange to him, like walking under water. All the colors were neon bright, with an afterglow when he turned his head. His body felt light, his breath was a fluttering in his chest. He'd never felt so good and so wired in his entire life.

So he didn't care that as they passed through Hell's Gate

into Soho in the golden morning light she'd let go of his hand; or that she seemed to forget him as she climbed up Gutierrez's fire escape and into the Studio, making her grand entrance, the hero returned. He didn't care that she let Ash make a tremendous fuss over her—while simultaneously bitching about how True Bloods should never venture into the flatlands, he wouldn't do that again for love nor money. . . . Every time Linny caught Hale's eye she grinned. For once it was their little secret that the elves weren't in on.

Ash had been waiting for them both in an agony of concern. The transportation of the paper had gone like clockwork; they'd collated the pages in the Mock Avenue chapel and then Billy and the Bloods had taken over the operation. Bear was now taking a nap on Hale's balcony. Robbin was carefully reading a copy of their paper, the cigarette in his hand the only indication he might have been worried about Hale and Linny too—Robbin only smoked when he was nervous. "Checking for spelling errors?" Linny asked him sweetly, peering at the paper over the elvin boy's shoulder.

Ash was saying, ". . . so then you dumped the coppers and went for a *walk*? Shit. We thought the Suits had gotten you for sure. We were going to give it another hour, then Bear wanted to go over the river with that gun of Buttons'."

Hale made the mistake of catching Linny's eye. They both burst out laughing.

"Shit," Ash repeated disgustedly, miffed that his concern was such a joke.

Linny winked at Hale, and tugged affectionately at Ash's silver hair. "Come on," she said, "let's go to one of those fancy-assed cafés on the Promenade, get some breakfast and watch people buying our paper."

"Using what for money?" Robbin asked, looking up from *Nightlife*.

"We'll borrow some from José," she said. "We can bring him something good back from the Hill."

"Aw," Hale told her with his newfound familiarity, "you just want to go picking through rich people's trash bins again!"

"Shut up, asshole." Linny punched him in the shoulder.

And so Ash was right, and Linny was right: the Mock Avenue Studio show at the Dancing Ferret, so well reviewed in the city's best hoax of the year, became the arts event of the week.

The fraudulence of their edition of *Nightlife* was quickly discovered, of course. (What became of the original issue no one knew—and the Bloods weren't telling.) But in this trade city between two worlds, itself built and sustained on cunning entrepreneurship, the substitution made instant folk heroes of its anonymous authors. And the bogus reviews brought people down to Soho to find out what was *really* going on. Already it was rumored that a Dragon's Tooth matron had asked Taco Hell to cater her next party. The *Nightlife* theater critic had supposedly been seen helplessly wandering up and down Carnival Street, waiting for the Squatters' Theater to spontaneously happen. And one hour into their own show's official opening, the Dancing Ferret was packed.

Ash was in his element, decked out in a satin smoking jacket, his hair a silver cloud around his face. He held a glass of champagne in one hand, graciously greeting his public, punk and nabob alike, as they strolled through the door of Farrell Din's club. The pudgy wizard who owned the place was nowhere to be seen. Ash held court here, master of all he surveyed.

There was little to connect this languid, elegant, high-elvin young man with the frantic boy panicking in the Church of Saintliness driveway—or the surly youth of only two hours ago, framing pictures at the last possible moment, hanging pictures as the first patrons arrived, convinced beyond a doubt that no one would come. Druienna, restored to favor for the event, glowed on Ash's arm in a beaded dress of elvin red. Her eyes opened wider and wider as the luminaries of Bordertown paraded past, inclining their heads to Ash as if he were One of Them.

They had pulled it off, from start to finish. Billy Buttons was so smug there would be no living with him for a month. On the street, the word was that the Bloods had somehow gotten hold of the Pack's famous sawed-off shotgun. Some said they'd broken it; some that it had never worked at all. It didn't matter to the Pack. They were hot to get it back, and the Bloods were holding on to it. Hale could see this going on for years. It reminded him of birthday-party games.

Hale had washed his mutating-fish shirt for the occasion. He hung around the edges of the show morosely, not really wanting to talk to any of the people who came streaming in the door. For him, all the fun had been in setting it up; now, in this crowd, he was just uncomfortable. He saw Gutierrez come in with a really stunning girl, fresh from the World by the look of her. She was wearing Hale's "Hell's Angels" jacket. Shit! Now he'd never get it back. The girl bumped into an immaculately tailored woman and swore loudly and fluently. Hale relaxed a fraction: this might be fun after all.

Robbin was wearing his usual studio clothes, which still managed to make everyone else's finery look tawdry. He was introducing elves to each other as if he were in his own living room. Billy Buttons was talking animatedly with a well-dressed crew of older elvin women in the corner. Hale wondered what sort of deal he was putting together now.

Bear and Linny had volunteered to go out and get more champagne—in fact, they had practically begged to go. It was clear to Hale that Linny, of all people, Miss Elvin Cool herself, was not enjoying the opening. She'd been snappish ever since the first strangers had started coming in. When Ash suggested that she hang around near the paintings based on her verses so he could find her more easily, she practically took his head off. The poems, she said, were already hanging on the wall next to the pictures; she didn't see why she had to join them.

The Ferret itself looked pathetic in the afternoon light without the glitter of fairy-dust, the driving rhythms of rock'n'roll. The elegant men and women descending from Dragon's Tooth Hill only pointed out the shabbiness of the building more painfully: the paint hanging in peeling strips from the ceiling, the floor stained from too many years of wine and beer. But against the drab, cracked walls, the paintings themselves shone like windows into Faerie: bright, vivid, jewellike visions of the artists' minds.

The patrons from the Hill and the Promenade all spoke in loud whispers, so that everyone could hear what they were saying. One elvin critic was heard to sniff, "It's a disgrace to the traditions of high-elvin art." Shortly after, Druienna managed to trip and spill most of a glass of champagne down the front of his pants. A human buyer cornered Robbin and complained that he had come to see Hale's paintings of Soho streetlife, like those sketches in the paper, not "this True Blood bilge."

Ash didn't care what they thought. He had his champagne, his attention, his circle of rich girls from the Hill all trying to catch his roving eye. Hale didn't care either—for him it was worth it all for the spectacle of Hill snobs and street scum standing side by side, passing canapes around on Dancing Ferret beer trays. He thought now that Ash should have gone ahead with Bear's joking suggestion to serve beer and popcorn for that authentic Soho feel. It would have made the show for these people. Hale's fingers itched to sketch. He'd never seen so many rich people before in his life. There was something about their faces, the way they stood, the way they moved. . . .

There was a commotion at the door. Bear, his arms

loaded with fresh champagne bottles, was trying to get through the crowd without dropping any. Right behind him came a tall girl in green velvet murmuring, "Excuse us . . . excuse us . . ." to everyone.

It was Linny. But not the Linny he'd seen an hour ago. Not any Linny he'd ever seen. She was wearing the traditional elvin dress from Gutierrez's store. If you knew what to look for, you could still see the dust marks around the knees. But, this time, you could also see that there was nothing else on beneath the dress. No boots, no biker's trousers. She wore delicate golden shoes with heels that made her taller still. Her short hair was gelled with gold glitter, and gold highlighted her eyes and cheekbones. Her lips were painted a rich, deep red, like the forbidden berries of Elfland.

Across the room, she saw Hale looking at her. He raised both eyebrows in admiration and mimed a wolf-whistle.

She looked right through him, as if he wasn't there. Then she drifted over to Ash, kissed his cheeks, and took his arm.

They made a stunning couple. Hale found Bear and began on the champagne.

Linny felt Ash's arm tighten around her waist. He was half plowed already. His eyes were fixed on her in lustful admiration.

"Madam," he said gallantly, breathing champagne in her face. "You are the very Queen of Elfland. The *Punk* Queen of Elfland." The rich girl he'd been talking to shot Linny a dirty look and drifted away toward Robbin. "My dear Linny . . ." He stared drunkenly at her chest, breathing hard. She didn't say anything. "Your words have inspired my finest art; now your face will inspire my verse. Poetry. A woman who is both boy and lady, the male and female spirit trapped in every artist . . ."

Mercifully, an elf dressed in a very fancy World-made polyester suit tapped Ash's shoulder then. "Ah . . . Mr.

Bieucannon, excuse me. I'm Riven Laeriel. I, ah, was interested in one of your 'verse paintings,' ah''—he consulted his notes, written on one of their carbon-copied show "catalogs"—"ah, yes, umm . . . *When She Comes* is the name of it, I think."

"Indeed," said Ash suavely. "As you know, the painting was inspired by the verse posted on the wall beside it. Allow me to present the poet to you."

He squeezed Linny's elbow, and she nodded at Laeriel, her eyes modestly lowered. "Linny!" Ash hissed in her ear. Laeriel must be important. "What's with you? *Say* something!"

But she didn't have to say anything. Laeriel took her hand. "Enchanted, Miss . . . ah . . ." She hadn't let them put her name on the poems, just her initials. She saw Laeriel desperately consulting his program and did not enlighten him. "Miss Ah, may I say that you have the true elvin beauty: classical features such as one seldom encounters these days; the stature one associates with the queens of yore—"

"Thank you," Linny murmured. Laeriel kept hold of her hand, tried to draw her away, but Ash's arm remained locked around her waist.

"Linny," Ash said, "is one of the most promising members of the Mock Avenue Studio."

"Oh?" The older elf's eyebrows lifted in cosmic interest. "Do you paint as well, Miss . . . ah?"

"Oh, no," said Linny. "I really don't have Ash's talent. He writes, too, you know."

"Indeed?" Laeriel didn't look nearly so interested. He tugged a little on her hand. "Miss, ah, Linny, I have a small art gallery on the Promenade . . ." This time, Ash let her go. "Just a few choice pieces, you understand," the dealer went on; "some Fern collages, a few early Lillets. . . ."

"Oh." Linny looked up at him. "I just *adore* Lillet!

Especially those unicorns. There's something so . . . so . . . well, I'm just not sure how to say it."

Normally she couldn't have gotten through that speech without cracking up. But she wasn't normal now. The girl in the green velvet dress said things like that all the time. She didn't have the words.

"Oh," Laeriel gushed, "I know. I know. It's something indefinably . . . sad, perhaps. Wistful. Longing for another time. I sense a little of that in your poetry too."

"Do you?" she asked bashfully.

"Oh, yes." He had her backed up against a wall now, staring into her eyes, or trying to. "I see in you the spirit of one of the old bards. But instead of that, ah, modish thatch of copper, you wear a mane of silver curls . . . how I should love to see your hair grown out to its natural color! Palest buttercup, perhaps? Or true elvin gold?"

In fact, her hair really was red. She only hennaed it to give it body, and to be sure it looked dyed. She couldn't tell Laeriel that, though; it would break his heart to learn she wasn't a True Blood, just a halfie trying very hard. And she didn't want to break anyone's heart today. She didn't want to say the wrong thing or do the wrong thing. She just wanted to fit in.

All of these people terrified her. She'd decked herself out in her usual t-shirt and leathers to come to the opening; it was what she felt most like herself in. She'd helped hang pictures, helped calm Ash down, run out for extra wire and paper cups. It was her and the studio guys, working together as always. Then the people started coming in. Soho punks who knew her, knew the studio, they were all right. But the sleek, well-bred patrons from the Hill, brought down here by Linny's own scheme, these struck a nerve in her that wouldn't stop ringing. This was the background Ash and Robbin came from, descendents of elves who really did drink Dragon's Milk, who lived the life she'd only pretended to. This was the aristocrat's life her parents had dreamed of for their kids, why her poor confused folks had worked so hard to move them to Pleasant Gardens, a human neighborhood that had only barely tolerated her parents' "mixed" marriage, and sent her to a good school so that she and her brother could climb up in the world. . . .

In her leather and torn cotton, she'd suddenly felt grubby. Suddenly all her cleverness had seemed brittle, her poems silly, her toughness a shell that would crack at the slightest touch.

In the weird afternoon light of the Dancing Ferret, surrounded by people she didn't know, who didn't know her, she had felt the tough Linny slip away, deserting her like rats deserting a sinking ship. Oh sure, the Studio guys had accepted her—she'd proved herself to them already. But these new people streaming in to see the show . . . What was Linnea Garnett to them but a ragged punk girl who hung around artists?

> *I am as I am, and so will I be*
> *But how that I am, none knoweth trulie*

Linny had muttered the fragment of old, old poetry to herself as she grabbed Bear's arm and followed him out on the champagne run. She had always found the words comforting, but they did nothing for her now.

As they crossed Mock Avenue, Linny stopped. "Bear," she said, "I'm sorry, I've gotta go."

"What do you mean?" Bear protested. "I need you to help carry the champagne bottles."

"Oh," she said dully. "Yeah. Well, would you just wait a minute—wait two minutes—"

She bolted off in the direction of Gutierrez's store.

It was more than two minutes, and when she came back, stepping carefully in the golden shoes, she was transformed. Bear didn't ask her to carry any bottles.

This time, when she came into the Ferret behind Bear and the champagne, Linny felt all eyes on her. But this time it was all right, because it wasn't really her. It was a creation of glitter and green velvet she'd made up specially for the occasion.

And here she was, transformed indeed, from all she had wanted to be to all everyone else had wanted for her. It was easy, really. She was surprised that a person of her intelligence had never figured out how easy it was before. Just nod and smile, be interested in what he's saying, don't get sarcastic, don't state any strong opinions. Easy.

She saw Ash heading their way, coming to claim her.

"Oh, Mr. Laeriel," Linny cooed, "I've got to come to your gallery sometime. Ash and I just love to walk along the Promenade. . . ."

Change partners and dance. Ash's arm once again around her waist, pulling her close to him as he walked with airy unsteadiness over to a group of elegantly seedy-looking elves, dressed in elvin brocades that, like their wearers, had seen much better days. "I'm so glad you could come!" Ash told them, ignoring the girl on his arm while simultaneously stroking her hip with his thumb, just the way he used to do with Druienna.

"Well," a tall beautiful elf said with a melancholy smile, "it's certainly *different*, Ashkin. Not the way it used to be at home, of course."

These must be his emigré friends, political refugees and outcasts of Elfland, still holding on to their fey, tattered dignity.

Linny allowed her gaze to drift. A mistake: Hale was staring at her from across the room. Not Hale. Not now. He was the only one she couldn't be perfect for. He knew her too well. He'd see right through to the coward beneath the green dress.

"Ash," she murmured, brushing his earlobe with her lips, "I'm going to get more champagne," intending to dodge Hale at the same time. But it was a mistake. Hale traced her amid the press of people as though she were the only one in the room, caught up with her next to one of his own paintings.

"Linny," he hissed, closing his fingers hard around her waist, "what the fuck is *wrong* with you?"

Not now, she thought; please, not now. She felt brittle as old ice. She had to get rid of him now, explain later. . . . "Wrong?" she said, opening her blue eyes wide. "Why should anything e wrong?"

"Oh, yeah! Listen, Linny, I know what you're up to: flirting with that art dealer, coming on to Ash—"

He'd been drinking too. It made Hale stupid; it made him jealous. And that made her angry.

"Hardly," she said, giving him her ice-maiden prudish stare. "You hardly know what I'm up to."

"—only it's not *sucking up* to Ash anymore, is it? Here in Soho we've got another name for it, princess."

"I'm sure you do." She wrenched her wrist out of his grasp, feeling the skin burn. She turned and walked blindly away. Her battered senses took her to the nearest door, leading out into one of the Ferret's backstage passageways. She was walking blindly down it, cold and white, as close to out of control as she'd ever been.

Hale followed. "Linny!" he bawled. The walls rang with it. "Linny, get your ass back here. I'm not done talking to you!"

She kept on walking. Soon she was going to run out of places to go.

Hale took her by the shoulders, spun her around, and shoved her back against the wall. She was as big as he was. She should have been able to push him back. But in the green dress, she couldn't fight.

"You're a lie," he hissed in her face. "You know that, Linny, you're a big fat lie. Miss Elf Queen of Soho—but we know the truth, don't we, babe?"

"Leave it, Hale," she said. Even her face felt cold.

"Where did you get those poems Ash likes so much—copy 'em out of a book?"

"No," she whispered. She couldn't believe how badly someone could hurt you once you let them in. "I wrote them."

"No," Hale corrected viciously. "Only half of you wrote them. Elvin nostalgia. Fine elvin sensibility. I can't give them that, and you can. I can't do elf art, but even Robbin thinks you do just great. But remember, that's only half of you. The other half is mine: running through that stupid suburb, getting vengeance on that stupid school—that's *human*, Linny, that's *mine*, and you can't just wipe it away!"

Her lips were stiff with rage. She felt them coldly forming the words. "Don't tell me what I can and cannot do."

"Right," Hale said harshly, shifting his weight against her. "Right. Words are for *you* to use. They're off bounds for us dumb artists."

He was as hot as she was cold. He drove his mouth against hers, his teeth battering against her lips. She almost wished that he would tear the green dress off her, maybe then she would be free—

"Well, well," a familiar voice said coolly. "A little lovers' quarrel."

Billy Buttons stood in the corridor, hands in his pockets.

"Don't let me interrupt," he said. But Hale had already released her, jumping back, fumbling with his shirttails.

"I thought," Buttons said, "that it was time we all broke for a general meeting. Saw the two of you ducking out and thought, What a good idea!"

Bear came pounding down the corridor, Ash and Robbin close behind him. God knew what Billy had told them.

"Hale," Ash said blearily, "what's going on? You can't run out on the opening!"

"Not me," Hale said. " 'S Linny. Needs some looking after."

"Fuck you, Hale," she said, but it was too late.

"Oh," Hale said formally. "I don't believe you gentlemen have met Miss Garnett, of Pleasant Gardens, Willow-crest Academy. They don't let too many mixed breeds into Willowcrest—very exclusive school—but Linny gets such good grades they made an exception.''

She wouldn't beg him to stop. She wasn't even sure he *could* stop, now.

"What the hell are you talking about, Hale?" Ash demanded. "Linny's as elvin as you or—as elvin as I am!"

"The fuck she is," Hale growled. "Not all humans are short and dark, Robbin. Miss Garnett here's a fucking throwback: human dad, halfie mom. Amazing but true! Mix them together and watch it grow. Result: one genuine elf poet. Ship to Soho, C.O.D." They stared at him as if they didn't believe it. As if he'd gone mad. "Now here's the neat part: can anyone who's not an elf do great elvin art? Bear, what do you think?"

"Sure," Bear rumbled. "Anyone can if your heart's in it."

"I don't think Robbin agrees," Hale went on stridently. "I don't think even Ash agrees, not really. So how do we explain Linnea Garnett? Do we say she successfully fooled a panel of experts? 'Cause let me tell you guys, she sure fooled me."

"You don't have to explain anything," Linny said stiffly. This was all so different from the way it was supposed to be. She couldn't believe it was happening. Was she dreaming this; or had she been dreaming the peace of the Studio? The guys were supposed to be the unit; she was the outsider here. She'd wanted in because of the closeness she'd felt in the Studio—and, by a miracle, they'd let her in. Now Hale was tearing it apart, ripping all the fragile connections that had held them together, human and elf, male and female. He was forcing a breach where none should be—hurting her because somewhere along the line everyone had hurt him. She loved Hale, wanted him hurt least of all. And she hated him for doing this.

"Hale," she explained to the others, "can't help it. It's

in his blood. It's that copper brutality; just like his copper daddy. Maybe he'll outgrow it, get real romantic. Hale's romantic past is all a fake, you know. He'd never even been out of the suburbs till he met you guys." She turned to Hale, shaking. "Okay? All done? We even?"

Now Hale was staring at her. To her horror, tears stood out in his meadow-grass eyes. She turned away.

"Is it true, Linny?" Robbin had his hand half out to touch her, whether to test or to comfort she didn't know. "Is it true what he said?"

"If you have to ask," she said, "it doesn't matter, does it, asshole?"

And that was as much as she could stand. She turned and walked away down the corridor, feeling already the heavy boots back on her feet, the purring cycle under her, the weight of years ahead of her.

"Mr. Hale?"

Hale looks up from the painting he has long ago lost interest in, is completing only out of stubbornness, and grits his teeth. If he hears that earnest little voice one more time today, he is going to scream. Or kick something. Or hurl the cat and the student out the window.

The cat has knocked a jar of turpentine and two jars of river water onto the rug. It winds itself around Hale's feet, as if this will make Hale forgive. Hale sets his face in a bland smile, hoping the student won't pick up on the aggravation beneath. He's been living too long alone, that's his problem. Not the kid's fault. The boy only wants information—a face identified, a scene labeled, handwriting translated. And he is a workhorse—three weeks in Bordertown and he's already gotten halfway through the storage room. When he gets through that, Hale will break it to him about the attic.

"Mr. Hale, why do they stop?"

The question takes him by surprise.

"I mean, you painted them for so many years . . . and then they just stop."

That's funny. He's never thought about that really. About *why*. He hadn't intended to stop painting street scenes, he just . . . had. When the neighborhood changed beyond recognition. When all his old pals were dead, crazed, or gone. When all the women's faces kept turning into Linny's.

"Soho changed," he says. "Hell, we thought we ran Bordertown from down here, set the styles clear up to the Hill. But in fact it was the Tooth that gobbled us up; there's little to distinguish Ho Street from the Promenade these days. So what is there to paint? My own past? I've already done that. The present doesn't hold much interest."

The student's gaze goes past Hale to the stack of paintings Hale has made, paintings he does not want the University or the galleries to cart away. The painting of Ash. The entrance to Danceland; several other landmarks. Bear. Linny.

"What happened to all your pals, Mr. Hale?" the boy asks shyly, peering from beneath the dreadlocks. "I mean the kids in the pictures." Hale has finally persuaded him to leave the goddamn suit in his suitcase; now he wanders around Hale's house in bleached drawstring pants, his feet bare. Yet nothing Hale can say will get rid of the *Mr. Hale*.

"What do you mean, what happened to them? You're a specialist on the period, you know what happened to them!"

"Oh," the boy says with an elegant gesture of his slim brown hand. That's new: must have picked it up from the elves around here. Hale absently doodles the line of it with his brush end in the still-wet oil paint. "I know about Robbin Pearl, the famous art dealer, houses in Bordertown and Paris. Ash Bieucannon, famous recluse painter." He gestures at the stack of canvases. "But what about *them*, the kids they were when you painted them? What happened to them, Mr. Hale?''

Hale sighs, shifts in his chair. This kid's been living among the dust and ghosts of Hale's past for too long. The same characters turning up in sketch after sketch, becoming more real to him than his own life. He can imagine the boy trying to argue with the silent smile of Ash, wondering if he could get big Bear to like him, falling in love with Linny. . . . Not good, to live with ghosts.

"You mean, 'Is it going to happen to me?' " Hale says. "Yes, probably; if you keep working hard and caring about things. Look what happened to Linnea Dark Garnett. She managed to escape her Soho connection, went down to the World, and started the Elvin Revival craze that led to Ash and Robbin being such hot stuff down there. Have you found my first edition of her *Songs from Elsewhere* yet?''

The boy shakes his head mutely, eyes bright. "A *first edition*? Is it *signed*?''

"What? No. Oh, no. Not signed. I bought it up here, when it first came out.''

"I hear Robbin Pearl's supposed to be writing his memoirs now.''

Hale chuckles. "That should be a good time. Just don't take them too seriously. Now, Robin did all right for himself; started his business buying elvin artwork for World museums. Married a Bordertown girl—human, if you can believe it!''

The boy looks at him, uncomprehending.

"No,'' Hale says, "guess there's no reason why you wouldn't. I couldn't get *everything* into those paintings.

"As for Ash . . . hell, you probably know more Ash Bieucannon stories than I do. I expect most of them are true. The lovers. The drugs. I was there the time he tried to bring William Butler Yeats back to life. Ash always had a fetish for dead poets; but he was never very meticulous in his work. And so he had the poor ghost stumbling all over Bordertown for a good two weeks, Ash sticking pins in a map, trying to track him down.'' Hale laughs—not at the memory, which is still rather horrible, but at the story it makes now. ''The city finally paid a group of elf mages to lay the guy to rest. . . .''

Hale grows thoughtful, tapping his pipe against his knee. The elvin cat climbs into his lap, butting its head against the artist's hand.

''I don't see Ash anymore,'' he says finally. ''He, umm, doesn't want to see anyone. He stays up in that old monstrosity way on the other side of the Hill, with his guard dogs and his cute little model, can't be a day over nineteen. Ash looks old. Elves don't age like we do: they don't age gradually over the years, but all in a rush, like a tree losing its sap. Ash, well, he's lost it—though by their standards he's not old. Dragon's Milk, you see. He got rich, and then he could afford it all the time. For a while he was the Prince of Dreams, but now he's just plain crazy. He doesn't know me anymore. He's convinced the art critic for *Nightlife* is threatening his life—a sweet, earnest little halfie, wouldn't harm a fly. But that wouldn't be so bad if he'd only write, or paint . . . you won't see anything more from Ash Bieucannon.''

The student is looking hard at the study of Bear with the shotgun and Linny on her bike that's still pinned up on Hale's wall. ''So what about Bear?''

''Bear . . . you'd have liked Bear. Don't let's talk about Bear, now; we're discussing the road to success, remember? Billy Buttons, the halfie with the wonderful coat with all the folds, he's on that road somewhere, I'm sure of that. BB never liked to publicize his successes. José Gutierrez, tattooed José, you'll meet if you go to that big elvin surplus store up on Calameada. Druienna, now there's an interesting story—she's the pretty little elf-girl in that series of—''

''Yes,'' the student interrupts, ''I know which one she is. What happened to her?''

''Well, at first she looked to be a sad case: got married, got fat, had too many kids . . . next thing I hear, she's running the old Wheat Sheaf, looking like a million bucks, and her oldest girl's got a hot band playing around town. . . .

''But, hey.'' Hale catches himself about to begin another story of people this kid doesn't even know. ''There it is. They all grew up, and got rich and famous. And a nice student from the World came up to old Hale's studio and spent all his time cataloguing their pictures, until finally the poor young man went completely crazy and his hair turned white and all his teeth fell out from overwork.'' Hale eases himself up from the chair. ''So what do you say we knock off early today, go down to the Wheat Sheaf, and I'll buy you a beer?''

The kid grins and nods, dreadlocks swinging. ''I'll get my shoes,'' he says.

Hale hears feet pounding on the stairs as the boy runs down them, his excitement sharp in the air. Well, of course. Maybe it's not the Soho Hale remembers, but it'll be fresh and new to this kid—a Bordertown of his own. The magic place at the edge of the Elflands that he'd saved for two years to come to.

Hale can hear the boy talking to the cat. It's still odd to hear another voice in the house, he's grown so used to being alone. Thirty years of living alone. Almost thirty-one.

The first few years he kept hoping she'd come back. He *knew* she would. She belonged on the streets of Soho. After that he stopped waiting. Or so he likes to believe. He tells himself that living alone is just an acquired habit, like too much Dragon's Milk, or Linny's passion for coltsfoot. He gazes up at the painting of her, cig in her mouth, that cocky half smile.

So she's still telling people her father is an elvin lord. Some things never change.

Hale unbuttons his paint-covered overshirt, exposing the

Danceland t-shirt he wears underneath. As he tightens the laces on his boots, he can hear the Mock Avenue Bell Tower clock chime the time, incorrectly. He counts twelve rings. That means it's a quarter to ten.

Hale damps the spell lights as he leaves the room. The cornflower-blue gaze rests in shadow.

About the Authors

Emma Bull is the author of *War for the Oaks*, *Falcon*, *Bone Dance*, and a Borderlands novel, *Finder*, which features characters which first appeared in ''Danceland,'' her collaboration in this volume with **Will Shetterly**. Shetterly himself is the author of *Cats Have No Lord*, *Witch Blood*, *The Tangled Lands*, and two Borderlands novels featuring characters from ''Danceland'': the award-winning *Elsewhere* and *Nevernever*. After the original publication of *Bordertown*, Bull and Shetterly revised ''Danceland'' for publication in their joint story collection *Double Feature;* it is that revised version which appears here. They live in Minneapolis.

Midori Snyder is the author of a number of fantasy novels including the ''Queen's Quarter'' trilogy and the recent *The Flight of Michael McBride*, a 19th century fantasy set in New York City and the American West. She currently lives in Milan.

Ellen Kushner is the author of *Swordspoint* and the World Fantasy Award-winning novel *Thomas the Rhymer*. A nationally-known radio personality, she lives near Boston, Massachusetts. **Bellamy Bach** is a pseudonym.

THE BEST OF FANTASY FROM TOR

☐ 51175-1 *ELVENBANE* $5.99
           Andre Norton & Mercedes Lackey $6.99 Canada

☐ 53503-0 *SUMMER KING, WINTER FOOL* $4.99
           Lisa Goldstein $5.99 Canada

☐ 53898-6 *JACK OF KINROWAN* $5.99
           Charles de Lint $6.99 Canada

☐ 50249-3 *SISTER LIGHT, SISTER DARK* $3.95
           Jane Yolen $4.95 Canada

☐ 51099-2 *THE GIRL WHO HEARD DRAGONS* $5.99
           Anne McCaffrey $6.99 Canada

☐ 51965-5 *SACRED GROUND* $5.99
           Mercedes Lackey $6.99 Canada

Call toll-free 1-800-288-2131 to use your major credit card, buy them at your local bookstore, or
clip and mail this page to order by mail.

Publishers Book and Audio Mailing Service
P.O. Box 120159, Staten Island, NY 10312-0004

Please send me the book(s) I have checked above. I am enclosing $ _____
(Please add $1.50 for the first book, and $.50 for each additional book to cover postage and
handling. Send check or money order only— no CODs.)

Name_____

Address _____

City _____ State / Zip_____

Please allow six weeks for delivery. Prices subject to change without notice.

THE BEST OF FANTASY FROM TOR

☐ 54805-1 *WIZARD'S FIRST RULE* $5.99
        Terry Goodkind $6.99 Canada

☐ 53034-9 *SPEAR OF HEAVEN* $5.99
        Judith Tarr $6.99 Canada

☐ 53407-7 *MEMORY & DREAM* $6.99
        Charles de Lint $7.99 Canada

☐ 55151-6 *NEVERNEVER* $4.99
        Will Shetterly $5.99 Canada

☐ 51375-4 *LORD OF CHAOS* $7.99
        Robert Jordan $8.99 Canada

☐ 53490-5 *TALES FROM THE GREAT TURTLE* $5.99
        ed. by Piers Anthony/Richard Gilliam $6.99 Canada

Call toll-free 1-800-288-2131 to use your major credit card, buy them at your local bookstore, or clip and mail this page to order by mail.

Publishers Book and Audio Mailing Service
P.O. Box 120159, Staten Island, NY 10312-0004

Please send me the book(s) I have checked above. I am enclosing $ _____
(Please add $1.50 for the first book, and $.50 for each additional book to cover postage and handling. Send check or money order only—no CODs.)

Name _____
Address _____
City _____ State / Zip_____
Please allow six weeks for delivery. Prices subject to change without notice.